CITY OF ILLUSIONS

JUDITH WORKS

Booktrope Editions
Seattle, WA 2014

Cover Design by Greg Simanson

This is a work of fiction. Names, characters, places, brands, media, and incidents are either the product of the author's imagination or are used fictitiously. Any resemblance to similarly named places or to persons living or deceased is unintentional.

PRINT ISBN 978-1-62015-579-0

EPUB ISBN 978-1-62015-600-1

Library of Congress Control Number: 2014920260

*To Glenn who is not the model for the
dark doings depicted in the story.*

Rome is the city of echoes, the city of illusions,
and the city of yearning.

—GIOTTO, 1266/67 – 1337

JULY/AUGUST

WHEN LAURA RECEIVED the e-mail she knew it was time to confess.

Two months earlier when she was bored with editing a technical manual sent to her by one of her clients, she took a break to check out blogs by women who appeared to have more interesting lives than hers. She came across a site recounting the adventures of an American family who lived in Rome. The latest post told about their invitation by the owners of a small country inn near Siena for a dinner to celebrate the grape harvest. After rhapsodizing about the setting, the food, and the wine, the writer ended her story with: *"We're so in love with this part of Tuscany we actually bought an old farmhouse to fix up to use on weekends."*

Laura looked at her souvenir coffee mug with the London Tube map, a relic of the high school graduation present from her aunt. The long-ago trip had planted a seed of restlessness. Now, as her marriage became ever-more routine, the germ had begun to grow, to push, sprout and slowly turn into visions of a more interesting life somewhere away from Seattle. To find a life with possibilities. And to distract from the unpleasant incident a few months ago. Better to get as far away from the memory as possible.

The blog spurred her to look for jobs in Europe. She didn't bother to tell Jake since she was sure nothing would come of her search. It was just a pastime, she told herself. But if she didn't find anything interesting, another solution to the stagnation she felt creeping over her would have to be found.

After several weeks of looking she came across an ad for a one-year assignment as an editor working for the United Nations in Rome. Romantic Rome. She applied though she was sure the chances were nil. But someone had sent the e-mail arranging a telephone interview for today.

After she put the phone down, her mind was still racing. The woman who called had a thick accent. Was it French? Or maybe Italian. Some of the questions were hard to understand and it was always so difficult to tell what an interviewer thought. She rolled a pencil on her desk for several minutes to help decide what to do next – up meant take the risk to reorient her life, down meant put the idea aside. Up won. That is, if she actually got an offer and Jake was in agreement.

A year abroad, something she had missed out on during her university years. Missed out because she was living with Jake. And now there would be a chance.

She crafted her opening remark to ease into the conversation during the Italian-themed dinner, spaghetti and meatballs, his favorite. Jake had speared his second meatball when she said, "Hon, what would you think if we went away for a year?"

"What do you mean, go away?" He held the forked meatball midway between plate and mouth.

"Well, I keep hearing you complain about teaching and how boring it is, and I'm not getting anywhere much with the freelance editing, and I wondered…I wondered if I could get a job somewhere else for a while you could take a break and do some painting again? Like you have talked about." She held her breath.

"Uh, I don't know. Where?" His expression showed a combination of suspicion and interest.

She plunged ahead. "I didn't tell you because I didn't think anything would come of it, but I applied for a job in Rome, you know, where the sun shines all the time, not like here." She pointed her own fork out the window where raindrops blotted the view of their garden where blooms drooped in the damp.

"Rome? You mean in Italy? I don't know Italian. And you did this without asking?"

"There was no point in talking about it unless there was a chance I'd get the job. And I don't know Italian either. The work is in English anyway. But you could learn and teach me in the evenings. I remember you said you used to know some Spanish."

"But why should we move? I don't see any reason to move."

"Because I'm twenty-nine and I've never done anything interesting. And neither have you and you're thirty-four. Look at us. Same routine every day, same weekends with Netflix or your poker games and sports on TV. Like we're on autopilot."

"Uh, I didn't know you felt like that. You're right that we don't do much but ..."

"But?" Laura leaned forward to look at Jake, trying to catch his eye to be sure he was listening.

He put his head down to search for another meatball before fixing his attention on the television where a baseball game was on. When the winning triple-play for the other side was completed he said, "Guess I could ask for a sabbatical. But I need to think. I mean, you're really springing this on me. And moving to Rome sounds pretty weird. Are you thinking of becoming a Catholic, you know, with the pope and all that?"

Wary about pushing too hard, she let the matter drop after assuring him that the only reason she was talking about Rome was because of the job. She might not get an offer and it would all be for nothing anyway. She could look somewhere else if he was agreeable.

After their dinner table conversation Jake slumped in front of the TV watching ESPN recaps and munching tortilla chips. When the bowl of chips was empty, he twisted his wedding ring around his finger. She wished he wouldn't fiddle with the band although she could tell the gesture meant he was thinking about her proposal.

The dinner-table conversation continued over the next week. Pros: travel, better weather, interesting food, an opportunity for Laura to polish her credentials and Jake to have time to paint again; cons: their house rented to unknown tenants, and living with people who might not speak English outside her office.

She was at her desk again the following week when another e-mail from Rome arrived. It was a job offer. Time to make a decision. She and Jake read the offer over together. A one-year contract for more money than he was making as a teacher. The UN would pay for a small air shipment, some sort of help with rental costs, and money to help settle in an apartment until she was paid her salary.

"What do you think? It's a chance and it's only for a year." She made sure her voice sounded more certain than she actually felt.

Jake looked dubious and said again he'd think about it.

"Please, I want a change before we're too old. Before we have a family." When she saw his face darken, she regretted mentioning family.

But the next evening he surprised her when he said, "I talked to the principal. She said I could apply for a sabbatical."

"That means yes?"

"Yes. You're right. I need a break too."

Laura's gratitude at his response was tempered by his flat tone. She thought about how his liveliness when they were in school had slowly drained away into a premature middle age.

She accepted the offer to begin work the first Monday in September and finished her latest editing project. Jake wound down the art class for children at the community center. They ordered passports on a rush basis, bought a guidebook, watched movies set in Rome and *House Hunters International*. They looked at websites with photos of places for rent, apartments with views of churches or the Colosseum peeking through the lush vegetation on a balcony. Jake bought new paints and brushes to go into the few boxes of domestic items that would be shipped air freight. The days passed in a blur as they put some things in storage, found an agent who would manage the rental of the house, and tried to imagine what it meant to be expatriates.

A friend took them to the airport. As they drove away from their Mid-Century Modern house, Laura looked at her own gold wedding band and the engagement ring with a small diamond that briefly flashed in the sunlight of a late August day.

SEPTEMBER

"*...ALLACCIATEVI LA CINTURA di sicurezza.*"

Laura awoke at the torrent of words coming from the plane's PA system. What did they mean? As if in response to her question, the voice switched to English. "Fasten your seat belt. We will be landing at Leonardo da Vinci Airport in twenty minutes." Laura shivered briefly and held on to the armrest to reassure herself that she and Jake had made the right decision.

She watched the jet's shadow cut across green farmland sprinkled with red tile-roofed towns. Then sunlight spun around the cabin when the plane banked above two small lakes set in wooded hills before passing over a city of pastel-colored buildings bisected by the curves of a murky river.

"Look!" She poked Jake with an elbow. "Jake?"

He pulled out an earbud and, in disregard of the seat-belt sign, unlatched and hung over her to watch the next sight unspooling below, the ruins of an ancient city set in a greensward dotted with umbrella pines. Laura saw groups of tiny figures gathered around buildings or walking along paths. One person stood alone on the grass, no one else nearby.

She put her hand on Jake's arm. "Everything will be okay, won't it?"

"Don't worry. It will be an amazing adventure, I'm sure."

His brief answer wasn't quite enough to reassure her.

The plane bounced and braked along the runway, the finale to a rough flight.

"*Benvenuti a Roma*! It is exactly 4:28."

Laura turned her watch ahead nine hours as other passengers pulled out their cell phones. One-sided conversations in Italian began.

The only word Laura caught sounded like "*Mamma.*" When the plane rolled to a stop, she unlatched the confining seatbelt to stand and face the future. The doors swung open and the steaming heat of a Roman summer day flooded the cabin.

Two hours later, Laura and Jake threw their bags down on the bed in their seedy room in a second-floor *pensione* and stumbled back down a long flight of stairs to find someplace to eat. The energy bars Laura had stashed in her backpack weren't all that sustaining, but she and Jake were too tired and hot to walk far. At the end of the next block Jake spotted a food truck with an awning striped in red, white, and green advertising pizza, *frutta fresca, panini, gelati,* and *bibite.* He had no idea what any word meant except "pizza" but he recognized beer cans. The proprietor spoke a little English and helped him select two cans, along with a liter of water, a couple of oranges, and two warmed-over pizzas. Jake handed over a wad of euros, hoping he'd get the correct change. He and Laura juggled the food back up the steep stairway to their dreary room.

"What do you think now?" She licked crumbs from her fingers before pulling the tab on a beer.

"Well, at least I'll have a break from teaching, whatever else happens."

"I wish I'd booked a hotel before we left. This is pretty grim. Worse than where I stayed in London. Anyway, we're right in the city center and we have a couple of days to look around before I go to work."

He yawned. "I'm wasted."

And now, their first evening in Italy, they sat silent with the remains of the meal between them. She stared at the cracked plaster wall and what looked like a blood spot where someone had squashed a mosquito.

So far the little she had seen of Rome was nothing like the Italy she anticipated. Where were umbrella-shaded cafes filled with marvelous food, or the vine-covered terraces overlooking the sea that fueled the many blogs by American and British women who enthused about their Italian life? Nothing like the Italian magazines she bought at the international newsstand near Pike Place Market with their lush photos of elegant people dining in lamp-lit Roman courtyards or modeling the latest styles in Capri and Venice. All these publications made her dream of lounging in a gondola dressed for a fashion shoot as it glided along the Grand Canal, or sipping *limoncello* on the terrace of a small hotel with a view of the Bay of Naples and Mt. Vesuvius. They did not make her dream of stale pizza in a dark *pensione* with an odd smell coming from the plumbing.

Worse, the night before they left Seattle, Laura had come across a blog different from the others. Instead of paeans of rapture and self-satisfaction, it was a hard look at some of the pitfalls that might await the would-be expatriate: risk of alcoholism, difficult relationships with new acquaintances, homesickness, and issues that might come from what the author called a "trailing spouse," one who might become depressed at no longer having a job. Surely that would not be their fate because it was only for a year. She glanced at Jake.

He had already fallen into a deep sleep, his back to her and slow, even breaths coming from his half-opened mouth. She continued to sit up in the lumpy bed, thinking. Trailing spouse? What will Jake do? He said he wanted to do this, to take a break, finally get time for serious painting. And what about her? Tonight marked the beginning of her attempt to reset a marriage grown stale after seven childless years. A change of scene to recall the first happy years and perhaps encourage Jake to overcome his reluctance to have children by getting him away from the teaching job she knew he hated.

She fingered a five-cent coin with an imprint of the Colosseum she had found on the floor near an ATM in the airport. Back and forth the coin flipped as she moved it between her fingers. Each time the Colosseum on the face appeared, she considered whether it was a good omen or bad. She tried to stand the coin upright on the night table, but instead of balancing, it rolled to the floor, coming to rest under the bed, out of reach in the dust.

They missed the *pensione*'s breakfast. Baggy-eyed and feeling off balance, Laura plopped down next to Jake at a small table set outside the Bar Termini across the street, the name a homage to Stazione Termini, the nearby train station. The crowded terminal, where they had ended their journey from the airport the day before, had been jammed with people scurrying around, reminding her of the time she had poked a stick into an anthill at her great-grandmother's farm.

"Let's have a cappuccino – you order. And something to eat please."

Jake went inside and, taking his turn behind a short man in a shiny suit, he pointed to a tray of pastries and then said "cappuccino," while holding up two fingers. He paid and brought Laura her breakfast.

"Yum." Laura said when she sipped, ruining the leaf pattern made of foam. Jake wiped her white mustache, licked his finger and smiled.

The cream-filled pastry the man at the bar called a *cornetto* was a rich compliment to the coffee. She let her eyes close behind her sunglasses as she sat back to enjoy her breakfast, Jake's small gesture, and the sun on her pale face and arms. "Not bad – this is going to be fun."

Jake nodded in response but the smile lines were missing. "I'm looking forward to getting a decent place to stay. I didn't quite expect all this."

Laura agreed. "The train station was something else, for sure. And the place we're staying. I'm sure everything will be good as soon as we get organized." She moistened her finger to pick up the last bits of her *cornetto* in an attempt to hide her worries that life in Rome might be more complicated than she anticipated.

They set off to wander the narrow streets. Laura surrendered to the vibrant scene where cats ate leftover pasta from paper plates, Vespas careened through congested alleys, religious frescoes with flickering votive lights below graced pastel stuccoed walls, and courtyards revealed mossy fountains that dripped water into sunlit basins. The colors of the buildings made her think of food: caramel, apricot, cantaloupe, orange, lemon, pomegranate, and even eggplant, a color used to trim green-shuttered windows. The city wasn't at all like the London of her graduation trip, so orderly and with sober-colored buildings and people, or Seattle with its wood houses in neighborhoods filled with trees and gardens. It was better.

"Jake, don't you think this looks like some sort of food arrangement, with such tasty colors?"

"I don't know about that, but did you see all the graffiti? Some of it was really good, I mean creative like some of the painters I studied in art appreciation. Keith Haring I think."

She forced a smile and fixed the more pleasing sights in her mind to savor in the evening. The small statue of an elephant supporting an obelisk was her favorite.

The claustrophobic streets gave way to the Piazza Navona glowing golden in the late afternoon sun. The buildings emanated light absorbed over the centuries. Laura, dazzled by the romantic setting, saw the piazza as an enormous stage open to the world. The water in the piazza's three fountains sparkled in the sun, the drops turning into rainbows. She looked at the crowds as they strolled and chatted on their cell phones and with each other.

"Like you said when we were landing yesterday, it's amazing."

"Now I'm not so sure. It's so damn hot." He removed a drop of sweat from his chin with the back of his hand.

They found a gelato shop where they ordered strawberry for Laura and lemon for Jake. Laura squinted to create an indistinct dream of the grandiose buildings, fountains, and happy crowds. After she finished the last lick of gelato remaining on the tiny spoon, she dug out a blank journal from her backpack, ready to make the first entry. She wrote, *This is the first day of my new life!* But how to express her intense joy at the scene and her good fortune to be able to live and work in Rome? She had promised her friends she'd start blogging about her adventures. Best to wait until she had something to say other than touristy things. She tucked the book away next to her new passport, virginal until yesterday when a stamp proving her entry into Italy was added.

"Let's go to the Trevi Fountain. A couple of weeks ago I downloaded that old movie called *Three Coins in the Fountain*, with all those thin women wearing clothes from the 1950s with pointy bras and the men calling them girls."

"Like Madonna used to wear." He surprised her with a quick hug, saying, "You're my girl. And better looking too."

"Thanks. Love you." Laura stopped in the middle of the street to put her arms around him like lovers do, but when passing tourists bumped against them they parted to join the flow of sunburnt humanity hurrying along a street lined with forbidding Renaissance *palazzi*, the massive buildings built of dark stone. Chinese and Africans hawked junky plastic toys and fake Fendi handbags to the passing crowds, exhausted guides waved their folded umbrellas in an attempt to keep their flocks in order, and smartly-dressed police watched with bored expressions. At the far end of one street Laura could hear the noise of rushing water over the murmurings from tourists.

The theatrical fountain lived up to the claims in their guidebook, with Neptune riding in his chariot drawn by two seahorses guided by tritons amid cascading waters. Tourists shoved each other out of the way as they threw two coins over their shoulders and into the basin – one to return to Rome and one for a favorable answer to another wish. Laura cast in a dime she found in the bottom of her backpack, wishing for a happy life in Rome. She couldn't find a second to make another wish. Anyway, it was too soon to think of one.

She glanced up at the building supporting the fountain. An elderly woman, as motionless as one of the statues, leaned down from a window to watch the crowds below, her elbows resting on the sill. What does she see? Does she see me? Does she care about any of us? Uneasy at the woman's fixed stare, Laura squeezed back through the crowds to find Jake who had remained at the back of the piazza.

By now footsore and hungry, they began their walk back to the *pensione*. They came to a small shop with a sign advertising *pizza al taglio*.

Jake said, "What about this place? I don't know what *taglio* means but it does say pizza." An aroma of oregano, basil, and cheese wafted out the door, pulling them in to see large rectangular trays of pizza, so hot they were still bubbling. They each ordered a large square, Jake's with onions and sausage, Laura's with tomato and basil. They ate while standing in front of the shop like living advertisements.

"Awesome," she said between bites. She wiped the dripping cheese off her face with a tissue.

Jake became animated. "No kidding. When we get back home let's see if we can find a place like it. Maybe we could open one near the U – bet we would do well."

"That might be fun. But now we have a whole year to enjoy ourselves. And eat all this great food."

"Yeah. I hope everything goes okay."

"I'm sure we'll be fine. Other people do this sort of thing all the time."

"I don't know "other" people." He curled two fingers on each hand to make quotation marks.

Jake's doubts were momentarily contagious. What if it wasn't fine? Then what would she do?

After buying a couple of Cokes, they came to a newsstand. Jake picked a paper at random along with a bus map. Laura added *Vogue Italia* and a home decor magazine.

She thumbed through the magazines, dreaming again of her new life with designer clothes and high-style kitchens, before spreading out *Il Messaggero* to find ads for apartments. Other than the pictorial ads for clothing and wristwatches, the local newspaper contents were incomprehensible, although she did see the word *appartamenti* in a section near the back page. The word had to be the correct term, but neither she nor Jake could decipher the strange abbreviations like "150 mq". She gave up and turned her thoughts back to the Piazza Navona and what part it might play in their future.

Church bells reverberating through the warm air woke them Sunday morning. Laura got out the guidebook and paged through for ideas. "How about Trastevere? We could have lunch there."

They took their time walking to the Tiber and over the bridge into the cobbled streets. Following the guidebook's advice, their first stop was a twelfth-century church, Santa Maria in Trastevere, apricot in color with a frieze above the portico composed of tiny squares of glittering glass that depicted gift bearers kneeling at the Virgin and Child's feet.

They entered. Laura did a quick look around the quiet and dim interior before finding a chair. She watched as Jake studied the one-dimension scenes and saints, each coming to life as a slowly-shifting sunbeam gently glided over the glass.

"I'll be outside. Don't hurry."

Jake, absorbed in the scene, didn't hear her. She tugged his shirt and pointed to the door before she moved into sunshine not far from a group of young men sitting on the ground by a fountain. One plinked on a guitar while the others talked in what sounded like German. Thirty minutes passed before Jake emerged, blinking as his eyes adjusted to the light. Behind him a priest closed the church doors for the siesta break.

"Let's go hon. Sorry I took so long but it's interesting." He took her hand in apology for making her wait.

Restaurants lined the street. Families of all ages, from grandparents to infants, relaxed outside under large umbrellas. Laura watched as waiters uncorked bottles and patrons tasted samples poured into their glasses. And she watched the noisy children whose parents didn't seem to care about their behavior.

Although Laura and Jake searched for their place in the sun, every attractive venue was full. They eventually found a simple restaurant called Trattoria Giovanna, and were seated at a table near the kitchen instead of outside with the talkative families. So different from mine, Laura thought. What would they be doing right now? Then she realized that it was four in the morning in Seattle. Probably asleep, but daybreak wouldn't bring much of a change.

Laura glanced at a family of American tourists laughing and talking with each other as they dug into their meals before she said, "Do you think you should see your parents more often when we get back?"

Jake stuck his face into the menu.

Laura studied her own menu although her mind was lingered on Jake's perpetual reluctance to talk about his family. And about having a child. Always, "not now" or silence.

The menu offered strange foods like *trippa alla Romana.* Confused by the words, she turned her attention to a long sideboard, where a moth-eaten stuffed fox and an array of dusty wine bottles rested on the top shelf. Below, platters were filled with silvery sardines glistening in oil alongside grilled zucchini and eggplant. Bowls of black and green olives contrasted with the grilled tomatoes, red peppers, marinated artichoke hearts, and mushrooms. Snips of parsley and red pepper flakes dotted mussels and clams.

Jake caught the waiter's eye and pointed with a questioning expression. The waiter said, "*antipasti,*" and signaled for them to help themselves. He and Laura filled their plates and tucked in. "Fantastic," they said in unison.

Still hungry, Laura found *spaghetti alla marinara* on the menu. "Must mean 'marine,' like shrimp and stuff, don't you think? Like mariners or sailors."

"Hope so," said Jake, adding, "wonder how the Mariners are doing?"

"Probably another losing season. I don't think they play baseball here."

The waiter carried a container of grated cheese along with the pasta. The shallow bowls before them contained a tangle of pasta, a small portion of thick tomato sauce seasoned with garlic and oregano, and a sprig of basil on top. It didn't look anything like Laura's version of spaghetti, with more sauce than pasta. And there was no seafood.

"Do you think the cats we saw yesterday have cheese on their pasta?" She spooned half of the container on her portion.

Jake laughed at the idea. "I thought cats liked seafood. There's none in this stuff."

They tried to wind the strands around the tines of their forks using spoons, as they did in Seattle at Olive Garden. Laura said, "I don't think they cooked it enough."

"Yours at home is sure easier to eat, and it has food in it," Jake said as he chopped the strands into submission. "How do we pay? We really need more cash. Don't forget to get whatever you call it on Monday, you know, the money they're going to give you."

Jake got the waiter's attention. With a wave the man signaled he would be back. Ten minutes later he came to their table, surveyed the empty dishes, and scribbled markings on a piece of butcher paper. They both looked at the paper where there were words that looked like *coperto, pane,* and *aqua minerale,* along with the buffet and the pasta. The bill added up to twice what they expected.

Laura frowned and said, "Do you think they made a mistake? I don't understand these words."

"I don't know either. Just don't forget the money."

On Monday morning Laura's disappointment at an evening spent staring uncomprehendingly at Italian television was forgotten as she heard Jake mumble, "Good luck," before sinking back into deep sleep.

She followed crowds down the stairs to the Metro platform to begin her new job, her new and serious life. No more freelancing. The train arrived with a *whoosh* of hot air. People behind her propelled her into the car, so crowded with other commuters that even if she died she would have remained standing. The interior was as decorated with graffiti as the exterior. Even the windows were covered, making it hard to see the stops. Laura held on to a sticky pole near the door so she could be sure to get off at the right station. The train slowed, then halted with a jerk. It had arrived at Circo Massimo, the stop for her office. Other passengers, anxious to get out, pushed her from the car onto the platform. She climbed the stairs to street level and entered the building complex to begin her life as an expatriate.

After several hours of signing papers and discussion of pay and benefits, Laura's head was spinning with the overload of information. It was a relief to be escorted to her office deep in a warren of rooms with closed doors. She would share her space with two others who also worked in English. She was disheartened to find that she was the junior member of a team who collaborated with experts that prepared papers on fisheries, community forestry, and food production for meetings or publications. She didn't think that the work would be much different than what she had been doing in Seattle, although she had never worked in team. The most senior editor, Raj, was from India. He greeted her warmly with the rich, distinctive accent of his home country. The other, an Italian woman, Silvia, sounded as if she had taken language lessons in London. She eyed Laura with apparent distrust.

By the end of the day, Laura was exhausted but exhilarated with a combination of apprehension and excitement.

Laura was long gone when Jake woke up. He propped himself up against the creaky headboard. The heat and humidity reminded him of their honeymoon seven years ago, the single other time he traveled beyond the Pacific Northwest. Laura had wanted Hawaii and he was happy to agree. The tropical two weeks had made him think the rapturous sex would last forever. And it canceled out the memory of their embarrassing wedding ceremony. But Rome? For a year? Doubts crowded back into his mind. What will I really do for 363 more days?

Did I really find teaching so bad? Was there a hint that my job was on the line when they seemed so happy to agree to me asking for a year off? The pizzeria idea flitted back into his mind. Would they be able to save enough money to get the business going when they got back to Seattle?

By the time Jake entered the breakfast room, the last of the tourists had long since departed on their hurried rounds. The food and coffee were gone. Chairs were stacked, tables cleaned. The single sound came from a maid half-heartedly swishing a wet mop over the terrazzo floor. It would have to be Bar Termini again.

He stepped off the curb to cross the street and then jumped back as he heard a speeding truck bearing down on him. It missed him by inches. He waited some minutes for a gap before gaining the other side to open the door to the bar. A crush of patrons blocked the cash register. He wormed his way to the front, ordered cappuccino and a *cornetto*. He noticed the barista pouring shots of a clear liquor into several espressos. The waiting customers gulped the mixture in one go before they headed out the door.

With no goal in mind, Jake idly stirred sugar into his cappuccino. Returning to Trastevere, if he could find the church, was the only idea he could think of. The bits of colored glass, called tesserae, had captured his interest because of their architectural quality. Inspired by a visit to Seattle's Space Needle when he was in high school, he had briefly dreamed of becoming an architect.

The compositions in the church were worth another look, although the depiction of the Annunciation had disturbed him. The angel's wings were wrong: the one above his head waved in the air as if broken, with the other horizontally extended. Mary's body language made her appear to be recoiling. The portrayal had reminded him of his mother. She'd never been the same since his little sister died.

Jake was watching the chaotic traffic from the bus when he felt a light touch on his back pocket. He turned around to see a scruffy man pulling his hand away from his Levi's. He felt for his wallet. It was gone. He seized the man by his jacket and yelled at him to give it back. The man tried to wriggle out of the jacket but Jake held on and shoved the thief backward over an empty seat.

The man recognized defeat and pulled Jake's wallet from his front pocket. He held it out with a humble expression, his head down and his eyes pleading. Jake snatched it out of the dirty hands. He looked inside. Everything was still there. When the bus arrived at a stop, the pickpocket jumped off and ran at top speed. Jake shook with tension and anger as the bus came to a halt at his destination.

Another thirty minutes in the church, still distracted by the attempted theft, convinced Jake that he wouldn't easily gain understanding of the mosaics. The prospect of vacant hours ahead daunted him. He had agreed to do his best to help out with some shopping and cleaning like in Seattle where he'd pitched in while making sure that he didn't become an expert. But now he was a house-husband. One with no house.

He passed a bar with various kinds of sandwiches displayed in a glass case, ready for lunch. One tray held a selection made with carrots, eggplant, or spinach. He tried to imagine serving them to his middle-school students in Seattle. There would probably be a riot. He wanted a hamburger and fries. The server raised his eyebrows in question. Jake said, "Hamburger?" but the man shook his head. Jake then pointed to the ham and cheese and a beer.

Dried leaves fell from the plane trees as he walked back to the *pensione* in the late summer sun. Their brittle, yellow bodies crunched under his shoes. He entered a small bookshop. One shelf held dictionaries: Italian-German, Italian-French, Italian-Arabic, and Italian-English. He picked out the least expensive English edition, paid, and then continued his slow trudge.

When he reached his room he flipped open the English side of the book. It fell open at "Home: *casa, dimora, in patria.*" Next, he came upon "Foreigner: *forestiero* or *straniero.*" He set the dictionary aside and stared at the cracked plaster ceiling. That's what I've become, a *straniero*, a stranger. He drifted off.

Jake knocked the dictionary to the floor as he sat up with a start to see Laura. She looked happy. So happy she leaned down to give him a long kiss before she put her bag down and moved to the sink in the corner of the room to wash up. He watched as she ran a comb through her short blond hair, brushed her bangs off her forehead, and added a touch of lipstick. Still as good-looking as the evening he first met her; same petite figure and creamy complexion.

"What a day, spent most of the time filling out forms, but everyone's really nice and the work looks really interesting. A bit like Boeing or what I was doing freelancing, but the atmosphere is so different."

"Did you get any money? What about finding a place to stay?"

"Yes, they gave me the money and I found a flyer called *Wanted in Rome* with some ads. We can look at them at dinner. Do you want to hear about the work? I'll be helping a more senior person."

"Let's find somewhere to get a drink and then you can tell me."

To pass the time until restaurants opened, they found an *enoteca* nearby and proceeded to work their way through the cheapest bottle on the list. Laura slowly drank a glass between giving him a description of her office and the people she had met. When she ran out of stories, she asked, "So, how was your day?"

"It was lovely, just thrilling."

Jake's sarcasm alarmed her, and when she looked at him she saw his head was thrown back, eyes squinting and mouth turned down.

"What happened?"

"Forget it."

Laura looked at the apartment ads in the flyer to break the tension. She pointed out several prospects and said she'd call the agent from her office in the morning. Jake poured himself another glass.

"I'm sure a rental agent will find something good. I know you'll love our life here when we have a place to live and your paints show up. You wanted a change as well."

"Yeah, but I'm not sure if I wanted this much."

Jake tried what the barista called *caffè corretto*, espresso laced with a shot of *grappa*, the drink he saw other men down in a single swallow the previous day. The caffeine and alcohol gave him a jolt of energy making him pace restlessly back in the room waiting for Laura to call about apartments. She called an hour later with the name of an agent who spoke English and who would show him several the following day.

He had the whole day, again, to do something. But what? He decided on the historic center, the *centro storico*, where they had wandered on Saturday. Alone, with no one to share the excitement the wonders had instilled earlier, he was reminded of his former architectural aspiration and the high school counselor who told him he could be anything he wanted to be even if he wasn't good at math. If he could find the inspiration to begin painting once more, he could at least capture some of the sights to remember their time here.

When his feet began to hurt, he found a refuge in an ancient church near the Forum dedicated to a couple of saints he'd never heard of: Cosma and Damiano. Behind the altar, a monumental mosaic portrait of Christ floated motionless in the luminous void. Enormous dark eyes stared at Jake. Delicate sandals tied with bows protected His feet resting on orange and blue clouds. The otherworldly glass squares glowed as Jake tilted his head this way and that to catch the reflective light. He tried to imagine the atmosphere in the sixth century, with candles and smoky incense.

But Christ's stare discomforted him. He lost the stare-down and left the church to find a bar. He sat outdoors, watching the traffic and the people crowding the sidewalks. So many pretty girls all laughing, talking, and sweeping back their long hair, busy with their lives. None glanced his way.

After a second, and then a third beer, he returned to their room. He listened to country songs on his phone. When the plaintive music about lost love became tiresome, he turned on the small television to wait for Laura.

A smartly dressed woman driving a battered old Fiat Cinquecento showed up at the *pensione*. Jake could hardly keep from laughing at the tiny car, smaller than the old VW Bug he owned years ago. She introduced herself as Janice and said she was originally from London but had lived in Rome for donkey's years. She gave him a wide smile and said, "You'll love it here." Jake wondered what a donkey's year was but decided not to encourage the woman's inane remarks.

When they arrived at the first apartment he was disheartened to see a building where small laundry racks extended from windows over the street. The racks were festooned with large-size bras and underpants alongside men's tiny briefs. The apartment itself looked like a disaster zone, with torn-up furniture and sagging pull-down shutters. And it was about the size of Janice's car.

The second unit was better, or at least the *signorina* who showed him around encouraged him to believe. Around Laura's age, she was dressed in a white pantsuit with gold on her wrists, ears, and neck. Attractively flamboyant, she waved her cigarette, pointing to the various features in the apartment. She looked like the Italian women in old movies they watched before leaving Seattle: lots of dark hair, big breasts, sexy, emotional, and maybe available. He momentarily visualized her naked.

She held his eyes during her sales pitch. He responded to her heavily accented English by saying, "I have another apartment to look at." She looked disappointed so he cushioned his statement. "Nice place." But when he added that he wanted to bring his wife to take a look, the woman's smile disappeared for good.

The third apartment, on the first floor of a building, faced a gloomy, laundry-draped courtyard enclosed by two other identical buildings. He told Janice there was no way he'd live there.

When he recounted the results of his search to Laura, he left out the description of the *signorina* in the pantsuit. "Found one that reminds me of my sophomore year at university – small but okay for a while. The other two places were disasters."

"I guess we can check out the one you thought was all right. Wish I knew what other people found."

They set off in the evening rush hour, taking two buses since the agent said they would have to go without her because another client had called to sign a deal. Jake watched as Laura looked at the landlady, who blew puffs of cigarette smoke from her mouth and nose as she showed her around. Laura inspected the balcony with the gas water heater taking up most of the space, the bathroom so small there was barely room for the shower, the worn tile floors throughout the apartment, and the minuscule, poorly-fitted kitchen.

"No," Laura said. They offered a *grazie* and left. "I'm not living in a hole like that, and did you see that woman? All the jewelry and the smoke making the whole apartment stink. And the dyed black hair. Oh, God, what are we going to do?" She began to chew on her hangnail, one that never really went away. Thoughts of her friends' designer kitchens danced in her head.

"It's NOT dyed."

"What? You mean her hair? How on earth do you know that? And it looked dyed to me."

"I'm sorry – that was dumb. Of course I don't know. It's just that you're attacking her. We need to find a place to live. I don't care what she looked like. What do you expect *me* to do, knock on doors, or press those buttons at the entrance to buildings?"

Laura said, "I'll ask at the office again tomorrow. Honey, give things a chance, will you? We just got here a couple of days ago. I'm sure we'll be okay after we get settled."

Jake could hear an element of concern in her voice. He decided not to pursue the matter in case they had a real argument, which always reminded him of his parents screaming at him or each other. He pulled an antacid out of his toilet kit.

A week later Laura had news. "We're invited to pizza tomorrow with Doug, my new boss, and the people I work with, and finally I found an ad on the office bulletin board for an apartment that looks good. I called the owner and she wants to show the place to us now.

The owner, a stocky, middle-aged woman with thinning, bright orange hennaed hair, met them in the marble-floored lobby filled with tired potted plants to escort Jake and Laura to her apartment for a look around. They saw the rooms were tidy and serviceable, with a living room furnished with a sofa, overstuffed chair, desk, and a dining table with six chairs. An amateurish picture of the Appia Antica hung over the sofa. A television sat on a small table. Although the kitchen wasn't much bigger than the other apartments they'd considered, it looked clean and functional. No dishwasher though. The bedroom had an *armadio*, or armoire as Laura called it. The second bedroom, furnished with a hide-a-bed, could be made into an office or accommodate a guest or two. The woman pointed out the balcony, furnished with a small table and two chairs. Laura saw the space was big enough to enjoy evening meals, a real plus.

Jake walked to the desk. The woman followed him sensing what he was thinking. "Good for computer. Internet available. Other Americans like."

Laura looked at Jake briefly before saying, "We'll think a bit and call you tomorrow."

They walked around the neighborhood looking for a place to eat while they considered what to do. The discussion of pros and cons continued over wine and *fettuccine con scampi* in a neighborhood trattoria. By the time they finished the last shrimp on their plates, Jake said, "Let's do it. I don't want to look any further." Laura looked into her empty plate. Her dream of living in an ancient villa with painted ceilings and antique furniture disappeared. At least for now. The idea of staying on had already implanted itself in the back of her mind.

At Piramide station they left the Metro to join crowds of people hurrying to get to their commuter trains or to the buses and trams waiting in the piazza in front of the station. It was already dark and beginning to drizzle, the moisture mixing with auto and bus exhaust to make a soup of pollutants in the heavy air. They saw a massive old brick gateway standing alone in the center of a traffic circle where five roads came together. Traffic was at a standstill. Horns blared. The siren of an ambulance trying to squeeze around the gate and through the mess assaulted their ears with a yodel sounding like *boota loota loo, boota loota loo*.

Jake spotted a triangular shape across four lanes of one road. They aimed for the indistinct shape, managing to squeeze through the stalled cars to reach the other side of the road. Instead of a restaurant, they found themselves in front of a dirty marble pyramid with plants growing out of cracks between the eroded blocks. Jake stopped to inspect the strange sight looming over them.

Laura leaned over the railing to see a few scrawny cats lurking in the undergrowth around the base, many feet below ground. "Do you think we could get a cat? There are loads of strays dozing around all the old monuments. I could feed it spaghetti."

"Fine with me, but remember you'll have to get rid of it when we leave."

They crossed the next road, dodging cars and crowded buses and then, between two rows of trees lining a wide boulevard, they picked out the terrace of a restaurant with a sign: Taverna Cestia. The lights were on. Despite the fine rain people were sitting outside under awnings, smoking, talking, and drinking wine.

"This must be it," Laura said when she saw a table with six people and two empty chairs, one at each end. They threaded through the other tables to reach their dinner companions.

Doug stood up. "I'd like to introduce you to Helena." Laura extended her hand to an attractive woman wearing a beige cashmere sweater and slacks, and chestnut-colored high-heeled boots. She wore gold jewelry, two bracelets, earrings, and a ring with a good-sized diamond. Raj introduced his wife, Chandra, similarly well-dressed but with more flashy jewels. Silvia, another co-worker, had invited Giorgio, who introduced himself with a forceful handshake and a cloud of cigarette smoke. Laura and Jake sat apart as the vacant seats demanded.

The menu was written by hand in illegible Italian, but their dining companions offered advice. If they didn't want the usual Friday night pizza, they might try a grilled cheese dish called *scamorza alla griglia*. *Risotto ai funghi porcini* was also an excellent choice because mushrooms were in season. For greens, they were all having *insalata di rughetta* which Helena explained was arugula. Jake decided to stick with *pizza margarita*.

"I think I'll just try the spaghetti with *ragù* sauce and the salad. Sorry we're a bit late. Jake tried to show me those old ruins across the street, but what I'm really interested in is the food."

"Well, we're fascinated with the history here," Helena said. "It's what makes Rome *our* Rome. And if you're talking about the pyramid, it was built by someone called Gaius Cestia around 12 B.C."

Embarrassed, Laura squirmed.

Helena decided to take pity on Doug's new recruit. "Are you a food writer?"

"I'm thinking about writing my own blog about life here as soon as I can get organized. And when I learn more I could add about the food."

A waiter put bottles of white and red wine, along with still and fizzy water on the table. The bubbly kind was *"con gas,"* Laura recalled one of her Seattle friends telling her, using the term to show she knew all about how to order water in Rome. When the waiter returned with baskets of hot flatbread perfumed with resinous rosemary and olive oil, they ordered their main courses.

The talk grew even more animated as they competed with other diners to make themselves heard above the noise. But Jake, always reserved, inspected the contents of his wineglass as if he expected the liquid to carry on the conversation for him.

Questions were beamed Laura's way: "Do you like living in Rome?" "Have you found an apartment?" "Do you have children?"

Raj interrupted. "Well, if you haven't already found out, you'll find that living in Rome is either a one or two, or a nine or ten. Not much in between. And some days it's both."

"Oh, I'm sure it will be on the high end of the scale." Laura tried to smile as she responded, but she was taken aback at this piece of news.

"So what are you going to do while your wife is working?" Raj turned toward Jake to look at him directly. The others ceased talking.

Jake looked pleased to be included. "Uh, well...I'm not actually sure although I've already seen some great subjects to paint. I'm an artist."

Laura noted that he didn't mention he worked as a school teacher.

"What kind of artist?" Raj pressed.

"I usually do abstract scenes, but the old buildings here are compelling." Jake poured himself more wine to avoid any further interchange. Laura understood that he did not want to reveal he was uncertain of his talent, and his painting had been limited to a few weekends when there wasn't much else to do.

Raj turned back to Laura. "Nice view from the office terrace, don't you think? I never get tired of looking at the sight."

"It's heavenly. I could look at the scene for hours." Her mind's eye retrieved the umbrella pines, cypress trees and buildings all floating in the gauzy air, but her actual eye watched Jake twist his wedding ring. When the waiter served her meal her lips smiled at the taste of the meaty *ragù* on her own plate, so much better than the meatballs she cooked in Seattle. The aroma of Helena's selection of grilled cheese and risotto with bosky-smelling mushrooms came her way to mix with the perfumed richness of her own meal. She thought about making some notes. And she thought about Raj's remark and Jake's discomfort. Maybe his rural background made it difficult to relax. She convinced herself that he would soon adjust.

After they said their goodbyes and headed back to the *pensione,* she said, "I loved the evening. All the wonderful food and wine and interesting people who can talk about Rome."

"Pizza was really thin. I like it thicker. But your friends are okay, I guess."

The rain had stopped earlier and a moon had risen above the trees. Laura watched the cool shadows bring the old gate and hard angles of the pyramid into sharp relief.

OCTOBER

ON A BRIGHT Saturday morning Laura and Jake packed their suitcases, paid the peevish owner of the *pensione* and left for their new home. Their new landlady gave Jake a brief handshake and handed Laura two contracts, both in Italian: One for a low legal amount and the other for the remaining larger amount, the "foreigner fee." Although Laura could not read either of the documents, she signed. No point in worrying now. But Jake's humiliated expression at being ignored, hands in pockets and head drooping, made her uncomfortable.

They unpacked their suitcases before moving to the balcony to sit on the two rickety metal chairs. Laura saw white marble heads beyond the rooftops of the neighboring buildings.

"Let's walk over there." She pointed to the heads. "I think those are part of a big church that Raj talked about the first time we had coffee on the office terrace. He said it was called a basilica. San Giovanni or something. We can get food for lunch and dinner on the way back."

"Good idea." Jake stood up, ready to go.

They set off, peering in shop windows along the way. Displays of stylish bathroom fittings competed with offerings of shoes, books, and lacy underwear. Bars, a pharmacy, a barber, drycleaner, pizza to go, and a few small trattorias were tucked in between the shops.

Laura paused in front of a window filled with a pleased-looking plastic stork, cribs, strollers, and tiny dresses and suits in the window. She thought that after this year she'd give it another try even if Jake didn't want her to. Wherever they were living.

They joined throngs of tourists and worshippers on the immense, grass-covered piazza in front of the basilica San Giovanni in Laterano. Majestic statues of Christ and Fathers of the Church scowled down on the sinners below.

The interior, dim with dust motes dancing in the shafts of light that streamed from high windows and chandeliers to illuminate frescoes, mosaics, more gigantic statues, and reliquaries, was filled with the noise of tourists walking and talking. The elaborate coffered ceiling competed for attention with the floor set with curling, colored marble pieces. It was dizzying and far more than Laura could absorb.

"I heard about a market near here selling new and used clothing really cheap, or so they told me at the office. How about I meet you in an hour at the obelisk we saw on the way in?" She showed Jake the picture of the monument in their guidebook.

She followed a mob of people through the remains of the Aurelian Wall and into Via Sannio to find herself transported to yet another country. An old gypsy wearing a black head scarf and dirty black dress hunched on the sidewalk, a basket holding a few coins in front of her. A listless baby lay in her lap. The wizened crone muttered and held out her hand in supplication. Laura hurried by with a shudder, concerned that the baby was drugged. Didn't Italy have any child protective services?

Near the market entrance a crowd milled around vendors selling cut-rate goods out of delivery vans. Crates and boxes were stacked in the street and on the sidewalk. Laura dove into the market, a covered area filled with stalls where more vendors sold underwear, fancy stockings, leather jackets, and shoes. Sunlight slanted through the dusty air. At the back, where the ruins of the adjacent ancient city wall abutted the market, beat-up trestle tables were laden with used clothing heaped in disarray. The jumble was presided over by swarthy men and women who stood on the tables shouting out the bargains.

Laura was mesmerized, the vendors capturing her attention as the snake charmer captures that of the cobra. She picked over the cashmere sweaters, perfect for winter. A few even looked new. She bought one for Jake. Then she found a pair of perfect party shoes with platform soles and stiletto heels, and at the next stall, a stylish pair for walking. Nearby, patterned hosiery was displayed on legs dangling from a wire strung above as if they were a chorus line. She bought four pairs. No more editing in pajamas like in Seattle.

When Laura glanced at her watch she realized that an hour had long passed. She hurried back to the church and on to the obelisk where a few tourists with guidebooks in hand were puzzling over the hieroglyphics. No Jake. She waited fifteen minutes before returning to the church. The crowds were now too thick to pick him out, even though he was tall and wore blue oxford cloth shirt, khakis, and sport shoes in contrast to other tourists in torn jeans and tee shirts.

She walked back to the apartment, assuming he would be there. Where else could he be? She juggled her bags of bargains with the key to open their apartment. Empty. She tried his cell phone but there was no answer. She left a message.

There was nothing to do but assume he'd show up soon. She sat on the sofa, riffling through her nearly empty journal with its cover depicting ruins. It was a gift from high school friends at a lunch at the Space Needle shortly before her departure.

She thought back to the lunch. A year in Rome working for the United Nations as an editor, what an opportunity! But the happy talk and unwanted advice about crazy traffic, good shopping, and dirty streets was mixed with nosiness about her marriage. Most of her friends were busy commuting to Amazon or Microsoft, or to a tech startup with long hours and low salaries but with the hope of becoming multi-millionaires. A couple of them juggled children into their schedules. Laura had attended their baby showers with the silly games and gifts in pink or blue. Several other friends were in no hurry to have a family, either planning to wait or skip the whole idea entirely with their husbands having a vasectomy.

One friend was divorced and unhappy. Laura had listened to her laments over several years but another two had shed their husbands and appeared to enjoy their lives, happy to have no permanent commitments.

Throughout the lunch party Laura detected disdain mixed with effusive comments about her move. She saw their words to be a summation of their view of her life: left out of the tech world, she couldn't make it in Seattle, and Jake was a failure settling for a low-paying teaching job, social studies and art, not even a serious subject like math.

One friend asked, "What's hubby going to do?"

"Paint."

Even though they all said how interesting that would be, Laura sensed that they were thinking: *I wouldn't let my husband on the loose in Rome for a year.* When they parted, they assured her that life would be fabulous and would make them envious when she blogged about her *dolce vita.* If any of them was ever coming to Rome after their kitchen remodel got finished, or they made partner, or school was out, they would be sure to let her know so they could meet up. Laura knew that they would never come.

Her reverie was interrupted by the sound of their door opening and closing. Jake looked pleased, not at all what she expected. Even more unusual, he smelled of cigarette smoke.

"I thought we were going to meet. I called but you didn't answer. I'm sorry I was late. Anyway, I got you a sweater."

Jake held the sweater up to his chest to check the size before thanking her and saying that he hadn't heard the phone or seen her text. It was as if his mind was far away.

They ate a couple of sandwiches at the local bar before braving the grocery store. After the staples went into their cart they moved to the pasta section. Laura selected a package of spaghetti, one of *farfalle* that looked like butterflies, and one that resembled little ears, *orecchiette.* She was reminded of the last time she cooked pasta, spaghetti and meatballs. The magic effect of pasta had transported them into the sun.

Her mood darkened when she inadvertently pushed the cart into the aisle where baby food was shelved. Boxes of tiny pasta were lined up next to the usual jars of pureed vegetables and meat. Besides pictures of lamb and chicken, other containers evidently held trout, rabbit and horse. She tried to imagine feeding her child horsemeat. She recalled that Jake said he'd had a beloved old mare named Dolly when he was a kid. Best not to bring the pictures to his attention.

The produce department was also full of unfamiliar foods. Laura thought about the bloggers who wrote about *rapini, fichi d'India, and nespole.* She would try whatever they were soon but she stuck with grapes, tomatoes, and broccoli, not wanting to put Jake off with things he would not eat. "This is sure better than Seattle."

"Yeah."

"Can't you say anything else?" She knew she sounded snappish but couldn't stop herself.

"Sorry, but I'm worried I'm going to be bored out of my mind. A whole year of pizza parties and grocery stores where I can't figure out what the stuff is."

Laura gave him a peck on the cheek and said, "Just remember, you said it would be amazing."

After they put the food away in the apartment they moved to the balcony with glasses of wine, the bottle a gift from their new landlady. The air remained warm although the sun was beginning to set, washing the neighboring apartment windows with golden light and brightening the stucco facades. Flocks of swifts swirled above the buildings before settling down as night fell.

Laura put down her glass. "Tell me about what you saw in the church." She didn't remark on his smoky odor.

"I followed a tour group with an English-speaking guide. Lots to see and I want to go back."

Laura looked at the skyline, the birds, and the distant statues on the church while she contemplated his evasive answer.

The news on the television came on at eight. Laura curled up on the sofa to watch, not that she could understand anything. Jake, who had showered, sat by her side. One segment showed pictures of handsome men wearing dark uniforms with red trim and silver braid, gloves, peaked hats, and leather belts with a strap across their chests. The men were standing behind a long table laden with small sculptures and broken pottery. Next, a picture of several scruffy types with lines drawn between the photos appeared on the screen.

"Looks like some sort of a gang. But what do you think all those pieces of junk are? Love the uniforms the police are wearing."

Instead of answering, Jake began kissing her mouth and fondling her breasts. She relaxed and responded eagerly, the first time she felt wanted since they had arrived in Rome. The worries of the day were left behind. Afterward, they nested in bed together like spoons, like they did in the first years of their love affair and marriage when energetic sex at six in the morning could be counted on. Laura was content and drowsy with pleasure. Everything will be fine, she convinced herself.

Jake could not sleep after their love making. His mind clicked into gear to turn over the events of the day. He sat up in his usual posture of hands behind his head to review his response to Laura's question about his late appearance. He assured himself he had nothing to feel guilty about and put the small prick to his conscience aside to relive his encounter.

After he and Laura had separated in San Giovanni, he poked around until he came to a kiosk where visitors could buy postcards and books about the church and Rome. He bought a booklet describing the church's architecture and art. He paid the fee to enter the cloister to take a break and peruse his purchase for recommendations on the most important treasures.

A woman strolled by reading the same booklet, also in English. She paused to regard him and his book.

"Enjoying your visit?"

"Yes, very much. But there's lots to learn." He pointed to a page describing the mosaics and asked if she knew anything about them.

She moved closer, saying, "Do you have a special interest?"

"I'm an artist. First time I've ever seen any of these except for pictures."

"Let me see."

They stood side by side next to the low wall surrounding the cloister garden while she looked more closely at the information he had pointed out. He felt her nearness, the warmth of her body, and the smell of a musky perfume.

"Do you want a cigarette?" She had an alluring voice.

"Sorry, haven't smoked for years."

She shook one from a pack of Dunhills for herself.

"Here, let me."

She smiled while handing him her gold lighter, as though she normally expected such service. After she drew in the smoke they stood in silence, each looking across the cloister with its grass and ancient well in the center.

Jake tried to study her profile without being obvious. Well-groomed, maybe even wealthy. Probably nearing forty, blonde with a few black roots, and beginning to show some extra padding. Cheeks a bit pouchy. Shoes and handbag like the designer stuff he saw on his walks. She wore a short, black skirt and a tight, black sweater decorated with sequins.

"Perhaps we should take a tour of the best ones in Rome." She exhaled and the smoke softly drifted around their heads.

"Ones?"

"Mosaics."

Before he had a chance to respond further she added, "Be at Santa Sabina on the Aventine Hill on Tuesday at eleven." She flashed an inviting smile before flicking her cigarette onto the cloister grass near a no smoking sign and walking away.

The languid smoke carried the scent of her perfume.

Her feeling of contentment remained when Laura awoke at sunrise on Sunday longing for coffee. Still in her pajamas and slippers, she went to the kitchen to get out the package of Lavazza and find a coffeemaker. She pulled out the pots and pans, the dishes and glasses, trying to see something familiar. On the highest shelf she found a two-part contraption with a filter on top and a little hole on the bottom.

"Jake, I need help. There's no coffeemaker but I found this thing. It says Moka on the side. Come and help, please."

Jake, in his briefs and only half awake, joined her to inspect the Moka. "Looks like you stick water and coffee in, but I'll be damned if I know how the thing works." He saw the little hole. "Must be for the safety valve. Maybe you just fill up the bottom with water and put coffee in the top where there's the filter. I'll try it."

"I'm standing back because it reminds me of my mother's pressure cooker. I always expected the chicken would end up on the ceiling instead of my dinner plate."

"Let me fool with it. I'll figure it out and bring you coffee in bed for our first Sunday here."

Laura crawled back into bed. She could hear him puttering around followed by the sound of steam. The rich aroma accompanied his footsteps. Jake climbed back in bed with two cups of coffee.

"Mmmmm, thanks. For last night, and for Rome, too."

"Let's do something. How about a walk in the park at the Villa Borghese?"

"I'd love it. Love you too."

Jake looked at the silt in the bottom of his cup.

On Monday, Jake found a video in Italian showing how to use their espresso maker properly. Afterward, he walked to the local *giornalaio* to get a paper. He sat at their table, coffee cup in hand and dictionary at the side, slowly translating a few short articles about art exhibits and auto accidents.

The reviews reminded him of mosaics, which reminded him of the woman he met and his date to meet again. Best to find Santa Sabina today so he didn't get lost and miss his meeting the next day. If he went to the meeting. He poured another cup of coffee and contemplated the situation. Surely there was no harm in meeting someone who would show him things he was interested in. Laura was probably eating lunch with Raj or her boss. Who knew what was going on in her office, anyway?

He found the church on his map, not far from Laura's office. The bus took him near her office building where he quickly crossed the main avenue away from the buildings to walk up the Aventine Hill. He was looking at his watch to check his timing when a voice startled him.

"Hi. I think we met earlier. Aren't you Laura's husband?"

Jake halted in front of a man who stood outside the gate to the entrance of an apartment building, his dog straining on the leash, eager for its morning walk. He could feel his heart beginning to pound as he realized it was Giorgio from the pizza get-together. Not wanting to be seen lurking in the area, Jake said, "No, don't know anyone named Laura."

"Sorry, must have made a mistake. You look like someone I recently met." Giorgio's curious expression told Jake that he didn't believe him.

Jake wasn't sure why he didn't want to admit who he was. He had as much right as anyone to be there and nothing else to do but sightsee anyway. It was none of Laura's business where he walked. He checked his watch. It didn't take much time to get to the area. The fall morning was cool with a few clouds marbling the sky. Perfect weather to meet someone who might make his stay unforgettable.

He walked the winding, cobbled streets past several churches before entering a park set with orange trees and cypresses overlooking the Tiber and Saint Peter's. The view, which included several pairs of entwining lovers, made him happy. A whole year to do what he wanted as long as he made a show of helping out from time to time. He watched as an old man filled a plastic water bottle from a fountain outside the park. He poured it on the windshield of a battered car before attempting to remove the grime. One thing for sure, he needed a car.

The doors of Santa Sabina were open in welcome. But Jake soon saw that the church had few mosaics in its columned nave.

When Jake saw the rain clouds on Tuesday, he toyed with the idea of staying in the apartment instead of slogging up to the church. The meeting wasn't as compelling as before, but he convinced himself that the woman was looking forward to it. Worried that he might run into one of the few people he knew again, he took a circuitous route to the church, walking down the far side of the Circus Maximus. He ran up the hill but still arrived ten minutes late. The only sound in the church came from his breath. Not another soul in sight. He returned to the covered entry to wait. A priest who acknowledged his existence the day before gave another curt bob of his head as he walked by. After he passed by several more times on his duties, the glances became stares. On his last pass, the man in his black robe stopped and asked him in Italian if he needed help. Not quite sure of what he said, Jake hesitated. The priest switched to English.

Jake responded, "I'm waiting to meet a woman. A friend."

The priest disappeared back into the church shaking his head.

Jake waited an hour before he retraced his steps down the hill. He returned to the church the following day and again on the following Tuesday. Giving up on the church, he haunted the cloister at San Giovanni, nervously picking at the bits of colored glass making up the design on the twisted pillars supporting the roofed walkway surrounding the garden.

He reverted to a low mood as the days passed, watching television all night and sleeping until noon. In the afternoons he continued to walk in his own neighborhood and in the *centro*. He saw the crowds all busy with their lives. No one else seemed to be lonely. It was as if he was in a bubble that only dissipated when Laura returned to tell him about her work. And now that she had started bringing work home and talking about setting up a blog, his time with her was even further reduced except for their weekends looking around Rome. The air shipment with his paints hadn't arrived and he was at a loss, a situation he had never encountered.

One day he passed a small sign advertising Italian and English lessons and climbed the two flights to find the office. The man at the desk said he could get a small fee if he would work one-on-one with a student who needed to learn English to pass his university exams. Despite not wanting to teach, Jake agreed and was assigned a pimply faced youth as disinterested in lessons as his younger charges in Seattle. They arranged to meet once a week. "I found a student to tutor," he told Laura.

"Why don't you sign up to teach at one of those schools in *Wanted in Rome* instead? They always need teachers and I'm sure they would pay better. We don't have as much money as I thought we would."

"I thought you'd be happy to know I had a kid to tutor. I'm done with classrooms. At least for this year."

"You can paint when our stuff arrives. Maybe sell some pictures. That would be fun."

"If it arrives. I thought it would be here before us. And I don't know if I'm good enough."

"You are as good as a lot of the pictures I see around."

"Thanks a lot."

"I didn't mean anything. The ones I've seen are really, really good. It's just you haven't done anything for so long I don't know what your style would be now."

Laura got out her Kindle to close the uncomfortable conversation but couldn't concentrate on a new memoir about living in Sicily.

Jake's meetings with the student were infrequent, neither party having any enthusiasm. But he found he was beginning to understand much of the TV and the newspapers. He practiced on the barista near the apartment and local vendors, although the niceties of pronouns and the subjunctive remained elusive.

Jake came back to the cloister at San Giovanni several more times, still burning over the woman's apparent rejection although he wasn't sure why he cared. Three weeks after their first meeting he found her loitering in the same location, again reading.

He hesitated to approach but decided he had nothing to lose.

"Hello, again," he said, trying to disguise his ire.

"You were late. I don't wait for people."

"Only ten minutes. Took longer than I thought in the rain. I didn't think Italians were very punctual anyway."

"You should have left earlier."

Jake could not think of a plausible rebuttal. He didn't want to tell her he took a longer route to avoid running into anyone he knew. She didn't say anything more but buried her head in the booklet, which Jake could now see was just a ploy. He began to walk away, despite knowing he wouldn't reject her if she persisted.

She looked up and said, "What do you really want?"

Jake turned back while thinking about what he wanted. He tried, "To see Rome."

She smiled and shook her head. "Come now, let's be real. Do you want to be a tourist, or are you wanting something more interesting?"

Surprised that she seized the upper hand so quickly, he stuttered that he didn't have much to do while his wife worked. It was as if she was casting a net over his emotions and pulling them toward her. He would hate to play poker with her.

"Where does she work?"

"Her name's Laura and she has a one-year contract as an editor with the United Nations."

"Does she have a commissary card?"

"Uh, yes," he said, thinking about the occasional frozen food she toted home.

The woman took his arm. "Let's walk outside."

Her possessiveness both suffocated and flattered Jake.

They came to a trattoria on a street with the Colosseum peeking out at the far end. "You can buy me lunch here."

Jake steered her to a table at the back where he faced away from the entrance. There were no other patrons. The owner scooted up. Air kisses were exchanged.

"*Ciao, Stella!*"

She responded in Italian before switching to English to order a bottle of red wine and *penne alla vodka* for the first course.

Jake now knew her name. One step forward in this interesting situation. "Stella, a nice name."

Despite the no-smoking signs, she lit a cigarette without offering him one and laughed.

"So, you want to know more, don't you?"

"Well, yeah." Not wanting to appear overly interested, he surveyed the restaurant. The walls were covered with paintings and old photos of presumably famous people. He saw a black and white photo of a man in Roman dress and woman with heavy eye makeup looking like an Egyptian. He had a vague memory of some old movie called *Cleopatra.* Surely the stars didn't eat in this place. He looked at the canvasses and saw they were as amateurish as some of his. Doubts that he could really sell any killed his desire to pick up his brushes when the air shipment arrived.

The wine arrived and she poured instead of waiting for him. "I'm needing help with a project. I have friends who are interested in art, like you. Maybe we could get together and look around before you decide if you want to help us."

"Look around?"

"Yes, they're interested in mosaics and frescoes and other old pieces, like you. I think you would enjoy their company. Let's meet here for lunch next week and I'll introduce you."

On the crisp fall day the *penne alla vodka* with creamy tomato sauce with a faint hint of alcohol invited him to eat. The owner poured more wine before bringing him the *secondo,* a huge *bistecca alla Fiorentina,* the meat taking up the entire plate. Jake watched Stella as she lit another cigarette and toyed with her selection, a veal chop. She wasn't bad-looking for her age and seemed a lot more sophisticated than Laura.

Stella's cell phone rang. She took a quick glance at the incoming number before answering, "*Pronto.*"

Jake heard her end of the exchange, although she spoke in a low voice and faced away from him. But even with his new Italian vocabulary, the words didn't sound Italian. They must be a dialect, which he'd learned could still be found in isolated rural areas or used by a few Romans.

Stella turned back to him. "Everything is arranged for next week. We'll meet here, same time."

"Good. But I'd rather you didn't contact me." He said it before remembering he hadn't given her his address or cell phone number, anyway.

She ordered a couple of espressos and the bill. The owner returned with a tray carrying the coffee and bottles of liqueurs, which Stella told him were called *digestivi*, for the digestion following a large meal. She poured some evil-looking brown liquid into a glass and handed it to Jake along with the bill. "*Amaro* means 'bitter.'"

Jake checked the bill as he tried to avoid gagging on the pungent drink. Even through the fog in his head from too much food and alcohol, he understood the total, about what he had in his wallet. He didn't want to use his American credit card for fear Laura would ask about the expenditure when she saw the statement. He counted out the last of his cash, not enough to include a tip.

He saw Stella flash a smile at the owner before she said to Jake, "*Ci vediamo.*"

Jake understood that meant "see you later." He didn't, however, yet know how to reply in Italian, "I can hardly wait."

Stupefied by the heavy lunch, he vegetated in front of the TV in the apartment until Laura came home.

"How did your day go? I've got an interesting new project." Laura was all smiles and excitement as she told him about the editing she was doing to help Raj.

"Italian lessons going good. I'm learning and the kid, Mauro, took me to lunch."

"Was the food good? What did you eat? I can make some notes. And I'd like to see the textbook. Maybe I can learn in the evenings. You'll help me, I hope. We'll practice together."

"Damn, I forgot to bring it. I'll get it tomorrow. Hon, I need some money and there's none in the drawer. The kid is a slow learner and his parents haven't paid me yet. I'm running short – got a little until you get paid?" Humiliation coming from having to ask for money made him look away from her as he asked.

Laura handed over some euros from her wallet before turning to the laptop to work on a blog post she'd been trying to write with no success. Describing her new life diplomatically wasn't all that easy and doling out money to Jake wasn't a scene she wanted to describe.

The rest of the week Jake reluctantly did household chores, not that he could meet Laura's exacting standards for dusting and drying the glasses to remove spots from the rock-hard water, or cleaning the cold terrazzo floors, so different from the yielding water and carpeting in their Seattle house.

He kept up the pretense of tutoring in between the domestic chores when he was either sunk in front of the television or walking in the *centro* among the brooding Renaissance buildings and ancient ruins so resistant to time. His mind wandered as did his thoughts, alternating between resentment at Laura for dragging him here and hungering for another meeting with the mysterious Stella. The scent of her perfume on the soft wisps of cigarette smoke when they first met had now metamorphosed in his mind to a message: *Here is an opportunity you've never had before.* A dangerous thought, but interesting all the same. After all, Laura said she wanted him to enjoy himself in what he saw as a sphinx-like city where nothing was ever quite clear; a city that exuded temptations to experience all that was on offer.

When Jake arrived early at the trattoria the following week, a sign saying *chiuso*, closed, for the weekly *turno*, day off, hung in the window. He was sure the sign hadn't been there the previous week but nevertheless stood by the front door trying to appear unconcerned. A half-hour passed before a black Lancia pulled up. Stella emerged, draped in a mink coat. His anticipation began to rise again until he saw two men in the car, one in the driver's seat and the other a passenger. Stella waved them over to meet him. They looked like loggers from his hometown with muscled arms and protruding guts. One of them had a broken nose; the other, an ominous scar running from below his left eye to his chin. They each wore a *corno* hung on a gold chain. The coral horn nestled in graying chest hair visible above the necks of their cheap-looking sweaters. Their shoes were unlike any Jake had seen: yellowish cracked patent leather, narrow with pointed toes and thick heels.

"This is Marco," said Stella, pointing to one of them, "and this is Gianni." She waved at the other one. They each flashed an insincere smile.

"Let's have lunch. I know a good restaurant down at Fiumicino." Stella's suggestion sounded like an order. Jake climbed in the back seat next to her. Gianni rode shotgun. Marco slid into the driver's seat and pulled away from the curb in a screech of tires. They wound their way through the traffic maze until they reached the Via della Magliana, where Marco floored it as if the cops were on their tail. They followed the Tiber toward the airport and the sea, Jake marveling at his new adventure as they overtook fast-moving taxis taking tired tourists to their outbound flights. The journey was nothing like his ignominious arrival nearly two months earlier. He grinned.

The car threw a spray of gravel as it skidded into the parking lot of a restaurant set alongside the quay lined with fishing boats. Marco slammed on the brakes so hard it made their heads snap forward and back. Jake wanted to rub his neck but decided not to.

He lost his appetite when he saw the prices on the menu, all seafood and enormously expensive. Stella laughed at his expression and said, "Don't worry. I'll pay this time."

They were seated in a closed-off smoking section of the restaurant. The conversation was entirely in Italian sprinkled with the foreign-sounding words. Jake understood enough to get a vague idea of their meaning. He listened closely, picking up the words for "marble" and "fresco." He also thought he heard the name of a town he had seen on a map, Viterbo. The two men slurped their oysters, picked at the prawns, and waited impatiently while the waiter deboned a large fish Stella had selected from the refrigerated display case earlier. Jake tried to look as if he regularly dined on such lavish lunches.

"Marco and Gianni here think you could be a help to us. We need a driver once in a while, and instead of paying you, we will give you art lessons."

"What? I'm not planning any art lessons. I'm already an art teacher." In truth, he taught social studies, which included a weekly period on basic drawing and art history to his middle-school students. "And," he continued, "I'm not working without money – real money."

Stella responded with another smile and blew a lazy smoke ring his way. "You have already told me you wanted to learn more, and the driving won't be hard, some in Rome but mostly outside. You'll like getting out in the countryside."

"I don't care where I drive. How much will you pay? It's expensive here."

"Well," she said as she glanced at the other two men, "if you don't want lessons five hundred euros a month is more than enough for what we have in mind."

Jake did a quick calculation. It sounded like easy money and he was already tired of asking Laura for handouts. "Shit, that's not enough. I want more. I want two thousand. What kind of lessons?" He was surprised at himself for showing some backbone.

Stella's plucked eyebrows shot upward at his response. "We have a small art restoration lab. We repair old ceramics and bits of sculpture and mosaics that nobody wanted. International collectors and museums are interested after they are fixed up. If you can learn the fine points, you will be able to work for a museum when you return to the States."

"Yes, but what would I be driving?"

"Just a car or a small delivery van to pick up or deliver the artworks to our dealer after they are repaired. Hard to find reliable workers here." Stella looked at him with an expression that might promise more than a strictly business arrangement.

"Could I use the car for a few weekends? And the two thousand."

Jake thought she must have liked his initiative asking for a higher salary as a counteroffer because she pulled out her phone and punched in a number before leaving the table. Jake watched her walking back and forth, one hand holding the phone close to her ear, the other waving a cigarette to punctuate the animated conversation. The smoke filling the air was as if a priest was swinging a censer filled with incense.

When she finished the call she said, "Fifteen hundred or forget it. You won't have much to do."

"Okay, let's do it." He tried to look reluctant although he was gratified Stella had agreed. They must really need someone to help. She and her companions didn't fit his idea of art dealers, but then he didn't really know any. And everything was different in Italy.

Business arrangements concluded, Stella pulled her sunglasses down from her hair and stubbed out a Dunhill in the remains of her fish. "How about getting me some cigarettes from the UN commissary? Marlboros are fine, but Cartier will be even better." Silent Marco and Gianni sucked on their cheap local brand, placing the cigarettes into the center of their mouths like pacifiers.

Jake, restless and excited by his new prospects, started to prepare dinner. While he peeled vegetables, he noticed Laura had left a half-full coffee cup on the counter that morning, a habit he found annoying since the day she moved in with him a few months after meeting at a dance. They were both juniors, although he was several years older. He'd decided to further his education, including some art classes, after realizing several years of work in the wheat fields, vineyards, and ranches of eastern Washington held no long-term attraction.

Jake hadn't cared much about marriage, and Laura told him she was content with life as it came along, with plenty of good sex and no permanent commitment. But when he got the teaching job in a school district near Seattle it seemed best to marry. Sometimes single men were suspect.

They wanted something casual at the local courthouse – as casual as their decision to make their arrangement legal. But only formal would do for Laura's mother. Jake hated to remember the inauspicious day: a true Seattle downpour, he dressed up like some eighteenth-century footman minus the wig, and Laura looking uncomfortable in an elaborate white satin gown that didn't suit her, a style selected by her mother. Jake's parents, ill at ease in new clothes from their local dry-goods store, attended. His gut ground throughout the ceremony and during the reception as he worried his mother would get drunk or his father would get angry. His sister and her family, along with a few aunts and uncles, made up the guest list from his side of the family. They all wore street clothes. Laura's side was filled with men in dark suits and women in cocktail dresses and extravagant hats. Jake hated them on sight.

After the honeymoon, Laura placed their wedding picture on her bedside table. He felt like a fool every time he glanced at the stiffly posed figures.

She found a job at Boeing as a technical editor. When Boeing had one of its periodic layoffs she began to freelance, slowly building a small clientele. Life drifted along at an even pace. Jake hung a few of his paintings done in university on the walls of their home. But his creativity and ambition had diminished after he graduated. Occasional trips to the coast, watching the local football and baseball teams, or dinner with friends filled most of the time during weekends. He often played poker on Friday evenings. Good at bluffing, he frequently won.

He knew Laura wanted children, but after his baby sister's death and putting up with his annoying students, he was unsure about whether he would make a good father. His own father failed as a role model with his violence and overbearing attitude, yelling at him to "man up" and play football when he wanted to try out some of the concepts his high school art teacher talked about. A skinny kid who didn't fit in, who sat alone in the school bus taking him into the small town in the far northeast corner of the state up near the Canadian border. Then, when Laura told him about going off the pill and the miscarriage he was even more reluctant. It was all so messy. There was still plenty of time.

His musings were interrupted by Laura returning from work.

He took the initiative. "I'm going to take art restoration lessons, learn to piece together old stuff. Think it will be interesting. Free, too. And once in a while I'll drive for them around here. They'll give me five hundred euros a month for the work. And I'll get to use the car for us sometimes."

"Hey, that's wonderful news." She hugged him. "The money will really help, and I'd love to go out into the country. We could have lunch and find a place to stay. I'll ask Doug and Raj about the best hill towns to visit. Can we go next weekend? I can't wait to see Florence."

"Let's wait a while. I'm not sure how this will all work out. Don't plan anything yet. I don't even know what day I'll get started. And it's not much money."

He saw her face fall at his rejection before she moved to the kitchen to finish preparing dinner. The silence was like a lead weight as he thought about his lies.

NOVEMBER

STELLA AND JAKE faced each other at a table outside a bar halfway across the city from his apartment. "Want one?" Stella pulled out a pack of Marlboros, obtained courtesy of Jake's visit to the commissary. His excuse to Laura had been that he was purchasing a carton for the boy he was purportedly tutoring.

Jake hesitated but decided it was time for a little independence. He took one. "Like I said, gave it up a long time ago, but it's kind of relaxing, you know." He lit his with her lighter first.

"Here's the plan. Tomorrow I want you to go to the cargo area at the airport and pick up some packages. We'll try that for a few weeks and, if it goes well, you'll go to Zurich as soon as we're ready. This is where you can pick up the car. Then we'll see if your services are satisfactory. I'll text you whenever we need you."

Jake, put off by the thought of being on probation, reluctantly looked at a hand-drawn map of the area near the Via dei Coronari's many antique shops. The building where the car awaited was marked with an "X." Stella handed over the map to him. "I'm telling you now about Zurich so you can tell your dear wife and maybe let things settle if need be."

He held out the map to her as if to give it back. He added, "What makes you think I have trouble with my wife?"

"If you want all the money we're going to pay you, you're going to have to work, *caro*. And, how do I know about your wife? You're always looking guilty."

"Okay, okay, I'll let you know." He folded the map and stuffed it into his inside jacket pocket.

"I need to know about the trip by Monday for sure, in case we have to find somebody else to do the work. For tomorrow, be there at nine sharp for your trial. Otherwise forget the money. *Capisci*?"

Jake got out the dictionary back at the apartment. *Caro* meant "dear" or "darling"; *capisci* could be translated as, "do you understand, stupid?"

Before he could tell Laura about his assignment, she opened the dinner table conversation with her own news. "I forgot to tell you. I invited everyone for lunch on Sunday. We've got to get to know people better. And I want them to invite us. I want to see how they live. We've been here for over two months and never been invited to their homes. Maybe they are waiting for us to invite them first."

"How could you do this without telling me? I hardly know them." He didn't want to risk meeting Giorgio again after the encounter on the way to the church on the Aventino. And he hadn't yet figured out how to bring up the subject of Zurich.

But after thinking about it, he realized that Laura would be distracted with her party plans on the weekend and probably not fuss when he told her she would be alone for a few days. But why would she care anyway? She wanted him to have a job.

On Saturday Laura and Jake shared a coffee and *cornetto* at the corner bar near their apartment before heading to the Testaccio market for the weekend shopping. Laura said she wanted to eat out for dinner to avoid messing up the kitchen before the lunch for her coworkers the next day.

The market was crowded with shoppers jostling each other in the morning rush. Jake and Laura made their way past the fish to the meat stands to select chicken breasts before going on to the fruit and cheese to be served after the luncheon's main course. She bought a kilo of almost transparent green grapes. Jake asked the vendor to select a melon for a light dinner after the lunch party. The vendor sniffed several and handed one over. "*Perfetto*," the man said. The cheese monger suggested all Italian: truffle-studded *pecorino;* crunchy, nutty *parmigiano;* and strong, milky, blue-veined *gorgonzola*. For their lunch, Laura bought two balls of the velvety and drippy *mozzarella di bufala,* a luxury they'd discovered not long after their arrival.

She made a *caprese* for lunch, slices of tomatoes interspersed with the mozzarella made of rich water buffalo milk. She dressed the dish with salt, pepper, and olive oil before carrying it outside, where she decorated the arrangement with sprigs of fragrant basil snipped from a pot on their balcony. While they sat in the sun enjoying their meal, they watched their neighbors across the street where housewives were hanging out laundry or watering a few plants on their own balconies. A soprano's trilling voice carried through an open window, the notes floating their way on a light breeze.

She washed the dishes while she listened to Jake's running commentary on a soccer game between two second-tier teams. He shouted, "*dai, dai,*" whenever the team he favored made an effort to score. She was impressed with his Italian, but the game's noise, which competed with the *motorini* outside revving their engines and, worse, the annoying din from upstairs, where neighbors were remodeling, gave her a headache. The sound of tiles being chipped from walls and floors carried into their apartment, an incessant *chink, chink, chink,* like some form of torture. Seeking refuge, Laura locked the bathroom door and sank into a warm bath. She held her journal just above the waterline, flipping through a few pages to see if she agreed with what she wrote earlier. She was disappointed at how few entries she had made and how banal they sounded. If she didn't get in more emotion, her life would never turn into a memoir or even the blog post she kept drafting but never sending. But she was afraid to write about her emotions. They weren't what she expected them to be with constantly vacillating views of the expatriate experience. Love, hate, frightened to be here, wanting to stay forever. Love. And always in the background, baby.

Jake's team lost the game 2–0. He grumped, complaining about the star player who seemed to be faking his injuries to avoid attempting to score. Match fixing he suspected.

They left for the restaurant in the city center with a stop by Piazza Navona, Laura's favorite place, for a glass of wine before they ate. But the domestic day unraveled with the weather, the sunny sky now covered by wet clouds, harbingers of winter. As she raised her glass to her lips, Jake looked toward the obelisk in the central fountain and said, "I'm going to be gone for several days sometime in the next couple of weeks."

"Gone? Where?"

"I'll tell you later. Let's go eat."

"I thought you were only driving around Rome. You never said that you would be going out of town."

"I'll tell you in the restaurant. I'm hungry."

After they arrived at the restaurant, which had few patrons so early in the evening, Jake ordered a half-liter of the house red before they considered meal choices.

"Where are you going? With who?" She drank some of her wine before carefully placing the glass back on the table.

"Zurich and it's my job."

"But what will you be doing?"

He tore off a piece of bread and rolled the dough between his fingers. He responded to her questions while arranging a row of bread pills on the table. "I told you earlier, we'll have use of a car once in a while if I drive for the lab. They like my work. And I'm going alone."

"I don't want to be alone here yet. What will you be doing? Why haven't I met these people? I've introduced you to my coworkers."

"I'll be back, don't worry. Remember, you wanted me to have a job. Why should you care if I'm gone? You never cared in Seattle." He rearranged his bread pills before gathering them up in a wad and folding them into a paper napkin.

Laura could feel her stomach give a distress signal as her mind returned to Seattle and the memory of what happened the last time he was away without her. The miscarriage was now eight months ago. She wished that she hadn't told Jake when he returned from the school trip to find her in bed and crying, but she was miserable and needed comfort. She could not forget his lack of regret about a lost baby.

She said softly, "It's just that I remember what happened the last time you were gone."

"I remember too, but it was months ago now. He looked at her closely before adding, "You're not pregnant again, are you?"

"No, I just don't want to be alone. Everything is still so new and confusing."

Most of Laura's chicken remained on her plate and half of Jake's lamb on his by the time they finished the wine. A narrow trail of smoke from the spent candle wick curled upward, as if to pass on an obscure message written in an unknown language. She examined the lazy coils, trying to decipher the meaning. In the end there didn't seem to be any.

The waiter inspected his nails while he waited for them to signal for the check. Jake raised his hands in the universal gesture: finger writing on the palm of his other hand. The waiter approached with the bill. Jake threw down a fifty and left. Laura remained, picking at the drips of wax on the tablecloth and watching the dregs settle in the bottom of their empty wine glasses.

When the candle extinguished itself, she slung her coat over her shoulders and walked into a rainy Roman night. Without an umbrella, she headed for the stairs leading down to the Metro, dodging under awnings on her way.

She arrived back in their apartment soaking wet. Jake's usual spot, slouched in front of the television, was empty, and he wasn't anywhere else in their few rooms either. Her journal waited next to the bedside lamp. She crawled under the bedcovers and reached over to retrieve it, even though she had read her entries earlier in the day. She reread her triumphant first words yet again: *This is the first day of my new life!* Correct, she thought, but I should have added this is the first day of a new life that will bring more changes than I could ever have dreamed.

She awoke with a start at three o'clock thinking she heard Jake come in. But the noise was only the next-door neighbor who had slammed a door. Wide awake, she puzzled again at Jake's surprise news, but the idea of being left alone in a still-unfamiliar city unsettled her. And another thing, why did he unload his news in her favorite place, especially knowing her nervousness about entertaining her office partners?

She drifted off again, only to awaken with the sun shining in her eyes. She put her arm out to the right side of the bed. No familiar lump under the covers. She checked the hide-a-bed. It was empty. She picked up her phone to call him. No answer.

Her guests would be arriving in a few hours. *Pazienza,* she said to herself, cheered she could think up a suitable word in Italian. She hadn't yet learned much of the language, her work being in English, although she listened to her fluent colleagues and had managed to pick up some of the basics. There would be time after she got settled.

Laura tried to set aside her worries while she dressed, but the photo by her side of the bed only fed them. Their air shipment, held up in customs, had finally arrived the previous week with the wedding photo mixed in with dishes, silverware, placemats, napkins, cool-weather clothes and Jake's painting supplies. She had set the photo in its accustomed spot on the bedside table. She picked it up to study the picture more closely than usual. Jake wore a strange expression, unreadable. And her own smile looked forced, too. The ceremony should have taken place in the courthouse like they wanted, instead of a cathedral. Why did her mother make all the fuss? And, why did she allow her to do it?

She got out the plates and silverware and began to prepare the meal. If Jake showed up she would rearrange the seven settings to eight. If not, she'd just say the student he was tutoring was desperate to prepare for exams and needed him right away.

When she checked the time it was already 12:30. Where were they? She had told them 12:30.

Shortly before one o'clock, the *citofono* buzzed. She lifted the receiver and said "Yes?" before changing to, "*Sì?*"

Doug said, "We're here."

"Fourth floor, turn right at the elevator, we're number eighteen." She pressed the button and could hear the front door to the building opening with a loud click.

Her boss greeted her at her door. "Hi, Laura. You remember my wife, Helena."

"Hello, Helena," she smiled.

Helena smiled back, all perfect makeup and clothes. Standing behind Doug and Helena were Raj and Chandra, and behind them, Silvia with Giorgio, who held a lit cigarette with ash in imminent danger of falling.

"Do you mind?" he asked.

Laura tried to erase her frown. She hated cigarettes. "Of course not. I'll find an ashtray for you." It was too late, but she ignored the deposit on the carpet out of courtesy.

Helena handed over a bunch of funeral-size red gladioli. Chandra offered carnations, and Giorgio presented a bottle of Chianti. Laura found a vase for the showy red flowers. The modest carnations went into a water glass. She got out an ice bucket for the Chianti. When she turned around, she received the impression her guests had been looking at each other and smiling.

Laura urged them to sit down to lunch immediately. Instead, she saw that they were assessing her clothes bought on visits to Via Sannio, the apartment, and the lack of Jake.

In turn, she observed Chandra, who said she had just come back from Delhi but wore Italian designer clothes like Helena, with logos on scarf and handbag, and a row of narrow gold bracelets up her arms. They jangled and glittered as she moved. Silvia dressed in a more subdued fashion, with sunglasses on top of her hennaed hair.

"Jake needed to go out. I think I told you he tutored. He'll try to get back in time. Do you want wine? I've Orvieto, Montepulciano d'Abruzzo, and the lovely Chianti."

"I don't drink alcohol," said Chandra. The others selected the Orvieto. Laura managed to uncork the bottle and pour without dripping, hoping it was acceptable despite it being the least expensive brand in the market. She poured a glass of tap water for Chandra, who held it up as if to see if bugs were enjoying a swim. "Don't you have bottled?"

"Sorry, we ran out and I forgot to get more."

They finally sat down to gossip about office politics until the subject wore out. Then Doug said to Raj: "Are you going up to your place next weekend? I've got a lot of work to do on mine, but if you're around Sunday, maybe we could get together." Raj responded and the two men began to talk.

Laura heard the word "pots." Maybe they were interested in cooking. "Oh, do you like to cook? Maybe you could convince Jake to learn."

They both turned toward Laura momentarily before continuing their conversation.

Giorgio said, "Nice apartment. How did you find it?"

Relieved to have a subject to talk about, she began her tale, trying to make an interesting story, knowing her audience listened only out of politeness. She cut it short by saying, "Let's eat."

The chicken was overcooked, so dry their knives and forks could hardly make a dent. The olive oil, drizzled on the salad too early, turned the leaves limp and heavy, and the *tiramisu* she had made great effort to cook correctly from a recipe found online, was more liquid than solid. At least she had enough wine, and the fruit and cheese plate went well.

Doug and Raj resumed their conversation. Helena and Chandra talked about the best shoe stores and the shops near the Via Condotti. Giorgio lit another cigarette. Every time she looked his way he was staring at her through the smoke. Confused by the scrutiny and with nothing to add to the table talk, Laura busied herself with serving while trying to interject the odd encouraging remark through the fumes.

To her relief, her guests finally left at 3:30. What a flop. She knew they'd never invite her in return. And Jake? She wondered if she should call the police. But what could she say beyond they had a fight? That surely would get a laugh. She picked up her phone to call him again but saw a text message saying he was going to work all weekend with his student at his country home and not to bother calling. She shoveled the remains of the meal into the garbage can.

Wanting her own getaway, she took an aspirin to alleviate her headache and fired up her Kindle to read another of the sunny Italian memoirs she'd purchased before leaving Seattle. Reading about other people's delightful lives, however, only brought an unwelcome comparison, and the aspirin didn't work, either. Thoughts of the never-completed blog post added to her distress.

Despite the vendor's promise, the uncut melon they bought the day before was past the stage of perfection, and fruit flies began to hover. She threw it out, too, and got out a piece of bread and spread an extra-thick portion of Nutella on top for her dinner. She went to bed early with her journal. Picking up her pen, she wrote:

I don't know what is the matter with Jake. We never seem to have any fun. I'm trying to get along with him but ever since we got here he's been so...

So what, exactly? She put the book down, unable to think of the right word.

Laura didn't want to go to work on Monday, the day that inevitably followed the miserable party. Jake hadn't returned, although he'd sent another text that he'd be back later in the day.

The traffic near her office was the usual nightmare. While she waited to cross the road full of cars attempting to maneuver past one another and outwit the pedestrians, she watched as a man carrying a briefcase unsuccessfully tried to dodge a car. It brushed him, leaving a mark on his suit pants. The enraged man swung the case at the car, an expensive Alfa Romeo, smashing the tail light in revenge. Laura smiled at the comic-opera scene. Maybe it would not be a bad day after all. Jake would be home at dinnertime, and work would go well.

But it was a bad day. Sitting on her desk were Doug's comments on her latest manuscript revisions, the first one she had done on her own. He must have printed it out to work over the weekend. Probably the disastrous lunch put him in a bad mood. The marks were in red, and there were a lot of them. She saw that her suggestions, done in the same style as her editing work in Seattle, were all crossed out. She hesitantly knocked on Doug's open door to offer an apology. She could hear his half of a phone conversation.

"Yes, I know the deadline. You'll have the draft on your desk by seven this evening. I'm sorry for the delay."

Doug hung up and waved her in, pointing to a chair in front of his desk. "Now then. Raj must have corrected your work more closely than I thought before I saw it or I would not have assigned you this project. I understand that you are new but that is not UN style." He gestured at the offending manuscript in her hand. "We don't write so directly in the introduction, and your suggestions have radically changed the normal layout. This manuscript isn't for some tech manual but will be used by community foresters on the Indian sub-continent, and they follow British style."

"Why didn't you say so earlier?"

"I'm busy and I assumed you would have sense enough to check with Raj, at least. It's pretty obvious where he comes from."

"Give me today and I'll use your suggestions. I'm sorry."

Laura slunk back to her computer to enter the crushing red edits into the document without questioning them. She knew the others had heard every word through the open door. Too humiliated to talk to anyone, she kept her head down and ate lunch at her desk, her face aching with tension. It was after seven before she completed the work. She forwarded her revisions to Doug, who remained in his office, gathered up her bag and coat and walked out into the evening.

She opened the apartment door to find Jake hunkered down in front of the TV. He had a beer in hand and an empty beside his feet on the coffee table. Her journal lay open beside him.

"Where have you been? How could you do this to me? You made me look like a fool and scared me out of my wits. I nearly called the police until I saw your message. And how dare you read my writings?" Her anger bounced off the terrazzo floors and into the neighboring apartments.

"What do you care? I tried to call but you didn't answer, so I texted," he shouted back.

"Jake, who is this person you're tutoring and why couldn't you have gone to see him another time? Your student *is* a "him," isn't he? And I don't understand what this job is that you have."

"You're at work all the time, and when you're home you're reading stuff from the office. What do you expect me to do?" He grabbed the empty can and threw it toward the picture of the Appia Antica, knocking it askew.

Laura was so frightened she grabbed her handbag and left. The elevator took her to the ground floor, her destination a small pizzeria a block from the apartment. Cold with rage, she found a table near the pizza oven and its glowing wood fire. She ordered a *quartino* of red and a *quattro stagione* pizza, not caring how many calories she consumed. The wine and carbs subdued her anger while she tried to think of what to do. Lock him out of the apartment? And why was she so upset? He did go with friends on weekend fishing trips in Seattle, although not without telling her. And the occasional teacher's retreat, too. But here in Rome the city had seemed to cast a spell over them, changing their relationship from one of trust to one of wariness and at times even foreboding.

When a shadow fell over the table to interrupt her thoughts, Laura raised her eyes to see Jake. "Hey babe, let's not get carried away. Okay?"

They observed each other silently, hoping to find a clue to their future.

When Jake had fled after his disagreement with Laura at the restaurant, he had walked aimlessly until he came to one of the many Irish pubs in the area. All of them were noisy and decorated in fake Irish memorabilia, with beer on tap, Irish and Scotch whiskies lining mirrored shelves, televisions blaring sports programs, and anonymous drinkers guzzling or sipping according to their moods.

He sat on a stool and nursed a beer, and then another.

The tattooed barkeep, busy wiping glasses with a stained towel, stopped in front of him.

"Need another yet?" His accent sounded as if he was from Chicago. A compatriot.

Jake downed the last of his second, wiped the foam off his mouth with the back of his hand, and said, "Yeah, I'll take another."

When the barman slid the full glass toward him, Jake said, "I might need some help."

Cocking his head, the man asked, "What?"

"Had a fight – you know – with the wife. Know of somewhere to bed down tonight?"

"Well, you know those bitches, nuthin' but trouble most of the time. There's a storeroom with a cot in back, but you don't get it for free. Nuthin' free in this world – I know."

"So what's the deal? I don't have much money with me. Don't want to use a credit card either."

"No credit cards. You'll have to make yourself useful. Need a barkeep to tend late at night and muck out in the morning. By the way, name's Sean."

"Call me Carl. Can't work – don't have any papers or whatever."

Sean laughed. "You think the *polizia* come around here to check? They come all right, but all I need is a twenty once in a while and they decide they'd rather sit over there and have a few. They don't even care if we smoke." He gestured with his head toward a corner where two Italian men sat with whiskies and cigarettes.

"Okay, no problem." Jake smiled to himself with relief. Maybe he could stay a while. Avoid the lunch. Even the whole weekend.

He worked the bar for a few hours and then slept in the beer-smelling room stacked high with kegs and supplies.

Sean poured him a beer late on Sunday morning. "Here, hair of the dog. A real fight, huh?"

"Yeah. I'd like to stay again tonight and then I'll go. Okay?"

"Need to talk?"

"Nah. But my phone battery is starting to die. Give me a minute to make a call and I'll get to work." He put in a quick call to Laura before he picked up a broom. She didn't answer so he sent a text.

He came home midday Monday and called Stella. She didn't answer either, so he left a message. "Jake calling. I'm on for the trip. Let me know the day. See ya." Then he added, "*Ciao.*"

Although he had no intention of telling Laura what he'd been doing, he realized he'd better clean up and prepare for the inevitable confrontation when she got back from work. He headed for the bedroom to get a change of clothes. He saw Laura's journal on the bedside table. Curious, he carried it into the bathroom, balancing it on the edge of the sink to read while he washed up. He popped a couple of aspirins, opened a beer, and carried the book to the sofa to continue reading the few entries. He hadn't liked what he read. And now when she came home he had thrown the beer can at the wall, making the situation even worse.

Jake considered his precarious situation. Stella and her pals might provide interesting tales back in Seattle, but he knew he'd better patch things up with Laura before he left town. Who knew what she'd do if she was really angry. He remembered that the lease was in her name.

He walked down the street to see if he could find her after the argument. He saw her in a pizzeria. The air between them was dense with recrimination. But after neither could stand the silence Jake sat down and signaled for a glass and more wine. "Laura, I'm sorry – it's just that I need to have my own life. I can't continue to hang around like a kept man. Please, Lor, let me get settled in my own way. I do love you, but…" His words trailed off into emptiness.

"But, what?"

"Oh, I don't know. This whole change has made me do a lot of thinking. I did want a change, *do* want a change I mean, but going from the ranch, to university and then Seattle, and now I'm in the middle of Europe, Rome for Christ's sake. Do you really expect I'll just relax and sit around with nothing much to do and wait for you every evening? There's hardly any trees or open space and our apartment is so small. I need space."

"I don't understand why you can't paint or do all the other things people do here. We never went out in Seattle, and we don't go out here. It's not like we're old yet, you know. I thought things would change but they haven't. Can't we go to some exhibits, or up on the Via Veneto for drinks, or something?"

"Don't worry, I'll just take this one trip out of town to help these people out. Probably leave in a week or two. Then I'll just drive locally or work at their lab like I told you and start painting. And yes, my student is a young man. Mauro is his name, like I told you earlier. So I have two jobs, like you wanted."

Laura swirled her wine without looking at him in case her face revealed disbelief. "Okay, but please, please don't embarrass me again like you did yesterday."

Jake raised his own glass in a salute before taking her hand. "You don't have to worry about me. We're a pair."

The following Saturday Laura suggested taking the bus to Hadrian's Villa and Tivoli.

Despite the map and pictures in their guidebook showing the villa's layout of baths and pools, temples and libraries, she found it difficult to imagine what the complex had originally looked like in the emperor's time. But it was a pleasant escape from Rome.

It was noon by the time they completed the tour of the crumbling ruins. They decided on lunch in the town before visiting a second villa and gardens, one that belonged to Cardinal d'Este in the sixteenth century. A sign for a small restaurant attracted their attention. A shop with copies of antiquities arranged in its window was next door. As they passed, Laura glanced at the display through the dusty pane. "Wait, I want to see something." Her eyes locked on the figure of a naked youth with a goat's tail. He played a double flute, his cheeks puffed out with the effort. The bronze statue, about a foot tall, had a green patina, as if it had been buried for centuries before discovery. "Could I have it for Christmas, please, Jake? A perfect souvenir of Rome, and I always wanted to play the flute but I got stuck with the oboe because everyone else wanted the flute."

He looked at the price tag – about three hundred dollars. "Laura, how'll we afford such a ...?"

"You said that you were going to earn five hundred euros a month."

"Let's have lunch and see the gardens first."

The restaurant menu offered winter dishes to warm patrons' hearts and stomachs. Laura selected rigatoni with chunks of sausage and *broccoli rabe*. Jake ordered *lasagna al forno*. She watched him dig into the layers of pasta, cheese, and ground beef while thinking about the layers of their life. Jake's lasagna contained plenty of meat filling, but their lives had very little, and what there was didn't have much seasoning.

They entered Villa d'Este to walk among the ancient cypresses, cedars, and sequoias, looming black against the intense blue winter sky. The paths led them under a cascade, along the Avenue of the Hundred Fountains, past a water organ, pools and water jets. Delicate mosses, maidenhair ferns, and other moisture-loving plants flourished, and the jets of the taller fountains reflected rainbows in the lowering sun. Laura was entranced with the whole park, which she remembered from *Three Coins in the Fountain*. "What a dream this is."

"Yeah, but I wonder about some of the dreams. Did you see the sphinx pouring water out of her breasts? Those Renaissance guys were something else."

On their way back to the bus stop they passed a stall where a local artist sold small watercolors on papyrus. A picture of a blonde in a pale blue robe driving a chariot pulled by two hermaphrodites with fancy upswept hairdos, red wings, and male attributes caught Jake's attention. He bought it for her. "Probably not what you'd see in Seattle, is it?"

She agreed, but added, "You couldn't find the statue in Seattle, either. Please Jake."

Jake dragged his feet as he accompanied Laura back to the shop. The shopkeeper took the figure out of the window and told them about the original. Found in Pompeii, it was a representation of a faun playing music for dancing slave girls.

Back in the apartment, Laura moved their wedding photo aside to make room for the statue in their bedroom. Despite its small size, the figure was much heavier than it appeared.

Laura approached Doug and asked for another meeting, saying she needed more guidance. He agreed to meet with her the next day. She reviewed examples of published work, trying to find the best to use as a model, cross with herself for not doing so earlier.

She arrived early the following day feeling unsettled because of her apprehension about the meeting, a second shot of espresso, and the uncertainty of her marriage that veered from lukewarm to cold with little compensating warmth.

Doug was relaxed and friendly. He came around his desk and sat next to her. She wished she had put on better clothes and more makeup, but in her worried state she had thrown on yesterday's outfit.

"Laura, you still need to take a little more time with your work. I'd like to be able to support you, because I know you like life here. But I don't like getting calls from the head of the department criticizing my staff. So, think about my earlier editing suggestions and what I've said, will you? I know some of the style is arcane, but such is life."

She took a chance. "Could we have a quick coffee before I get back to revising?" She saw her coworkers slide their eyes in their direction as she and Doug walked by.

They reentered the office after an extended discussion of how her unit operated and who was who. Her colleagues pretended to be diligently working, eyes now focused on their computer screens.

By 6:30 only she and Doug remained in the office.

"You want a drink?" he asked.

Pleased, she switched off the computer. Jake could say whatever he wanted when she got home.

They headed for a bar across from the office. UN workers and Italians from nearby banks filled the space as they shared bottles of wine and plates of olives. The conversations were in Italian, French, and English. Laura saw the crowd as sophisticated, better dressed than she, and showing a studied ease – a style she wanted to emulate. For sure she would go shopping while Jake went to Zurich. Maybe having him gone wasn't such a bad idea.

"*Salve!*" Laura looked up to see the head of the department. Doug introduced her as his newest protégée, remarking what a great addition to the team she had become. Laura was worried by this statement. Could he be blaming another editor for her mistakes, or was this simply a joke? She smiled at the department head, an Englishman named Derrick Clawson. In response he shook her hand and held her eyes.

A group left a nearby table. Derrick moved in and pulled out a chair for her. Without asking her preference, he ordered her a *spumante* and glasses of Nebbiolo for himself and Doug.

Laura sized up Derrick. Probably in his late fifties, younger than her father. Pretty handsome for an old guy. She wondered if he was one of those older men who has a mistress. The word sounded so European and erotic.

She moved her eyes to the procession of bubbles rising from the bottom of her glass. She let the two men converse about a meeting, halfheartedly listening to the words in case something might be useful for her career. She wished again she had put on better clothes.

Derrick turned her way. "How are you liking Rome? Are you settling in? Food's good, isn't it? Can't think what it would be like going back to Yorkshire after this life."

Laura responded that she loved it and the job, carefully avoiding mention of her husband.

Derrick began to carry on about his old house near Viterbo. "Water system packed up. Damned plumbers, never show up when you need them. I should have hired Poles. They know how to work and for half the price. The town planning people are a bunch of crooks – had to pay them a thousand just to get approval for the new heating system. Should have just told them to piss off." Derrick briefly flashed a tight-lipped smile.

While trying to find an opportunity to tell him that she visited London once, Laura turned her watch to check the time. Almost 7:30. She finished the last of the fizzy wine before saying, "Sorry, but I've got to go." She tried to call Jake on her way out, but he didn't answer.

Jake was slumped as usual in front of the TV with a beer and the crumpled remains of a bag of potato chips. She couldn't think of anything to say other than, "Sorry I'm late – lot of work to do. I tried to call you."

Jake roused himself and said, "Whatever." He grabbed his jacket and left the apartment.

She found a piece of cheese and sat on the sofa, nibbling and writing a few notes about her day and Derrick. If Jake snooped again that was his problem. Then she opened their laptop and pulled up the draft blog post. After rereading it, she added the story and photo of her little flute player. She described the meal they had eaten at Tivoli but didn't think the words were much better than reading a menu. It wasn't easy to write about food. The post was still short so she added a teaser at the end: "Life is full of surprises here. Today I met another interesting character from the office. This one is from England and he knows all about Rome. I'll tell you about him in the next post." She hit "send."

Except for the seafood restaurant at the beach and the visit to Tivoli, Jake hadn't been outside Rome since they arrived. Two weeks after their last lunch together, Stella called to tell him to report for work. She waited for him in a big Lancia blocking a narrow alleyway in the *centro*. Behind that car sat a Mercedes, anonymous-looking with a coating of dust and a dent on the front fender.

"The car's already loaded. You are to drive straight through – should take about nine hours. I know Americans are used to such long drives. The weather forecast is good. I'm going to fly up tomorrow morning to do some business and will return with you. Here's a map to the art dealer's villa and a copy of your hotel reservations. Got your passport?"

"Yes," Jake said as he hoisted his duffel bag into the back seat. "But where's the stuff?"

"Don't worry, all taken care of. Don't want to be obvious. Don't want you hijacked on the way. Whatever you do, if you stop at all, do not forget to lock the car. And do not start poking around."

"Are you sure this isn't risky?"

"Don't be worried. Nothing has ever happened. We need to keep our shipments safe from other people who might want them. Other dealers, I mean."

Marco came out of the doorway and handed him the keys to the car, a package of euros, another of Swiss francs, and maps of both Italy and Switzerland. Jake experienced a *frisson* of trepidation, followed by a leap of excitement.

It took him nearly an hour in heavy traffic to reach the A-1, the *autostrada* heading north. He drove with care, staying within the speed limits, which he soon saw was a poor idea. Drivers coming up behind him pounded on their horns, flashed their lights, and passed him in a blur, barely missing his wing mirror. He sped up to match the traffic moving at eighty miles an hour or faster in the slow lane.

The car handled like a dream, nothing like the old Corolla they sold before leaving Seattle. He saw groves of olive trees, houses and villas, and a few cattle and sheep tranquilly grazing in fields bordering the highway. Small towns appeared as if they had grown out of their rock foundations in the Middle Ages or even earlier. He passed a city perched on top of a cliff. He could see a cathedral and several towers. The road sign said it was Orvieto, where the white wine he and Laura liked was produced. Signs to other locations, Siena, Montepulciano, Cortona, tempted him to turn off the highway. Distracted, he had to swerve at the last second to miss a car he was passing.

Traffic over the Apennines from Florence to Bologna was jammed with slow-moving trucks. From Bologna through Milan the route became another nightmare, with fast-moving trucks constantly overtaking him. Dusk had fallen by the time he reached the border near Lugano. He lowered the window and held up his blue passport. The guard gave him and his duffel bag on the back seat a once-over. "Where are you going?"

Following Stella's instructions, Jake replied casually: "Just to see my uncle near Zurich for a few days before I go back to Rome and then home to the U.S." He must have looked innocuous in jeans, a sweatshirt, and old Nikes because the man waved him on without bothering to take more than a cursory glance at his passport before swiping it into the data base.

Jake found the hamlet marked on his map as his destination an hour later. The house hid behind a high, ivy-covered brick wall at the end of a dark lane. He got out and stretched his stiff limbs. The tension and long drive made his neck ache. He rang the intercom at the gate with one hand while massaging his stiff muscles with the other.

"*Ja?*" said a voice.

"Hi, I'm Jake."

The gate swung open. Jake drove in and set the brake. A harsh sodium light cast angular shadows over the buildings in the yard. Two men came out and told him to remain in the car. He looked in the rear-view mirror to watch as they opened the trunk and then removed the back seat. A dozen packages of odd sizes were wrapped in burlap. The workers carted them toward a garage without a further word. Jake's curiosity was overpowering but he didn't dare follow the men. He'd ask Stella in the morning.

After they slammed the trunk lid, he could now see a large half-timbered house in the mirror. A man stood on the porch observing the action. The light reflected off his round glasses, his face without expression.

Jake drove to the place Stella had booked for him. As he ate a *wurst* at a fast-food joint nearby, he became resentful that he hadn't been put up in better accommodations. He knew she would never have stayed in a one-star hotel.

The following morning he parked not far from the main railroad station. A scattering of obscure art galleries dotted a side street not far away. He pressed the bell beside the entrance to one of them. An elderly man dressed in a suit and tie opened the door. His gray hair was close cropped, and he wore round rimless glasses that gave him a severe appearance. He had a tic below his right eye. Jake couldn't stop watching the flickering flesh. All the man needed was a monocle and he'd pass for a Nazi. The man coolly inspected him. "What do you want?"

Wondering about an appropriate answer, he hesitated. Stella came up from behind the man and intervened by waving in Jake's direction. "This is Jake Miller."

Jake didn't know she knew his last name. He never mentioned it, but like everything else about him, she knew anyway.

The Nazi continued to stare. Stella said, "He is my new assistant. He is very knowledgeable about our business. You need not be concerned. I trust him." The man managed a small bow as if not quite sure he accepted the reliability of her statement.

Stella continued: "Jake, meet another Miller, although he spells it Muller, Herr Karl-Heinz Muller. Maybe you're related." She laughed.

Jake started to stick out his hand but changed his mind when the dealer's glasses caught the light, making his eyes vanish. The same man as the previous night.

Jake walked around the gallery. No antiques were displayed. Instead, the stark white walls were hung with garish-colored designs based on graffiti not so different from his own work. In the center of the showroom floor, one of the artists the gallery represented had erected an installation: dirty mattresses topped with several videos, each endlessly cycling a couple having sex. Jake stopped, riveted with curiosity and lust.

Despite Stella's words of confidence, she and the Nazi went to a room in the back of the gallery, ignoring him. Jake watched the video for a few more minutes before turning his curiosity to what were evidently business dealings.

"Just trying to find the toilet," he offered as an excuse to enter the back room. Stella and the gallery owner were seated next to each other, going over some papers. Behind them stood a wall of shelving filled with marble figurines and fragments, as well as pots, both painted and plain. Now he knew about the contents of the packages.

"We'll meet at the coffee bar around the corner." Stella didn't smile as she ordered him out. Forty minutes later she showed up. "Sorry we were so long," she said. Her expression didn't match her words. She continued: "Don't describe the artworks to anyone – don't want competition from other dealers, you know. But Herr Muller is very pleased about the delivery. He has buyers for almost everything already. He's invited us both to lunch – just a quick bite at the Odeon. You know, the café where Lenin used to talk revolution."

The café was crowded with a combination of well-dressed business people and bohemian students, some perched on the red leather barstools and others at tables. No one looked like they were plotting revolution. Herr Muller had managed to arrive before them and waited at a table with a beer. Now, out of context, he looked like any other old man, slight stubble on one cheek and a spot on his tie. Every time Jake glanced in his direction, he saw the tic continuing to wink.

Stella selected white wine, Jake a Sudwerk, the beer advertised on the mat sitting under Muller's perspiring glass. A sturdy waitress with blond braids brought plates of sausage and kraut. No one said anything until Stella started a conversation in German. Jake, cut out again, stared at the gray-and-black marble walls while daydreaming of becoming an art dealer, returning to the present only when he heard chairs scraping back from the table. Muller paid. Jake pocketed his damp beer mat as a souvenir.

Jake dropped off Stella at her hotel, the Baur au Lac. The imperious doorman in his uniform laden with gold braid sniffed at the dirty car as he helped Stella out and signaled for a flunky to get her case. Jake felt sure the man looked down his long nose at him, too.

Stella said, "Be here at nine," as she walked into the luxurious entrance followed by a man carrying her luggage. Jake's anger from the night before returned when he thought about her hotel while he was stuck in Spartan accommodations. Still, he said to himself, this is interesting. Far better than walking around Rome.

They headed south in the morning. Stella smoked silently without offering him a cigarette. As the *autostrada* descended into the Po Valley and its now-bare orchards, the weather brightened, except for patches of fog hanging over the damp ground, leaving pointed church bell towers poking up like floating obelisks. By Florence the sun was shining in a crystalline winter sky.

Laura returned to the Piazza Navona while Jake was away. She wanted to revisit the scene that caught her fancy on her first day in Rome. Taking the same table where she and Jake sat licking spoons of gelato in the sun, Laura ordered a prosecco in an attempt to brighten her mood and regain the sentiment of wonder and promise she felt that first time. But the last visit to the piazza when she and Jake argued crowded into her thoughts to compete with those of her happiness.

She twisted the delicate stem of her wineglass back and forth as her thoughts swung from one visit to the other. The waters of the Fountain of the Four Rivers, enchanting in September, were now only background noise to her concerns about Jake and their relationship. Reading the hieroglyphics on the ancient Egyptian obelisk in the center of the fountain would have been as easy as coming up with answers to her questions.

The glass stem snapped under the pressure of her twisting motion. The half-filled bowl crashed to the stone paving, leaving her with splashes of liquid on her clothes and a cut finger. A few tourists among the swirl of people admiring the fountain's Baroque exuberance paused to watch her wipe the blood with tissues before they turned back to ogle the naked muscular statues lolling around the obelisk. A waiter scurried up to remove the mess and replace Laura's glass. The drips on her jacket and pants dried as she stared at the new set of bubbles rising to the surface of the flute before they burst into nothingness.

Her attention was redirected when she felt something bump against her ankles. She looked down to see a small child reaching for a soccer ball that had rolled under her table.

"*Mi scusi, signorina.*" A smiling young woman knelt to gather up her toddler, who screamed with delight when he retrieved his errant ball. The woman saw Laura's uncertain expression and switched to lightly-accented English. "Sorry – my Arturo is so active I can't always control him. I hope he didn't disturb you."

Laura was pleased by the unexpected chance to refocus her thoughts and meet an Italian, especially one who spoke English and who had a child. And she was desperate to talk to someone, anyone other than Jake or office workers.

"Would you like to sit down?" She pushed the other chair back from the table with her foot. "Can I get you a coffee?"

The woman hesitated for a moment before sitting. Arturo squirmed out of her lap and wobbled a few steps away to try kicking the ball again.

"I'm Laura."

"Stefania, and yes, I'd love a coffee." She extended her hand to Laura, who grasped it, sending a jab of pain through her wounded finger.

The coffee arrived and Laura's untouched replacement flute of prosecco was removed. "Tell me about Arturo," she said while checking out her new acquaintance's elegant attire. With spike-heeled boots, short skirt, and a jacket she saw in a Prada ad, Laura thought Stefania, like Helena, was a perfect example of Italian style. A style she wondered if she could ever successfully copy as she gradually accumulated shoes and outfits from local shops, fast fashion within her budget.

Stefania, delighted to have an audience, began a story about the marvels of her son and his father, who was teaching him to play soccer. As she talked, Laura reflected on her own childless marriage yet again. Maybe that was the real reason she now lived in an unfamiliar city and needed to talk to an unknown woman, a lucky one who had everything Laura desired.

Arturo began to cry. "Nap time," said his mother as she scooped him into her arms. "Nice to meet you."

They disappeared into the crowd before Laura could reply or even finish her wave of farewell. No invitation to meet again and no chance to exchange confidences. Laura felt bereft, overwhelmed with a sense of yearning for a true family life. She touched her wound, a minor cut but painful all the same.

She left a few coins on the table. Time to return "home," as she now called their small Roman apartment. As she washed up after dinner, she looked at her hands, a wound on her right and the rings on her left. The wedding ring was engraved on the inside with their initials and date. Surely they were meant to connect directly to her heart. She thought back to the day they had gone to the jewelers to order the engraving during the summer they had graduated. Jake had looked like a true Westerner, tanned and muscled from his regular summer job bucking hay and working livestock at a ranch not far from the school. Handsome and competent. Not a jock but someone who had artistic aspirations. She loved that look and attitude, but somehow they had slowly faded away when they moved to Seattle. He seemed conflicted, alternately content with teaching and other times restless and dissatisfied, wanting something undefined. Always taciturn and laconic, those characteristics had become magnified since their move.

Jake showed up late that evening. "How'd it go?" Laura asked.

"Good. Zurich is super interesting with all the art galleries and those rich people. Shoulda seen the A-rabs with their wives all covered up with black sheets walking along behind them."

"So, who were you with?" she probed.

"Just delivered a bunch of old junk to a guy named Muller – funny, huh – might be a long-lost relative. Never heard of him though, must be a coincidence and he spells it different anyway. Reminded me of a Nazi. I'm tired." He closed the bathroom door behind him without asking her about the bandage on her hand or how her time went while he traveled.

Laura was disheartened to be cut out, again. She turned her thoughts to the invitation she received that morning. Derrick had invited her to an office lunch in celebration of the approaching holiday season. Finally, the social atmosphere might be brightening.

DECEMBER

THE MAÎTRE D' showed Laura to a corner table in the restaurant normally reserved for visiting diplomats. To her surprise, only Derrick awaited. A pinot grigio rested in an ice bucket beside the table set for two. The Englishman stood up in welcome while the waiter seated her and poured the wine. Derrick said nothing about other guests.

"I thought we would have *spigola*, suitable for fish on Fridays. Did you know you should have *gnocchi* on Thursday and fish on Friday? Old Roman customs." Laura didn't know about either but smiled in acknowledgement at the lesson.

"How about *risotto ai scampi* for a *primi* and then a side dish of roast potatoes to go with the fish for a main course?" He raised his wine glass in a wordless toast.

Laura felt compelled to raise hers in response. She sipped. The wine was smooth and she sat back to relax. Maybe the meal would be something to blog about if she could remember everything and a good opportunity to introduce Derrick to her readers. At last, the signs were pointing in the right direction for her social life. Doug, her boss, was friendly and hadn't overridden many of her editorial suggestions, and Derrick was positive when she first met him after work the previous month. Now here she was, dining with him.

She was also happy with her new clothes. Two days before the party Laura had left work earlier than usual, telling Doug she would make up for any lost time. The bus took her to the main shopping area. Not the Via Condotti where Gucci and Fendi were located, but the nearby Via del Corso, where ordinary Romans went for the more moderate prices. She wished Stefania, the woman with the sweet little boy who'd kicked the soccer ball under her table, could be with her to help her buy just the right outfit.

Laura found a conservative black suit. As an afterthought, she bought new underwear and stockings to complete the outfit in a nearby shop selling *biancheria intima* such as lacy bras, panties, and nightwear, all so much more luxurious and revealing than the items she bought in Seattle. She spent more than she intended.

When the day of the lunch arrived Laura slipped into her new lingerie before Jake awoke. They felt silky on her skin. If Jake asked why she was wearing her suit, she would just say truthfully that she was going to attend an office lunch and she saw other people dressed up for such events.

Raj and Silvia glanced her way when she arrived at the office. Laura detected a knowing smile on Silvia's face. No one else wore anything other than their normal attire.

Laura surreptitiously glanced at her watch every few minutes, unable to keep her mind on her task. With one o'clock nearing, she told Doug she might be late back to work. He looked displeased. She ignored him.

Now in the restaurant, her tablemate chased thoughts of Doug, shopping and Jake from her mind. An attractive man but for a few tiny broken blood vessels near his nose, hair graying around the temples, and bright blue eyes like her father's. He wore slacks, a sweater over a striped shirt, an expensive-looking tie, and a well-tailored tweed jacket, the ensemble making him appear assured and so English she half-expected him to bring out a pipe.

"Tell me, how long ago did you come to Rome? And I'd like to hear about your country home. In Viterbo, I think you said the other evening."

"I arrived twenty-five years ago. Just a lad, you know. Times were jolly good then, everything cheap. As I said, can't imagine how I would ever be happy in England again, Yorkshire born and bred that I am. Too much rain and no fun. The neighbors were too nosy. The UN has been good to me – you might want to consider a career here. Lots to do in Rome, you know."

Laura found the last bit of news encouraging. "How could I begin a career here if I've only got a one-year contract?"

"There might be a vacancy coming up soon. It would be for three years. Why don't you apply? I'll let you know when it comes out."

Their first course arrived, the rice just tender, the scampi on top perfectly cooked. The conversation lapsed until she said, "I'd love that but I don't know about my husband. He might not like staying here."

"Well, why don't you both come up for a weekend and I'll tell him about all the advantages."

"We don't have a car, I'm afraid."

"Don't worry, I'll drive. We'll leave from the office on a Friday and come back Sunday evening. I'm not planning to go to England for the holidays. Instead of a weekend, how about over the New Year's break?"

Laura hesitated. She had no idea what Jake wanted to do for Christmas and New Year's, now only a few weeks away.

"Thank you for the invitation. I'll talk to my husband."

"What does he do in Rome?"

"Well, he's doing a bit of tutoring, and he recently went to Zurich – he's working with people who do antique restoration."

"Oh? Who are they? Do you know who he saw there? I'm planning a trip to Zurich one of these days and I might want to pop in."

"All I know is the man's name, Muller, nearly the same as mine. Funny."

"Interesting." He abruptly changed the subject. "We'll have a great time over the holiday." He closed the conversation as if all arrangements were settled.

The waiter served the main course, expertly boning the sea bass with its glistening golden skin, before sliding half on each of their plates, the lower piece for Derrick and the top for Laura. He added grilled zucchini and roast potato wedges decorated with rosemary.

When the last bite was gone, she put her fork down. "This is the kind of meal everyone dreams about eating in Rome."

Derrick smiled in satisfaction before saying, "Do you want a salad now or dessert, or shall we have a coffee on the terrace – it's a beautiful day."

"Coffee would be great, and then I have to get back to work soon. Got to keep Doug happy."

They stood on the side terrace near a pot of oleander, looking at the extensive ruins making up the Baths of Caracalla. Laura was enjoying her cappuccino when Derrick gave her advice: "Italians don't drink cappuccino after noon. But rules are made to be broken, aren't they?

Laura tried to think how she could maneuver Jake into letting her go to Derrick's country home if he would not. Maybe he would be off on one of his wild goose chases and wouldn't be around.

"Do you have a family here in Rome?"

"No, my dear. My wife has a shop in London. She shows up once in a while for antique fairs. Never had any wee ones. Pity, don't you know? Anyway, summer will be coming around and we will see if there will be any performances at the Baths. There were many years ago, but the Culture Ministry became worried the whole place would fall down – so no more elephants in *Aida*. Shame, what?" He gestured toward the Baths with the pipe he'd pulled out of his jacket.

Laura smiled inwardly at the sight of the pipe but the pressure to spend time together made her apprehensive. Maybe he was just helpful. Or lonely, without a family.

"Time to get back to work, I guess. Thanks so much. I really enjoyed the food and our talk."

"So soon? Well, until our next meeting. I'll ring you." He put the unlit pipe back in his jacket.

"Yes, that would be very nice," said Laura as she walked away. She caught a heel on her new shoes and stumbled.

"Careful, my dear." He placed a hand on her lower back for a moment.

Silvia invited Laura for a drink after work. Laura knew her co-worker's interest was limited to prying but accepted anyway, hoping for more progress in her social life. Doug, Raj, and Silvia had briefly thanked her the Monday after her lunch party, but there were no return invitations except for occasional Friday night pizzas in restaurants near her office. Jake refused to attend. She knew by the office conversations that her colleagues all enjoyed active social lives. She could not decide if it was because of Jake's absence at the Sunday lunch or the sickening slop she served. Whatever the problem was, she hoped it would be overcome soon.

Silvia carried the wine to the table while Laura waited for the interview to begin.

"Did you enjoy your lunch?"

"Yes, the food was lovely," Laura responded in what she hoped was a neutral voice.

"Need to be careful with him – likes them new to the UN and lots younger than he is. Bit of an old goat, you know." At this she fingered one of the tiny diamond studs in her earlobe. Her action reminded Laura of Jake unconsciously rotating his wedding ring when he was deep in thought. She had noticed that he did that now even more than when they were in Seattle.

"Oh, I'm not worried because I know what the signs are. He's just being helpful, which is more than I can say about a lot of people here."

Silvia's eyes widened with pretended concern. "Please don't think people are unfriendly. We're all busy, and I have a few problems on the home front. You've seen that Giorgio never comes to pizza any more. Like your man. Doug's got a real job with the old house he and Helena bought a couple of years ago. Remodeling is always a problem in Italy, what with all the permits and unreliable workers. Raj's wife is always going back and forth to India." She finished with a flourish: "And you're only here for a year, anyway."

Laura downed the last of her drink and headed home for another weekend with no particular plans. Maybe she'd go shopping again. Jake could just hang around with his soccer games. She was tired and hoped he had started dinner. He hadn't; the apartment was empty. She found a note taped to the refrigerator saying he'd gone to a pub. She retreated to the sofa with a glass of wine. Why doesn't he do some painting? He said he wanted to take a break from teaching to visit museums and have time to paint. But he was so secretive, and she didn't believe his story about the weekend with his student the Sunday she hosted the disastrous lunch. Now she wondered if he ever went to Zurich. Silvia's remark about Giorgio not attending Friday-night pizza as an indication of her domestic troubles overhung Laura's mood like gathering thunderclouds.

Laura sat at her desk, staring blankly at her equally empty computer screen. Her thoughts were focused on Christmas. She needed to get her parents a gift. She hadn't contacted them for a while because her mother insisted turning their conversation toward babies and questions about when she would return to Seattle.

Her desk phone rang. Assuming the caller was Jake but hoping for Derrick, she answered. As though thinking about her had been a summons, it was her mother who began, "How are you dear? It's been so long since we talked. Your dad and I just got home. This time we did Shanghai to Singapore instead of the Caribbean. Deluxe as always, especially with the butler bringing us afternoon tea. You should go on a cruise. All the fabulous food and Las Vegas shows every night. Anyway, we want to come to Rome to see you for a change."

Laura's first reaction to the news of a visit was a silent *oh no*. The pause in the conversation lingered a beat too long before she asked, "When are you thinking of coming?"

"Well, how about February? I know the weather will be nice. You're on the Mediterranean, aren't you? Can we stay with you? We want to see the Colosseum and the Vatican. Maybe you could arrange a visit with the pope."

"Our apartment's pretty small so we'll find you a nice hotel. It's funny, I was just thinking about you when you called. I'm making a Christmas list. What would you and Dad like?"

"A hotel is fine and just buy a trinket. We'll open it when we get there, no use shipping anything. It will be enough just to see you. We thought we would stay only ten days. Jake can show us around and we'll see you on the weekend and in the evenings. Your dad and I want to hear all about your life as a diplomat. It must be very exciting with all those parties. Let me know by next week. Hugs and kisses." Her mother abruptly cut the connection.

Laura was left with the dial tone. Diplomat? Where did that come from? She should have been at my so-called luncheon.

Laura hadn't spent any extended time with her parents since she graduated from high school. Anxious to become independent, Laura insisted on moving to central Washington to attend university instead of applying to schools on the east coast as her mother wanted.

Laura had put off telling her father and mother until a week before the flight, not wanting to give them news that would make them unhappy. After she called to make sure they would be home, she drove to their house rehearsing all the while what she would say to minimize their distress. When she arrived at a large home in a gated community overlooking Lake Washington, she knocked before letting herself in. Her parents were waiting in the living room. Her mother was perched on a blue velvet sofa, her father in front of a large studio photograph of Laura as a baby and her proud mother. The picture took up most of the space on the mantel. She didn't like the photo because it was a glaring reminder that she had no children and no doubt had the same effect on her mother.

Laura's mother patted the cushion next to her but she declined to sit, opting to stand to deliver her news.

"Oh." Her mother's hand flew to her mouth. She put her head down although Laura could see her watering eyes and trembling lip. After her mother wiped her eyes with a handkerchief that had been tucked in the sleeve of her blouse, she recovered enough to ask questions. "Did you say when you are leaving? I hope we'll be able to visit you, but I don't know anything about Rome. Is it safe? But what will Jake do? Does he have a job?"

"I'm sure he'll find something. And of course you will visit as soon as we get organized."

Her mother looked even more distressed. Her father, Hank, tried to comfort his fluttering wife. "Now Dorothy, don't worry. She'll be fine, I'm sure. She's no worse than your sister, the one with the itchy feet. Never should have sent Laura off to London with her."

He put his arm around his wife. His normally smiling blue eyes narrowed as he looked directly at Laura with an expression of reproach. Hank, a wealthy retired building contractor, seldom had much to say about anything unless the subject included his former business or the new high-rises springing up in Seattle. He didn't comment any further on the news beyond, "I'll miss you, sweetie."

Laura knew she had made a mistake in waiting when she saw her father was hurt by her desertion and by the short notice, which left him insufficient time to prepare her mother, who had now become so distraught she began to wring her hands. And she knew her mother thought the move to Rome represented the culmination of everything she didn't want for her daughter: first a husband from a low-life family from the wrong side of the mountains working as a poorly-paid school teacher, and now a man, if she could use the word, with no job, wife as sole support in a foreign country filled with foreigners. Not how her only child's life should go at all.

After her parents had resigned themselves to her relationship with Jake they held their noses and urged her to marry because they made no secret of their desire for grandchildren, ones from a legal relationship. Laura's mother often made pointed remarks, although her father was more subtle. Laura sometimes wondered if it was all about inheritance, since Laura was her only success at maternity and it came in her early forties. Laura saw her as stuck in the past with her unstylish clothes. If anyone asked what she did, she described herself as "just a housewife," an expression that made Laura wince and wonder how the wave of women's liberation managed to stop short, leaving her mother's feet dry on the sands of change. Perhaps it was because Hank, her high school sweetheart, had done well and she didn't need to bother about working. What to eat that was slimming when she had lunch with her friends at private clubs was the biggest problem. That attitude and the disparity in their ages had made for an unbridgeable gulf between their viewpoints and Laura worried that if her own child or children were born too late she might suffer from the inability to cross the same insurmountable distance.

Laura's mind moved from her parents back to Jake and how she would tell him about their visit. Their dislike of Jake was too obvious with Jake responding in kind. What would he be doing when she returned from work to give him the news? Probably nothing although he did do some housework and shopping when he wasn't driving or engrossed in watching some game on the television or his laptop. The tutoring was no longer mentioned and he frequently smelled of beer and cigarettes. The paint brushes still looked unused.

She recognized the inertia of their marriage had been roiled by the move to Italy, although it wasn't in the manner she intended. Instead of coming closer, a centrifugal force had whirled them into seldom-intersecting elliptical orbits, hers energized, his wobbly. Whatever the difficulties of living in Rome were, she was becoming increasingly sure that she would find a more fulfilling life in Rome rather than Seattle. With or without Jake.

She turned back to her work, but the day passed slowly as she worried about him and her parents' visit. As she expected, the evening wasn't any better. Jake watched another inane *spettacolo* with bouncing babes on TV while they ate dinner. In an effort to appear as if married life was normal, after the dishes were done Laura said she was going to get ready for bed. Jake ignored the hint. She was washing her hands when she heard him come into the bathroom. She looked in the mirror to see his face hovering over her shoulder.

"It's not what you think. I delivered stuff to a gallery for sale. We might even get a cut of the profits. It's interesting to be a part of the action. I'll be helping restore a few old artworks so others have a chance to enjoy them. Otherwise they would just rot in some moldy old church or castle. You should be proud of me instead of picking all the time."

Laura tried a smile. Then she gave him the bad news. "Well, we've got a small problem: my mom and dad are coming in February for ten days. They expect the weather to be warm and that you will take them around the whole time."

"Are you kidding? No way – I'm not a tour guide. What were you thinking to agree to this? We don't have a car. And I'm busy. This is insane."

He marched off to his spot in front of the television, leaving Laura holding the toothpaste, squeezed in the middle instead of from the bottom as she liked. She carefully rolled the tube, flattening the used portions.

Before she left for work the next morning she shook Jake awake and handed him a mug of coffee. "Didn't get a chance last night to tell you, but we might have an invitation for New Year's. A guy at the office has invited us to his country home. He says he likes art and

I think you'd like him. What shall I tell him? I need to let him know, and I think it would be fun. Can we go, please?"

Jake, still half asleep, didn't register what she was saying.

Laura took his non-rejection of the idea as a "yes."

Laura worked long hours on her projects and frequently brought work home. Her editing came back with fewer critical markings. But concerns about Jake's remoteness and the arrival of her parents in the new year nagged. She worried that they would see the fault lines in their daughter's marriage, now so evident. She could not think of any way to explain the situation if they asked. And she and Jake needed to get a car and make plans to entertain them. Maybe Derrick would have good ideas. She called his office.

"Hi Derrick."

"Yes? How are you? Did you enjoy our lunch?"

"Yes, lunch was great. Actually, I loved the whole time – especially talking with you. I really don't have many friends here yet, and I want to learn more about the UN and Rome. And we would really like to come for New Year's Eve. But now I have a small problem I hope you might be able to help me solve."

Derrick listened to her story about her parents and no car. He invited her for drinks at an American-style bar near Piazza del Popolo, a long way from her office and apartment, where they could discuss her problems.

A piano player in a white dinner jacket worked over old standards, launching the set with "Night and Day" and "I Get a Kick Out of You," before moving into "I Left My Heart in San Francisco." The evening was dark and cold as they sat outside, not quite near enough to the heaters arranged in a row along the sidewalk. Derrick fiddled with his pipe, filling, tamping, lighting, and puffing, as they both sipped a warming Sangiovese. Artistic types and businessmen streamed into the bar for an *aperitivo* before dinner. Laura contemplated a floodlit fountain in the piazza with its four lions surrounding an enormous obelisk.

Derrick took her gaze as a cue to begin a history lesson – how the obelisk was brought to Rome by Augustus and set up in the Circus Maximus and then transported to the piazza in the 1600s. The reference to the Circus Maximus reminded her about the job Derrick had mentioned. She ignored his commentary to consider whether she should apply and what would happen if she was selected. And what about Jake? Maybe the next tidal change in their lives would lift their marriage off the rocks.

Derrick's voice joined with the music as background white noise as Laura's thoughts turned to the obelisks she'd encountered, thrusting into the sky. First, the funny one on the elephant. Then the one in the center of the Fountain of the Four Rivers in the Piazza Navona, her introduction to the beauties of the city, and where she returned to unexpectedly meet Stefania and little Arturo. She had been sure that obelisk heralded a happy stay in Rome until Jake told her about his trip to Zurich just before the lunch party. Then the one by San Giovanni, where she didn't meet Jake that first day in the apartment; and at Tivoli, where she bought the bronze youth now standing guard by her bedside. And now, here she sat with Derrick looking at yet another obelisk while asking for favors and knowing something would have to be offered in return, willingly or not. Maybe they pointed at answers floating somewhere up above that she could not see.

The view and her musings were punctuated by buses crowded with commuters, their blank eyes staring out the windows without seeing. Taxis, motorbikes, and Vespas competed for space. Laura sighed. So hard to settle here, yet her determination to remain grew rather than diminished with every setback. Her attention moved back to Derrick when she thought she heard him say, "Did I tell you that you are beautiful?"

She looked at him in surprise, grateful that he could not see her blushing in the dark. No one had said that to her since she and Jake first got together. If there was an appropriate response to a man she hardly knew she didn't know what it was other than a brief, "Thank you."

"I mean it."

She was gratified but sensed dangerous waters and steered the conversation back to her parents.

"Here's my problem. I haven't seen my father or mother since I left and Jake, you know – my husband – has never been fond of them, and now they are coming in February for over a week and I don't know what to do with them and we haven't got a car. Do you have any ideas of how I could get a car? Also, I need a hotel. Not far from us over by Via Gallia."

"Ah." Derrick blew a few breaths into the pipe stem. Laura watched the bowl glow like the braziers used by the chestnut vendors now scattered about the major tourist spots. He appeared to be inflating with self-importance as he continued, "Let me think. How about lunch as soon as I have some ideas? My secretary will give you a call."

He went on to suggest she plan to take a few hours off work. He would show her the hotels he selected and also discuss their New Year's visit and the use of a car.

"Do those ideas make you feel better?"

"Yes." She pushed her glass to the side, declining a third. Time to go home. On the bus she thought about Derrick's remark that she was beautiful and the second invitation to lunch. He seemed a little lecherous but she needed his help.

Lunch with Derrick was set for a few days before Christmas. In the interim an American, George Ferguson, who worked in another unit, invited Laura and Jake to share in his family's annual Christmas potluck. He assured her there would be a traditional turkey and trimmings. It would be nice if she would bring a bottle of wine and a dessert. She didn't know the other invitees but was overjoyed to have an invitation. Surprisingly, Jake agreed to the idea, since he would be with Americans.

The day of her lunch date, Derrick picked her up in front of the office in his new Mercedes. She relaxed in the plush and quiet car as they drove to a hotel on the far side of town. Its restaurant was famous, Michelin rated. Laura pictured herself as stylish and self-assured in her black suit and high heels as they were led to a secluded table in the opulent dining room, surrounded by gold-framed paintings, flowers, and crystal. A few discreet holiday ornaments decorated the tables. She opened her menu. None of the offerings had a price listed. She told Derrick to order whatever he thought would be good.

He selected *crostini* as a starter, to be followed by *pappardelle alla lepre*. The small rounds of toast were topped with pâté, olive paste, or a tomato mixture. Laura ate more than her share.

When the pasta dish was presented Laura asked what *lepre* was.

"Rabbit, or I should say, hare," he replied.

Despite misgivings about eating a relative of Peter Rabbit she enjoyed the wide noodles graced with a thick sauce made with bacon, onion, celery and small cubes of hare. When the main course arrived, an even richer *osso buco*, Laura only tried a taste of the marrow in the veal shank because she wanted dessert. Glasses of red and white wine accompanied each course, and by the time a chocolate tart covered with a blood-red berry sauce arrived, Laura felt woozy. The coffee didn't have any effect.

As they left the restaurant, Derrick said, "This is one of the hotels your parents might like. I made arrangements to check out a room so you can tell your mother all about the accommodations." He retrieved a room key from the front desk on their way to the elevator.

Laura saw herself in the elevator mirror. Her face and neck were pink and her features indistinct. She felt a little unsteady. She brushed back a strand of blonde hair hanging over her eyes but her vision didn't clear.

Derrick opened the door and extended his hand, palm upward, to usher her in. She didn't see him hang a sign on the door handle: *Si Prega Di Non Distubare.*

Instead, Laura saw not a room but a suite with an entryway, large bath, nook with a desk, and a bedroom with a balcony overlooking a garden set with umbrella pines and orange trees. How wonderful it would be to stay in the suite for a week. Alone.

Derrick said softly, "Let's rest a moment."

She forgot about Jake and her family as she sank down on the coverlet, knowing that the meal and wine combined to reduce inhibitions to near zero. She closed her eyes.

"My dear, you'll never know how much I have been waiting for this. From the first time I saw you, I knew you were the one to make me happy,"

At the sound of Derrick's words she sat up and opened her eyes to look at him. She could clearly see his lustful expression and it repelled her. "Derrick, I'm sorry, but I can't. I don't want to. I'm married. You're married. I...I just can't."

Derrick drew back as if bitten by a snake. "Well, if that's what you want. I thought you wanted some love." He knotted up his tie and tucked in his shirt. His face was flushed with anger as he watched her put her shoes back on and use her fingers to comb her hair.

She tried to find suitable words to smooth over the awkward situation. She ended up with, "I do, want to be loved I mean, but things are all messed up and I don't want more problems right now. Please don't totally reject me. I want to continue our relationship, but as friendship. Maybe in the future..." Unsure what she did want, the thought trailed off.

"I'll call a cab."

She'd already upset him so there was nothing to lose. "Derrick, I still need to know what to do about my parents."

Derrick hesitated before responding as if he was considering whether it was worthwhile to continue to help her. The decision made, he said, "I've got an old car I don't use much. I could lend it to you. When you come over New Year's Eve, you and, what did you call him, oh yes – Jake, can look at it. I know you wouldn't want to rent this room for your parents unless they're rich. Are they? If not, I've got other ideas. Let me know next week. What do you say?"

"Thanks, Derrick, you are a marvel. Please do find another hotel. And please forgive me." She didn't tell him they could have easily afforded the suite but the thought of them staying in this one was too unpleasant to picture.

Derrick gave her a forced but hopeful smile.

On the cab ride back to the office Laura breathed a sigh of relief and shoved the scenario depicting her actions to a corner of her mind where she hoped they would remain. Out of sight, but not forgotten. And definitely not something to put in a blog.

"Jake? We need to talk for a moment. We have to settle the arrangements for my mom and dad, and I have info about New Year's."

He turned away from the television only after waiting to watch the outcome of a penalty kick.

"I said I wanted to tell you about some good news."

He shrugged before muting the television, all the while keeping his eyes on the screen.

Despite the unpromising response, Laura commenced. "You agreed that we could go with the man in my office to his country house for New Year's Eve. Well, I forgot to tell you that his wife is an antiques dealer. You might be interested since you're working in that field now. And, he also said he would find a hotel and lend us a car while my folks are here. Actually I only know him a little, but he is kind to newcomers."

Jake's antenna quivered at the news. "Who is he? How do you know him?"

"Well, he's rather a big wheel at the office, name's Derrick, he's English, and, like I said, he likes to help new arrivals. Besides, we need to get to know more people. I don't know how many will be at the New Year's party, but it should be fun to see a villa. You'll laugh at his accent."

"Did you say his wife was an antiques dealer?"

"Yes. I understand that she has an antique store in London. You might like to talk to her."

"Might be interesting." He couldn't recall agreeing to the excursion but became intrigued with the idea. He thought Stella might be interested to hear about the man.

"Okay, but only for one night. I might have to get to the lab." He thought of Stella's still unseen charms. He hoped the information would warm her up.

On Christmas Day Laura got up early to make *tiramisu* for the potluck. This time it came out well. They shared slices of *panettone* and juice made from blood oranges for breakfast. Jake gave her a silk scarf and Laura presented him with shaving lotion and a bottle of Jack Daniels, his favorite whiskey, from the office commissary. She looked at the Valentino label on the scarf wondering how he found the money to buy such an expensive item. Or was it a fake?

"Let's go to the Vatican to see what's going on. I've seen pictures of the pope giving a speech in a bunch of languages. I think someone told me they call it *Urbi et Orbi* or something like that. And we need to be at the Fergusons' apartment by five. American-style dinner hour I guess. It seems strange. I like dinner later now. Italian style."

The crowds in front of St. Peter's filled the enormous piazza, barely leaving room for the obelisk, two fountains, life-size Nativity set, and Christmas tree. Neither Laura nor Jake could hear much of the speech, but it was exciting anyway to be with happy people from all corners of the globe, many waving flags and wearing national costumes. Following the speech they walked over the Ponte San Angelo to the Piazza Navona, which was crowded with booths filled with toys and balloons for children, who were running in circles on joyous overdrive. She looked unsuccessfully for little Arturo and his mother Stefania.

Laura remarked, "Lovely, don't you think? Not so commercial."

"Yeah." Jake's attention was directed to the sketches and paintings resting on easels manned by hopeful artists. He vowed again to begin.

When they arrived at the Fergusons' home, Laura thought it looked like a photo shoot for an American women's magazine with a large, decorated fake tree surrounded by opened boxes, the wrappings strewn about. There was a fire in the fireplace hung with stockings. A buffet table decorated with poinsettias was already laden with salads and vegetables, fruitcake and brownies. A bar with bourbon and scotch, along with the usual bottles of red and white wine, took up one corner of the room.

"Just put your dessert over there," George said, gesturing toward the table. "Mona will be out to say hello in a minute. Let me introduce you to the others."

Many of the guests were clustered around the television watching CNN's production of Christmas around the world, in between focusing on their wine and cocktails. Laura didn't know any of them beyond a passing "hi" in the halls or cafeteria, nor had she met any of their wives or husbands. She busied herself with introductions even though she could see Jake drawing back.

Laura felt a sense of dislocation listening to the hosts' and guests' nostalgic talk about American politics, American films and TV shows, and what they would do on their vacations at Disneyland or Yellowstone. They seemed intent on preserving their American culture to ward off the pull of Italy and Europe. She felt the opposite – glad to be freed from the daily grind in Seattle and ready for new experiences. There had to be some stray DNA in her genes that made her want to live away from her original home. Even her globe-trotting aunt came home from her travels before setting off again.

The other guests got around to asking about their experiences in Rome after exhausting more interesting topics like office politics. One of the women approached Jake with the expression of an inquisitor: "So do you like working for the United Nations? What did you say you did?"

"My wife works for the UN."

"Oh. What do you do to pass the time, then? I at least have my ladies' group. Otherwise I don't know what I would do all day. I find life here so difficult with the traffic, the noise, the dirt."

"I'm an artist."

"Oh my – maybe you'd like to come talk to our members." The woman rattled on about her friends as Jake turned toward the turkey now on the table. Already dissected some time ago, the meat was cold and the gravy congealed by the time he loaded up his paper plate. The vegetables were also cold and overcooked.

Every time Laura looked at Jake he was openly yawning. She made excuses as soon as the meal was finished. "Thank you so much but I'm not feeling well. I'll pick up my dish next week," she told Mona as she and Jake zipped up their jackets.

Myriad strings of holiday lights strung over the streets illuminated their way home.

"Isn't this beautiful?"

"It was a nightmare," said Jake. "At least you know how to get hot food on the table. If some old bag thinks I'm going to talk to her silly group, she's nuts."

"Jake, you're ruining everything. I thought we'd have a good time together here but instead it's worse than Seattle. Can't you make an effort sometimes? And what do you mean 'at least'?"

"You complain about me being gone but where are you all the time?"

Laura looked at the shuttered shop windows lining the street. A good question, where was she? And what was the answer?

The week between Christmas and New Year's was quiet in the apartment. After the uncomfortable dinner Laura was at a loss about next steps with Jake. Grateful to have work to do in the office, she managed to finish a big project early. Her comfort level steadily rose, along with her hopes for a future in Rome.

"Derrick will pick us up at noon. What clothes shall I take? Do you think people will be dressed formally? Maybe I should buy a cocktail dress. What are you going to take?"

"Just take your regulars, your Levi's and a warm jacket. I'll bet the place is just a cabin like up at Snoqualmie Pass, anyway. Quit going on and on."

"Don't be a jerk." She put her black suit, new scarf, shoes, and Italian underwear in the overnight case as she visualized yet another uncomfortable social event.

Derrick arrived on schedule. After Laura introduced Jake, he loaded their case in the trunk and climbed into the back seat where they sat as far apart as possible, each looking out their respective windows. The Mercedes purred along the Via Cassia. Derrick sounded as smooth as the engine as he filled the silence.

"Cottage needs a bit of work, you know, but don't worry – you'll be cozy. Hope the power doesn't go out – once in a while there's a problem. Bit of a bother, but nothing serious. Better half will show up this evening – coming from London. Got a car and driver to meet her at the airport."

Jake eyed the back of Derrick's head suspiciously. Why did he bother inviting people he didn't know? It didn't sound right. Surely Laura couldn't be interested in this old geezer, and he didn't want to cultivate Derrick's friendship, unless of course the bit about antiques turned out to be useful. Stella would want to know all about him, if he really had any. He closed his eyes to better concentrate on visualizing the party and how he could turn the subject to antiquities.

The car slowed as Derrick turned onto a secondary road and then on a succession of narrower roads until they came to a gate at the entrance of a winding drive lined with dark obelisk-shaped cypresses. Jake, lulled by the ride, had dozed off while wondering what Stella was doing, when she would need to travel with him again, and how long she would keep leading him on with no result, at least not the one he now wanted. Acting as a local delivery man after his one venture to Zurich was getting tiresome, even if he was getting paid.

They turned in at the open gate, passing olive groves and a pasture with a few sheep standing motionless in the cool mist that enveloped the valley in cotton wool. A large villa came into view as they ascended a hill. The main section with two stories was covered with a lichen-blotched terracotta tile roof. Dark green shutters flanked the windows, contrasting with an ocher-colored exterior. An enormous umbrella pine shaded a one-story garden room.

A man wearing rubber boots carried a pitchfork as he walked toward the barn. He touched his hat brim when he saw Derrick, who didn't return the acknowledgement. "Antonio will get your bag. Let's hope he's got a fire going – getting chilly. Frost tonight, don't you know."

Derrick took hold of Laura's elbow and steered her into a room with fourteen-foot ceilings, plump upholstered chairs, and a sofa facing a grand fireplace. The honey-colored, waxed terracotta floors were covered with antique carpets. Heavy draperies framed tall windows. French doors led to a terrace and a swimming pool covered for the winter. Beyond, a vineyard slept.

Jake followed behind filled with suspicion because Laura accompanied him so readily.

"Here's home. Not much, but I think you'll be comfortable." He smiled at Laura and ignored Jake.

Jake was incensed at the slight and at the overblown luxury of the decor. Damned effete Europeans.

"Let's have a sherry before I show you your room, where you can change. Better half should be here shortly." At the sound of his voice a maid came into the room carrying a tray laden with sherry, glasses, and an assortment of snacks.

"Oh, Derrick, what a super..."

Jake cut her off. "I'd rather have bourbon. With ice. Sherry's not my drink."

Derrick obligingly went to a drinks cabinet but apologized for the lack of ice when he returned with a full tumbler. Jake continued to ignore Laura, who he knew was silently willing him to be more civil. His attention gravitated to a row of shelves above the fireplace. They held several undecorated black pots, a few more with red figures of gods and goddesses around the bowl, two small bronze statues covered in verdigris, and several marble pieces, including a sandaled foot missing its little toe.

Jake was curious. "Where'd you get these? From around here, are they?"

"Yes, found them on my property. They're Etruscan – you know, those strange people no one really knows much about. Can't even read their writing, but you should see their tomb paintings. Did they ever know how to live it up!" He leered.

"Your property?"

"Yes, are you interested in them? Maybe you could help me find more. Your wife mentioned that you were in Zurich recently. There are so many dealers and galleries there, but I'd like to know a reliable one just to get an estimate sometime."

Before Jake could answer the door opened with a gust of cold air rushing in along with a tall, thin woman carrying a chinchilla coat. "Darling," she said, air-kissing Derrick near one side of his face as she threw the coat over a chair. "I'm shattered. A nightmare with all those tourists squeezing by me with their carrier bags and trash. One even knocked my drink over. Look." She pointed to a miniscule splotch on the sleeve of her dress.

Laura and Jake stood, waiting to be introduced, but the woman didn't notice them. She walked over to the fire to warm her hands. It took a full minute before she turned around. "Oh, I see we have company. Derrick, please do introduce me." Her voice was flat and disinterested. She frowned at their casual clothes.

"Darling, I invited my new friends, Laura and Jake Miller, to share our New Year's Eve celebrations. Laura works with me and Jake is interested in my tiny collection." He waved at the shelves before saying, "This is my wife, Livia."

Livia briefly extended a limp and ice-cold blue-veined claw to each of them. Her expression telegraphed scorn that Derrick had brought yet another pair of insignificant strays home as one did orphaned puppies. She then put the hand out for a sherry and turned away again to face the fire. Derrick prattled on into the silent room until the maid showed Laura where she could change her clothes. Jake remained, wordlessly contemplating the warm bourbon reflecting in the cut crystal of his tumbler as the fire cast flickering light. Noises from the hallway eventually broke the tension. Two sets of neighbors, all Italians, entered. Jake, and Laura, who had returned, stood again.

"Here are my delightful neighbors, Massimiliano Rinaldi with his wife, Oriana Colombo, and Salvatore Moretti with Cristina Zefferelli." They were middle-aged and well dressed, husbands in tailored suits, wives in modest cocktail dresses. They had comfortable demeanors, leaning toward each other to converse and welcome their partners' comments.

All four were talkative and wanted to know about Jake and Laura, politely asking questions in broken English without actually prying. Laura told them about her work after they expressed support for the United Nations. Jake warmed to them as he explained what paintings he planned and what sites had particularly caught his attention. He thought it best not to bring up anything about antiquities unless Derrick expanded on the subject. He didn't. Livia smiled and murmured as if she was interested.

The maid motioned to Derrick that dinner was ready. The table, set with silver, glowed in the candlelight. Laura was seated on Derrick's right at one end of the table and Jake on Livia's right at the other end.

As the maid was grating truffles over steaming bowls of risotto, Livia whispered into Jake's ear, "You'd best keep a close watch. That one never gives up." Her head tilted toward her husband to make sure he got the message.

A tsunami of anger swept over Jake as he visualized Laura and Derrick making love. He gripped the table to steady himself until he saw Livia's satisfied expression. He recognized she had intentionally created havoc, and tried to will his thoughts back to safe Seattle where life had always seemed under control and people were normal. His appetite vanished but he put up a pretense of enjoying the meal.

Midway through the fish course, Signora Zefferelli remarked to Laura that she had a son. "My Francesco is an architect with two other partners in Milan. I hoped he would be able to be here for the whole week, but he could only get away for two days at Christmas. Next weekend he will be skiing with friends at Cortina. I expect I'll see him shortly after. The train from Milan to Rome is so fast, he often comes for a weekend. Maybe you and your husband would like to meet him. He's about your age, not old like me."

"Yes, we'd love to meet him. I've been hoping to meet Italians instead of so many Americans at the UN."

Signora Zefferelli responded, "Shall I give him a phone number to call?"

"That would be nice," Laura replied. She didn't see Derrick listening intently to this exchange. Jake, his attention focused on toying with his food, didn't notice.

When the dessert of English plum pudding flamed with brandy was finished, Derrick looked at his watch. "It's nearly time." They pushed back their chairs and placed their napkins on the table before moving to the fireplace for the New Year's toast. They raised their glasses as their cell phones ticked over to midnight. Laura tried to kiss Jake, but he turned away. Rejected, she shook hands with the other guests and Derrick, wishing them *buon anno*. Livia ignored them.

Before the guests left, Laura dug in her handbag for a piece of paper and pen to write her personal cell number and office e-mail address. She gave the note to Signora Zefferelli.

Derrick drove them home on New Year's Day after breakfast. Livia didn't show. Jake was silent on the way, worn out by the effort of pretending he fit in and knowing that the other guests probably thought him rude in his jeans and heavy sweater. And he was upset with Laura, smiling and chatting with Derrick, obviously delighted with her new experience. His mind was full of unsettling thoughts: I don't trust her anymore. And who the hell is this guy and his nasty wife? What did she really mean when she told me to watch it? Laura couldn't, wouldn't. Didn't?

As Derrick deposited them at their apartment building, he spoke to Jake: "What did you say the dealer in Switzerland is called?"

"I didn't, but it's Muller."

"Ah, yes. Come to think of it, Laura told me earlier."

Jake glared at Laura in anger.

JANUARY

"PRONTO." **JAKE ANSWERED** his cell phone.

"Who is it?" Laura asked. He waved her off and took the phone into the bathroom, making sure to shut the door so she couldn't hear anything. When he'd finished the call, Jake said "I'm off to the lab. See ya'."

The street door where the restoration workshop was located swung open after he rang the *citofono*. Jake crossed a courtyard packed with junk: an old cart, boards and chunks of plaster heaped up in a corner, and several large green bottles encased in rotting wicker. He climbed stairs to a doorway on the top floor where Marco stood waiting with a cigarette dangling from his lip. He gestured for Jake to enter the room. Cold sunlight flooded through skylights, illuminating racks and boxes filled with tools, brushes, chemicals, paints, and trays of glass tiles in several sizes.

Several Asian women dressed in white lab coats and blue gloves bent over long tables covered in bits of sculpture, pieces of broken pots, a damaged fresco, and mosaic fragments. One woman was using what looked like dental tools. Jake shuddered at the memory of his last visit.

Marco said, "I call all of them Maria because they all look the same to me." They raised their heads for a moment at the sound of his voice before returning to their tasks.

Jake was puzzled. Maybe they didn't speak Italian or English, or were handicapped, or refugees, or – what?

"Just watch what they're doing with the things that came in with our latest rescue operation. Then maybe we'll let you try to help. If you get good we'll put you to work."

Jake obediently walked around the tables. But he couldn't see how watching the silent women would help him become anything other than a menial worker like them. He wondered if Marco would call him "Maria" along with the other flunkies. He thought about the strange lettering on a package he had collected at the airport one time. He turned to Marco, who stood next to him as if he was worried Jake would steal something. "Where does this stuff come from?"

Marco waved his hand in a vague manner and said, "From east of here, where no one wants it anymore. Maybe you'd rather help us in our rescue efforts along with driving?"

The idea that he could actually save works of art was compelling. Jake would really have a story to brag about in Seattle. "Yeah, that would be better. Don't think I could do this kind of picky work. Want to be in the big picture." And maybe earn more money, even a cut of the proceeds. He'd bring that up later.

When Marco turned away to dismiss him, Jake walked back out into the cold, bright day. He could not stop thinking of a Madonna's face in a ruined fragment. She stared at him reproachfully with one remaining eye.

Stella called the following week to say she needed him to drive to Ravenna to help with an incoming shipment.

"What kind of shipment?"

"Just part of a rescue operation. Odds and ends nobody wants where they are now. We save them, like Marco told you. Be ready on Thursday." She reeled off an address, which Jake scribbled down and plugged into his phone's navigator.

Jake was excited. He thought about the money hidden behind the picture of the Appia Antica in their living room, sure Laura would never check there. Soon there would be more. Thursday couldn't come soon enough.

Jake tried to sound nonchalant Thursday morning as he said to Laura, "I'll be in Ravenna for several days. I'll give you a call if I have a chance." He shut the apartment door before she could say anything. He jumped on a bus to get to the warehouse to pick up the delivery van, *furgone,* and get going up the road. After the turnoff from the A-1, Jake relaxed and lit up. As he breathed in the smoke, he saw indistinct figures in the road ahead. The figures became two policemen waving what looked like ping pong paddles. One stepped into the road to block him while the other remained on the side. Both had automatic weapons and wore body armor.

Jake pulled over and tried to rehearse answers to the obvious questions the police might have about an American driving a van with Italian plates.

"*Patente?*" Jake had no idea what the word meant. He pulled out his new UN identity card and the false papers showing he rented the vehicle.

"*No. Patente,*" the officer insisted. The only other document in his wallet besides a couple of credit cards was his Washington State driver's license. He handed it over. The cop looked satisfied. Sweating, Jake filed the word away for future use. The policeman carefully examined both sides of the card. Just as he began to confer with his partner a red Ferrari sped by them. Distracted, the officers turned to watch. More interested in the rapidly disappearing sports car than Jake in the anonymous van, the first man handed back his license and waved him onward.

Needing a break Jake pulled into a gas station to relieve himself, get fuel, and review his instructions one more time. He regarded himself in the washroom mirror. Same height, same brown hair as before, but now with a little sprinkling of gray. He'd added two days' worth of stubble trying to appear Italian. Despite his efforts, he still looked like a tourist with his American clothes. But his reflection also showed him a few frown lines on his brow and the intimation of lines from nose to mouth. He couldn't see the top of his head. He'd read in a men's magazine that hair loss often started on the crown. He raked his hands over his head and felt a small patch of unaccustomed smoothness at the back. He sat in the van for a quarter hour before pulling out of the parking lot.

Jake neared Ravenna thinking it shouldn't be difficult to find the hotel near Marina di Ravenna where a room awaited. But when he tried to locate the elusive road to the Adriatic, the winter night had already closed in and his shoulder and neck ached from the strain of driving on unfamiliar roads with a van that handled nothing like the Mercedes he'd driven to Zurich. He made several false turns before he finally came to an area near the water. Pine woods and small side roads with signs advertising beach resorts, all closed for the winter, lined the road. He continued north for a few miles until the sign for the marina came into view.

The nearby Hotel Adriatico was a shabby building with peeling stucco and shutters hanging at odd angles. A single car was parked in the graveled parking lot, well away from the intense overhead light.

A man sitting in the small entryway was fondling a porno magazine. He stopped running his eyes and hands over the photos when he looked up and noticed Jake.

"Hi, I'm Jake. Stella said to ask for Nando."

"Nando?"

"I don't know who he is – like I said he's the person Stella said I should see." Jake began to worry he was in the wrong place.

The man put down the magazine and rummaged for a cigarette. "You. Who?"

"I'm Jake, I already told you. I'm to meet Nando. Who are you?"

Without responding to his question, the man said, *"Momento,"* and walked out a door leading to the back of the building. Jake waited impatiently. He fingered the magazine. None of the models were like Laura or Stella. He liked their carefully posed, sexually aggressive appearance. They looked readily available and not liable to ask for commitments.

A muscular, unshaven man eventually showed up. Dressed in a heavy sweater, black leather jacket, and dirty jeans, he had the demeanor of a cold-eyed convict – like Stella's two other companions, only with more of an air of authority.

In heavily accented English the man said, "Sorry for the wait. I'm Nando. I'll need your help tomorrow morning. Take a break before we go to dinner when you can tell me all about yourself. Meet me here at eight."

"Okay, but I'd like a drink first. Long drive today."

"You'll find a bottle in the room. On the second floor."

Jake climbed the stairs with his duffel bag. Halfway down the hall a door stood open. He entered to find nothing but a narrow bed and an unsteady night table. A liter of Johnnie Walker Red and a smudged glass rested on the table. No TV. The dreary bathroom down the hall had a curtainless shower in one corner and a grimy sink and toilet.

Jake lay on the bed hoping there weren't fleas or bedbugs. Restless, he got up to take a shower. But the water soon became tepid, and then cold as the greasy suds reluctantly went down the drain. He dried himself with the thin, sour-smelling towel, dressed, and then poured a shot of the scotch. He glanced at his watch – an hour to go. He fell asleep, only to be awakened by Nando grabbing his shoulder. "Dinnertime." Groggy from the alcohol and the short nap, Jake got up and put on his shoes.

Nando's late-model BMW 5 Series came with a driver. They both got in the back seat. Jake didn't respond to any of Nando's questions about his journey and Stella other than to say everything was okay.

The restaurant specialized in seafood fresh from the Adriatic. Jake ordered a mixed seafood antipasto and *coda di rospo*, monkfish. Nando selected *spaghetti alla vongole*, clams, followed by *capi santi*, scallops. While they ate Jake noticed several tough men also in the uniform of heavy sweaters and leather jackets sitting with the driver at the next table. Bodyguards? Why would they be necessary? Probably just laborers. The men ordered course after course, all the while keeping Nando and Jake in sight. Nando signaled the waiter after they finished their espresso and *amaro*. The waiter gave the bill to the driver, who dropped a fistful of euros on the tray. They all left. Jake didn't see where the other men went. Back at the hotel, Nando said, "Be ready at six."

Jake spent a restless night thinking about Stella and her friends but convinced himself that nothing was wrong and that he would have good stories to tell his poker buddies when he returned to Seattle.

The wakeup call from Nando came early. The unnamed man at the entrance the previous evening, now even more unkempt, handed him a mug of steaming liquid, not as strong as espresso but four times the amount, *americano* or *brodo*, broth, the Italians called it.

Nando came in dressed for cold weather. He signaled to the other man to get Jake warmer clothes. Jake put on the watch hat, heavy jacket, and gloves the man collected for him. He didn't have any work boots, only the sports shoes he wore the day before. They set off for a harbor some miles further up the coast, Jake driving with Nando giving the directions.

"Where are we going? What are we going to do?"

"You'll see. Don't worry, hard work won't hurt you."

They came to a dock where Jake could see a small coastal freighter, its lights barely showing through the freezing fog. The men from yesterday evening's dinner were waiting dockside, stamping their feet in the cold. Nando went on board and climbed to the bridge. Jake could hear raised voices, an argument in some language. Nando eventually emerged, stuffing his wallet back in a pocket with a testy expression on his face.

"Let's get to work."

Jake followed him and the men up the gangplank and then down into the hold. Four large unlabeled crates were stacked up with the other cargo. Nando told Jake to help the men carry them to a truck parked near the dock. The heavy crates had to be maneuvered up to the deck, and then to the shore before lifting them into the truck. "*Porca miseria,*" the men complained. It was well past noon by the time they finished. Jake was worn out and famished. His toes felt frostbitten.

The group turned back to the hotel, Jake and Nando in the van, the others in the truck. One of the men was appointed to watch the truck. Jake wondered if he was armed. The rest of the group entered through the back door. A hallway led to a kitchen where a fat and perspiring woman boiled pasta while occasionally stirring a meaty sauce simmering in a large frying pan. Steam rose in a spiral from the pasta pot and carried with it the scent of oregano from the sauce. Jake's mouth watered as he watched her drain the pasta before pouring it into the sauce. The workers lined up, holding out their bowls like convicts as she served directly from the frying pan. Someone took a portion to the guard.

Nando stood up and flicked his head toward the door as soon as the bowls, and the glasses that had been filled from unlabeled bottles of red wine, were emptied by the silent group. They trooped out to the truck to store the crates in a shed behind the parking lot. When they were finished, Nando handed a map to Jake. His grubby forefinger pointed to a spot next to a tertiary road on the western outskirts of Ravenna.

"At four o'clock, drive to this place, park in the courtyard, and ask for Robert. Two crates will already be loaded in the van by my guys. Robert will take care of everything. You might as well take a break now – you've got a couple of hours. We will finish up early tomorrow and then you're done here."

Jake bristled at being treated as a servant again but kept quiet as he watched the man appointed as guard leave in the now-empty truck. He contented himself by mentally counting the money he would be saving up in the next few months. Two thousand, three, four? Maybe even more.

Jake found the van difficult to maneuver because of the weight of the two crates. He merged into the traffic and found his way around the center of the city and then to the dirt road leading to his destination. The medieval farmhouse and attached buildings took up three sides of the property and surrounded a yard full of rusted equipment, including the remains of an ancient Lamborghini tractor. One wing of the building had lost many of its roof tiles as if it had been bombed. Jake saw bare timbers over the upper floor as the last rays of the sun faded out.

A Doberman, barking in rage, rushed to meet him, saliva dripping from sharp fangs. Jake sat still, afraid to open the door. A light over a doorway went on and a man in tan corduroys and a quilted vest emerged. He collared the dog and attached it to a chain bolted to a doghouse. Jake lowered the window a few inches. "Are you Robert?"

"That's me. My men will unload. When we're done go back to the hotel but be back here by eight tomorrow." He didn't invite Jake inside. Zurich all over again.

Jake watched as the same men who helped move the crates earlier in the day came out of the farmhouse to open the van's back doors, remove the cargo, and lug it into the house without a word. Jake turned back to say goodbye, but Robert had already entered the house. The dog was barking again.

The hotel was enveloped in silence. Jake fell into bed without taking off his clothes. In the morning he was stiff and could feel his muscles aching even more than the previous evening. He switched on the light to see his watch. Six and pitch dark. He glanced out the window to see a hard frost on the gravel and surrounding shrubs glittering in the glare cast by the light over the parking lot. He went back to bed.

Nando shook him awake. Jake and the other workers tramped to the storage shed to load the two remaining crates into the van. The sun had risen by the time he headed back to Robert's.

The dog went into another paroxysm of barking. Robert came out. "Help me. The others aren't here yet and I don't want to wait."

He caught the lunging dog by the collar and wrestled him off. With only two to handle the heavy boxes, they staggered as they moved them into a well-lit wing of the house. The contents of the crates from yesterday's delivery, pieces of marble sculptures, winged feet, hands, and several heads, one missing its nose, dirt-encrusted smashed pots, and a few fragments of mosaics and frescoes, were spread out on a long table. Many were deteriorated, as though they had been carelessly handled.

"You can also help me crate this bunch up again. They go to our lab in Rome. With you." Robert waved in the direction of the pieces needing cleaning or repair.

Jake tilted his head towards several wrapped packages on the table. "So where do these go?"

"Ready for our dealer. I have someone else to get them to Zurich. We usually use Muller. They'll be in museums soon. Stella will come to check everything first before we transport them north. You met Muller, I think."

"Are you sure there's no problem with this? I heard there has to be something called provenance."

"No worry. Our dealers are very careful to make arrangements. Never been a problem."

Jake was comforted by Robert's American accent and by his well-dressed appearance. And some good news: Stella would be coming here. Maybe he would have a chance to see her. But he was jealous that someone else was also driving for her.

Two laborers showed up to help uncrate the remaining portion of the shipment. "Go into the kitchen," Robert said, waving in the direction of the main section of the house. "Have breakfast while I separate this stuff. My guys will box up the pieces needing restoration for you to take back to Rome with the others from yesterday."

The same fat woman from the day before now worked an espresso machine. Dry rolls and even drier Melba toast, containers of Nutella and honey, slices of ham, and hard-boiled eggs were laid out on a table.

Jake ate while he watched the workers load up the van and shut the doors with a lock. Robert waved his arm toward the vehicle.

"Go directly to the lab without stopping." He let the dog loose. Jake left, impatient to return to Rome and get rid of the cargo even though he hadn't seen Stella.

Marco and Gianni were waiting for him at the lab. Jake handed over the keys without engaging in conversation or volunteering to help unload or return the van to the warehouse. He found a bus to the apartment. Home again, he sagged on the sofa with a beer and went over the events of the past few days until he fell asleep. The beer can dropped from his hand, spilling the remaining contents onto the floor.

"*Merda*," he exclaimed when Laura shook his shoulder.

"How was the trip?"

"*Schifoso*. Lousy. I got stopped by the police."

"Didn't you see anything of Ravenna?"

"No time."

"You never called."

"Sorry, hon." Laura had been far from his thoughts and he knew his expression didn't express regret for his dereliction.

"You don't act like you're sorry and you smell like you need a shower."

"Just lay off, I'm tired and don't want to listen to all this nagging," he shouted.

"Jake, keep quiet, we have neighbors, you know."

"Listen, I don't give a damn about neighbors. It's your fault we're not in our own house anymore. You wanted to come here and you wanted me to have something to do, so I've got something. I'm using the car to drive like I told you and I'm earning a little money. So lay off."

Stella called the following day with congratulations for Jake's successful trip. She offered to take him to lunch. They met at the trattoria near the Colosseum. They sat at the same table as before. Jake again faced away from the window, his eyes on Stella. She removed her fur coat to reveal a tight, red knit dress, low on top and short on the bottom. She sat back to cross her legs, covered in diamond-patterned black stockings. One of her stilettos dangled off her foot as she jerked one leg back and forth, as if she was nervous. Jake could smell perfume, Shalimar, the scent a former girlfriend wore. Overly exotic for his tastes then, but now sexy, especially when mixed with the cigarette smoke.

They finished the wine and the *digestivi: Fernet-Branca* for her and *amaro* for him. Like the cigarettes and the Shalimar, the taste of the bitter liqueur grew on him. He hoped for a continuation of the afternoon, but Stella said she had an appointment. He helped her with her coat, trying to hide his disappointment. She air-kissed him on both sides while murmuring, "Next time, let's meet at my apartment. I'll call you."

He tried not to appear over eager but couldn't suppress a wide smile.

Keeping to their agreement to do some things together, Laura and Jake shared occasional walks around Rome, a gallery visit or two and a few dinners. They were careful to keep the conversation to noncontroversial subjects. The détente didn't satisfy her and she doubted it satisfied Jake, either. She now saw their marriage as an old toy whose wheels had fallen off and lay discarded in a corner. But she didn't know how to repair it, and wasn't yet ready to throw the remains in the trash. Best to continue on as is for a while.

At Laura's insistence, Jake borrowed the lab's Mercedes for a weekend trip to Florence. While he went off to shops to check the pricing of antiquities, Laura spent her time window shopping and enjoying espresso at outside tables in small piazzas where she watched Italian life unfurl around her. The warm greetings with cheeks touching or air kisses exchanged, the delighted examination of babies in strollers, the extended goodbyes with *arrivederci* and *ciao* accompanied by a beckoning gesture instead of a wave away. The old men moving like cats to find the sun as they gabbled on about soccer. The grannies carefully examining vegetables at the produce stalls. Laura recognized that her observations were superficial, but even so what she saw were lives so much richer than hers in Seattle, with the food, wine, scenery, people and history all blending into a harmonious culture.

When Jake declined to accompany her for weekend sightseeing around Rome, she began going for long walks alone on Sundays to enjoy the theatricality of the Baroque buildings and fountains and to attempt to put her thoughts in order. Often beginning in Piazza Navona with a coffee, she moved on to check out some of the Bernini and Borromini churches, wondering, as she stood in the back watching weddings, if their curls and frills of marble and gold transferred into happiness for brides and grooms. Other times, she concentrated on the hysterical mixture of saints and angels in swirling robes and naked little boys on the ceiling of the Gesù and other churches. She was repelled and fascinated at the same time. Would she ever begin to penetrate the intricacies of Rome?

One day she wandered into a church where there was a marble statue of a richly-draped woman lying back as if in a swoon. Her eyes were closed and her mouth was open as if in a gasp of ecstasy. A smiling angel stood over her holding an arrow pointed below her waist. Laura's guidebook said it represented a religious vision but she thought it looked more like the marble figure of St. Teresa was enjoying an orgasm courtesy of the angel. The statue only reminded her of her lack of love life.

She thought back to her high hopes for a happier marriage, a marriage made exciting and romantic anew by life in Rome. But she also remembered the day when the cabin attendant said to buckle her seat belt and a few minutes later when the plane flew over what looked like an ancient city as it landed at the airport. The figure of the person standing alone had concerned her. It represented the loneliness she could not yet escape.

When she arrived home still thinking about the solitary figure in the ruins and wondering how St. Teresa felt after she recovered, she saw Jake in sweatshirt and jeans engrossed in a soccer game. He hadn't washed up yet.

The thought of going to Stella's apartment was an impetus for Jake to get out his watercolor kit to begin a few rough sketches of his neighborhood and San Giovanni. He found using the brushes to apply color to paper relaxing, even though he knew his previous figurative work was amateurish. He thought about the artists showing their work around Piazza Navona and the Colosseum, hoping to pick up money from free-spending tourists. He'd try to sell his own as soon as he amassed a dozen or so pictures, a slow process. But he'd give one to Stella, the best one.

When she called about lunch, Stella told him to bring an overnight bag and his passport. She needed him to drive her to Ravenna and then back to Zurich.

Jake set off on a shopping expedition to become more Italian in appearance. He prowled the shops near his apartment finding a black turtleneck and a shirt that went with the sweater Laura bought him months ago. Then he braved the crowds in the Via Sannio market to add a leather jacket like those worn by Marco and Gianni, a pair of loafers – Tod's knockoffs, nothing like the style the two thugs preferred – and a new pair of high-style but cheap sunglasses. He tried on his new outfit at home. The mirror reflected a transformation. He had become an Italian, at least one who shopped in outdoor markets.

He told Laura he would be away again for a few days.

His heart rate ticked up as he rang the *citofono* outside the gate to Stella's apartment complex in Parioli. The call system had a video camera, so she would know immediately who wanted access. The *portiere* sat in his office watching him as he crossed the entry hall to the elevator. He smiled at Jake, who didn't notice in his haste to get to the fifth floor. If he had, he would have heard the doorman's accompanying snicker.

Stella stood at the open door to her penthouse apartment. Beautifully dressed as usual, she welcomed him with an air kiss, took his hand and led him inside. The decor was sumptuous, with Oriental rugs strewn on pale marble floors, white leather upholstery, walls covered with canvasses, and small sculptures on side tables. Jake thought if this is how art dealers live, count him in.

"*Buon giorno, caro,*" she said as she handed him a glass of prosecco. "Let's have a toast to our success." Their glasses touched in tribute, but Jake's spirits sank when he saw Marco and Gianni come out of a side room with their own half-empty glasses already in hand. They smiled at Jake, showing all the charm of twin sharks sensing blood in the water.

"Now," she said directly to Jake, "here's the plan: you and I are driving in my car straight to Ravenna where I'll check with Robert to see if everything is in order. Then we will head to Zurich to ensure Muller is ready to take another consignment, and to check out what he has left in inventory. My friends here will go to Ravenna separately to help with the new shipment, some extra-fine items from Cyprus."

Jake tried to look as if he was already current on the plans and agreed with them.

Marco and Gianni sat silent during the interchange. When Stella finally addressed them, she spoke in what he decided was their dialect. He wanted to know what she was saying. He'd ask later. If he was going to be in the business he needed to know.

When Stella said, "*Andiamo,*" the other men left without a word. Jake remained, waiting to be told what to do. Stella went into the same room Marco and Gianni had emerged from. Jake followed her into what turned out to be her bedroom, all pink satin with a few small religious works, one partially covered with silver so that only a Madonna's face showed. The bed was mussed as though it had been hastily made up.

Instead of an invitation for sex, she handed him a small Vuitton suitcase and slung her fur coat over her shoulders. They took the elevator to the basement garage where her Lancia awaited in its slot.

"I'll drive the first part," she said.

Jake maneuvered into the low passenger seat to be cradled in rich leather. Stella lit up and backed her car out of its space. Jake noted she didn't put on her seat belt so he left his off also, not wanting to appear cowardly. They sped up the *autostrada* as Stella blinked her lights to pass anyone in her path, swinging out at the last second and then as quickly back into the lane. Cars scattered out of her way. Jake wished he had buckled up. Stella switched on a classical music station and lit another cigarette. He lifted the pack lying on the space between their seats to look at it. Balkan Sobranie Black Russians, a brand he never heard of, one making her even more foreign. He liked the aroma until she picked a stray piece of tobacco off her lip. He turned away at the unpleasant sight, mystified by his attraction to her.

Disliking classical music, he put in his earbuds to hear country favorites on his phone. They took him back to eastern Washington where his life was less complicated, or so it now seemed.

The engine was soundless, the sky darkening, the music narcotic. He dozed until the car stopped at a roadside bar for a coffee break. Stella told him to drive when they were finished. Jake pointedly buckled up before changing the radio station to pop music. As he did so, a surge of aggravation engulfed him for listening to others make decisions while he remained a mere retainer cut out from the main action, reduced to changing radio stations, laboring, or buying cigarettes. He was glad he never did buy her the Cartier brand she wanted.

He seized the opportunity to question his captive audience. "If you want me to be your partner, I need to know more."

"Partner?"

Jake noted the verbal question mark but continued anyway. "Who are Nando and Robert? And I want to know about the Chinese working in the restoration lab. Why aren't they Italian? I'm not completely blind, no matter what you think. And what languages do you speak?"

Stella laughed and lit up again. She blew the smoke out her nostrils and put the cigarette back in the ashtray, now on the verge of overflowing. He glanced at her hands with their nicotine-stained fingers. Her nails were lacquered, the dark red clashing with the yellowed skin. He looked at his own hands on the steering wheel and decided he didn't want to smoke anymore, even though nearly everyone he met smoked incessantly.

"All right, *caro*. Nando and Robert are my partners. I'm a business person and I want reliable help. They are and I hope you are, too. If you want to progress you need to be cooperative and keep your mouth shut. This is a competitive business. As for languages, I do English, Italian, German, and sometimes Marco, Gianni, and I like to talk in dialect. Nothing you'd need for your job." She didn't refer to the Chinese.

He suppressed his anger at the vague response. His resolve had vanished as rapidly as it had appeared and, instead of pushing for more information, especially about who else could be driving for her, he lapsed into silence, fearful that if he pressed he would be thrown out of her circle. Even if he might be caught up in a shady operation, although he knew of no real evidence of illegality, the job was better than doing nothing, or even worse, teaching. Besides, he was an American. What could possibly happen to him? Anyway, despite the smoke, Stella was alluring after all. Nothing like Laura.

Stella approached one of the desk clerks when they reached the hotel. She returned to hand Jake an electronic room key in a folder. He didn't check it, although he hoped it was for the same room as hers.

"I put the rooms in your name, but I'll pay with my company's cash. I know you want to hang on to the cash we're giving you. Someday I want to know what you do with it. Got a piece of action on the side? Now, I want a drink before dinner. How about you?"

Jake followed her into the dimly lit bar. She ordered champagne; he asked for a 16-year-old Glenlivet, the most expensive whiskey on the drinks menu. They ordered another round before entering the adjacent restaurant. He scanned the menu to find dishes as pricey as his drink. He settled on risotto with truffles like the New Year's Eve dinner at Derrick's villa, followed by *bistecca alla Fiorentina,* even though the last time he ate the steak it took him days for his gut to process the slab. Stella ordered a plate of *olive Ascolane,* huge green olives stuffed with meat, breaded and deep fried, and a bowl of soup full of squid and langoustines. They shared a bottle of Barbaresco red.

Stella had a spot of the tomato broth on her lip. She dabbed it with a napkin and said, "Enjoying yourself?"

"Do you care? I still need to know a lot more or I'm going back to Rome in the morning." He didn't know how he would get there, but his resentment had flared up again at the news of two rooms instead of the hoped for one. And the scotch and red wine were going to his head. He gulped down the remains of his second glass of wine anyway and grabbed the bottle to pour himself the remaining drops without offering any to Stella.

"No, you're not – you're staying right here with me. So finish up and let's go to my room to plan tomorrow." She stubbed out her cigarette.

Go to her room? Maybe she likes to be threatened. Maybe that's the way Nando and Robert act to keep her in line. He licked his lips.

She pulled a couple of bottles of *grappa* from the room's minibar, poured them into two glasses, handed him one, and lay down on the bed. He saw her actions as the invitation he'd longed for and knelt by the bedside to remove her shoes. She took a gulp of the drink. "Long drive."

"Yes," Jake responded, "I'll help you relax."

She sat up. "Don't get any smart-ass ideas, *caro*. You're just an employee."

Jake's frustration at her inconsistency overcame his inhibitions and he snapped. He downed the grappa in one swallow before shoving Stella back down so hard that her head hit the headboard. Her carefully arranged hair came loose, the snake-like strands spilling out, making her into a Medusa. She tried to sit up again but he pushed her back. She struggled. He put one hand over her mouth, holding it there until she bit him. He yelped with pain as she tried to kick him between his legs, missed, and then connected with a hard blow to his thigh.

"Don't you dare call me dear one, bitch, and don't think you can keep playing games with me. You've been leading me on for months and don't think I don't know. We're going to finish what you've been wanting right now."

But he didn't finish. When he saw a look of naked fear in her eyes he sank back to the floor, head in hands. He remained there in a daze, not daring to think of his behavior and the crime he nearly committed. The vision of his drunken father punching his mother expanded in his memory. After a minute he got on his knees and then stood up to straighten himself and his clothes and get away. Stella wiped his blood from her mouth before grabbing her half-full glass of *grappa* on the bedside table and throwing it at him. The glass hit him in temple, the liquor stinging his eyes. She laughed and said, "Satisfied, Jake *caro*?"

Nearly blinded, he rushed for the door and entered the hallway where a couple entering their room stared as he struggled to find his room keycard in his pants pocket. He descended the fire stairs to the floor above the kitchens, hoping to remain unseen. As he ran, he panicked. Would she file assault charges?

He found his room without meeting anyone else. His bag sat on the luggage rack. He rushed into the bathroom, stripped off his clothes, and got in the shower. The hot water cleansed his body as he soaped over and over, but his mind was in torment, replaying the evening's events like a video loop. He had a lump on his head, a painful thigh and a bite mark as souvenirs. One of her teeth had barely punctured his skin. He examined the mementos of his shameful actions. He again thought about his father and his violent tendencies, beating him or his mother whenever he got drunk or life didn't go his way. The idea that he might have inherited the gene was frightening. Never again, he vowed.

His clothes were spotted with *grappa* and smelling of her perfume. The sight and smell made him sick. He wadded up the underwear, jeans, shirt, and sweater and stuffed them at the bottom of the duffel bag, intending to dispose of them in the morning. Then he decided he shouldn't wait. He put on his other set of clothes, grabbed the bag, and went out the door to the fire stairs, praying he would be lucky again and not encounter anyone. A back door at the ground floor led to the street. He walked four blocks until he saw a dumpster next to a parking garage. He was sorry to see the sweater Laura bought him disappear into the bin, but it had to go along with everything else. If she asked, he'd say he left her gift in the classroom at the language school and someone must have stolen it before he could return. He threw the soiled clothes in the bin and piled garbage on top.

He had finally fallen into a deep sleep when the incessant ringing of the room phone dragged him out of bed. He was in pain. Before he could say hello, Stella's voice ordered, "Be down in the lobby in fifteen minutes." She hung up.

He arrived five minutes late, desperate for coffee. Stella was as well dressed as usual, although he couldn't see her eyes with much of her face hidden behind oversize sunglasses, unnecessary in the dim morning light. "Marco and Gianni are waiting."

"I'm not moving until I get coffee." He was relieved when she silently acquiesced. Maybe he would be able to repair the situation.

They drank an espresso. And another for Jake. The second one hit his stomach like a bomb. He ordered a pastry to sop up the acid.

"Drive to the Hotel Adriatico first."

Nando came out to welcome Stella and acknowledged Jake with a brief dip of his head. Stella told him to stay in the car. Jake saw Marco and Gianni waiting patiently, as if they were beasts of burden. Like him. A half hour later Stella gave him his orders: "Let's go. I'm going to take a break. Pick me up at three. Need to go to Robert's. I'm finished here. We'll leave tomorrow at seven."

Jake drove her back to the hotel in silence, furious with himself again for being no different than her other two doltish helpers. Drained from the emotional overdose and the pounding headache, he switched on the television and took a beer from the minibar, settling in until it was time to pick her up. He visualized himself as Stella's personal chauffeur. All he needed was a dark suit and cap to complete the picture. He swore he would quit when he got back to Rome although he would miss the money.

Back at Robert's, he watched as Stella looked over an assortment of small sculptures along with paintings on cracked and worm-eaten wood depicting Christ and Mary surrounded by bishops or other functionaries. Several were like those in her bedroom with silver coverings leaving only faces and hands visible. He picked one up to examine the piece more closely before turning to Stella. "Are these worth much?"

"They're just icons. A few people collect them. Not much market, but Herr Muller might find a buyer. Nothing for you to be concerned with."

When her business was finished, Stella ordered him back to the hotel. "Nighty night," she said with the hint of a sneer.

Jake stomped off to his room in a fury at his dismissal. When he calmed down, he ordered a bowl of pasta and a bottle of wine from room service. The pasta was cold by the time the waiter finally came to his door. He scraped the mess into the wastepaper basket and opened the bottle before calling Laura in hopes of some solace. The phone rang for a minute before she answered.

"Where are you?"

"In Ravenna, like I told you."

"When are you coming home?"

"In a few days. I'm with the people from the lab. We're going to Zurich, too. I'll give you another call when we're done."

"Are you all right?"

"Yes, why?"

"Oh, I don't know, but you sound funny."

Jake hadn't anticipated her perceptiveness or the lack of reaction to the news that he would not be returning for a few days. "What have you been doing?"

"I'm just busy at work." She sounded vague

The conversation came to a dead end with "*ciao*" and "*baci, baci,*" kiss, kiss, words that were now meaningless.

The phone rang again, startling him. Maybe Laura had something more to say, but then he saw the sound came from the hotel phone.

"Are you awake?" Stella asked. "Do you want to come to my room?"

Jake, deciding to be forceful, said, "No, you come here, or forget it." To his surprise she agreed without argument.

When he heard a quick knock on his door, Jake threw on the hotel robe and opened the door a crack. She held out a bottle of champagne. "Let's do it the right way, *caro*. The bottle's cold so we don't need to order ice." Her uncharacteristically sweet demeanor put Jake on guard. Could she be interested even with what happened or is this all a bluff? Well, he could play too.

While he popped the cork and poured the foaming golden liquid, Stella lay down on the bed with a welcoming smile. She wore her mink, black stockings, and her usual spike heels. Nothing else. They drank in silence until she curved her body to him. He forgot about the painful wound in his hand and the bruise.

He awoke alone at dawn to think about Stella's confusing actions, first luring him on, then rejecting him, and now so compliant. She was fascinating and he didn't want to give her up despite his earlier decision. He speculated on his future. If he and Laura were to separate, he would have to find a way to stay on, although the lack of papers never concerned the thousands of illegal immigrants washing up on Italy's shores. No one bothered them except for an occasional roundup of Africans selling fakes on the sidewalks. And they were back ten minutes later. Would Stella help him stay on? Robert? Nando? He doubted they would bother. For now, he would reap the mental and physical reward of evoking Stella's willing reaction to his eager overtures and make plans to continue their relationship. Laura was so uncreative in comparison. But did he really want to leave her? Some of their good times also came to mind and, he admitted, she was right to push him out of his rut.

Laura and Derrick frequently shared lunch at one of the restaurants and bars along the Viale Aventino or met for drinks after work. She knew she would eventually succumb to his pleadings even though he wasn't someone she would ever have dreamed of being attracted to in Seattle. Too old, married, and in control of her fate in Italy. But he was solicitous, knowledgeable, and the epitome of European sophistication. There was no one else who took an interest in her and she needed someone to confide in, to help her at work and with the complexities of expatriate life in Italy. Jake was not, and she now saw, would never be that man.

One day when disillusionment with her marriage sunk her mood to its lowest ebb, she agreed to meet him at a hotel. The room was luxurious and Derrick an expert lover. Her thoughts about whether he really cared about her dissolved in a blur of pleasure. She didn't need to make a pretense of enjoying the event as she did with Jake on the rare occasions they had sex.

But after they both were satisfied, Derrick groaned loudly. He was panting and red-faced, looking like a strong candidate for a heart attack.

"Are you all right? You were wonderful."

"No worry, girl, I'm just out of practice. And there's a pill bottle in my jacket. Can you get it?"

Laura was alarmed. Maybe he had a heart condition, although he didn't appear that old. What were the pills for? What if he keeled over? She had read novels about men dying in the arms of their mistresses. The story sounded romantic, but the reality would be a nightmare. She grabbed the pill bottle and a glass of water before putting on her clothes.

Whatever was in the medication restored him enough to call room service for champagne to celebrate. Laura was amazed at his gratitude. Maybe his marriage resembled hers, with an uncaring, undemonstrative partner. Love certainly played no part in their meetings. He had never uttered the word and she didn't expect it and could not respond with her own declaration if asked. He wasn't lovable.

The room service attendant rolled in a table with the bottle in a bucket of ice and two flutes. Derrick poured with unsteady hands, spilling a few drops as they touched the rims of the glasses in a tribute to their new arrangement. But the words *adultery* and *assignation* expanded in her mind, blotting out the luxury of the suite and the pleasure of their encounter.

"My dear," he said with a small bow. "We'll make this a regular event, eh? I have an apartment just up the hill from the office. So much more convenient."

"I don't know, Derrick. Life is complicated right now." She inspected her hands, turning them over and back as if she could divine her future from the pattern of veins and creases.

He kissed her wrists, saying, "Ah, yes, life's complications. We all have them. Don't I know."

Laura found the right moment to overtly launch her plan to stay in Rome when Jake returned from Ravenna and Zurich. "I really don't want to leave when the year is up. And it's already half gone. You have talked about opening a pizza restaurant when we get back but what would you say if I tried to stay on a little longer? If I could get a longer-term job and maybe a promotion, we could buy a car and find a nicer apartment if you'd like. It'd be wonderful to have a fireplace, and a terrace." She was hoping he'd decline but the residue of their earlier happy days lingered along with a little hope for their future. The thought of launching into a new single life in Rome seemed too daunting.

"Well, it's okay if you want to look into it, at least for another year. Don't know after that," he responded in a guarded manner. "We'll have to see if you can find permanent work. Not sure about my job. Maybe I could go into business myself."

"Go into business? What kind of business?"

"I'm learning a lot about art restoration and galleries."

"I'll find out what I can about an upcoming vacancy." She embraced him, saying "Thanks, honey."

He responded with a hug little better than a handshake. Discomforting doubts about staying on, or staying on with Jake, swept over Laura. From what little she had gleaned it was very difficult to go into business in Italy, especially for a foreigner. But maybe he was talking about selling his paintings in a gallery. Artworks that didn't yet exist as far as she knew. Perhaps he was becoming settled in Rome and was making real plans. Perhaps.

Encouraged by Jake's response, even if it was less than enthusiastic, Laura called Derrick. "Derrick, can we meet? I'd like to talk more seriously about how I can go about arranging to stay on. Jake wants to stay on, too."

"Right-o. Let me know what day you're available for a long lunch."

She soon managed an opportunity to leave work. Derrick picked her up. He suggested they stop at a museum first. "Time to get you a bit more culture, my dear, now that you will be staying in Rome."

Laura murmured, "Derrick, you can't know how much I appreciate your help." She wasn't sure "how much" could be measured when she balanced his helpfulness against his occasional pompous manner.

As Derrick drove down the Ostiense to the Montemartini Museum, Laura, cocooned in his car, enjoyed the silence, the rest of the world shut out for a few minutes. Whatever Derrick's faults, having a sophisticated older man to guide her was the perfect European experience.

"This is pretty weird," Laura said, summing up her opinion after they took a quick tour of the museum, where ancient Roman statues stood in front of early twentieth-century industrial equipment. "Interesting, though," she added.

"Well, this was Rome's first power station, and there are a lot of leftover statues languishing in the basements of other museums to display here. I think the concept is clever."

"Yes, clever." She smiled at Derrick, adding, "I mean this is really interesting and I'd like to learn more."

"Well we'll do that, but now it's time for a real Roman restaurant." The restaurant, Checchino dal 1887, was located a few blocks away. As they came to the portal of a red-stucco building next to Monte Testaccio, Derrick explained, "This hill is where the old Roman sailors threw broken pots they had used for ballast. When I first came here, you could walk up the hill and pick up pieces. Now you can't get near. A shame, I think."

Laura glanced at the hill behind the building. Pots always seemed to be part of a conversation.

An obsequious head waiter recognized Derrick and seated them in a corner away from a noisy group of Japanese tourists.

"Now, my dear, this part of town is famous for traditional Roman food, the *quinto quarto*, the fifth quarter – leftover parts from the slaughterhouse that used to be just across the road. Just wait, you'll see. Sit back and let me order."

Laura wasn't a big meat eater and certainly not innards. Whenever her mother tried to get her to eat liver, she'd rebelled. She always picked out the disgusting giblets in the turkey dressing at Thanksgiving, leaving them on the side of her plate.

Derrick picked out a Barolo, which the waiter decanted after making a show of opening the bottle and smelling the cork. He poured a sample of wine into Derrick's glass. After he swirled, sniffed, and sampled, the waiter poured for both of them.

"*La signorina* will have minestrone for a *primi,* as will I. And for the *secondo, coda alla vaccinara* for the young lady. I'll take *rigatoni alla pajata*. After, the *insalata* of fennel and oranges. You're sure everything's good today? Have to keep my little friend happy." Laura was affronted at this portrayal, but Derrick didn't notice.

Derrick raised his glass in a wordless toast before telling her about the history of the restaurant and what he'd ordered for the main course: for him, the intestines of an unweaned calf fed only its mother's milk, stewed in tomato sauce and served over pasta. The oxtail, *vaccinara,* was for her.

Perhaps it was the heavy wine overcoming her concern, but Laura enjoyed her dish, although the thought of Derrick's poor calf in the *pajata* was worse than the rabbit she guiltily enjoyed before Christmas. She began to think that the meal would be a good subject for her never-started food blog. But writing about a meal with a lover might not convey the theme she desired to attract readers in the States. She would save it for later and wait for a more auspicious subject.

Wine and espresso finished, Derrick paid and stood to help her out of her chair, a gesture Jake never made in his life.

"We'll stop at my place for a few minutes to discuss your future, as you wanted."

Laura silently prayed she wouldn't meet anyone as they walked the few steps into the entrance of Derrick's peach-colored apartment building. The elevator took them to the top floor. He opened the door for her and she entered his apartment. It was nicely furnished but nothing special in her eyes when compared to the extensive, plant-filled terrace ringed with large pots of purple and orange bougainvillea that climbed up trellises to afford privacy. She stood by a small olive tree in a terracotta pot to dream of living in an apartment in this quiet neighborhood, with its elegant buildings and umbrella pines softly dropping needles on the cobbled streets.

"I do love your apartment. You're so lucky."

"Yes. Sit down inside and I'll be back in a minute." She could hear him in the bathroom.

Derrick opened the door. Laura glanced up at the sound of the latch. He stood in a silk bathrobe, looking eager. A half-steamed mirror reflected the back of his balding head, and a glass with a tired toothbrush. The pill bottle sat next to it.

Laura slipped past him to wash up. She dabbed a bit more perfume on her wrists and earlobes in the hope that the floral scent would encourage him to see her as a sophisticated and desirable woman, instead of an object Jake now wanted only on occasion and only for a moment.

Derrick's ardent embrace answered her desires.

Afterward he said, "I have some news. I quite forgot because you are so distractingly beautiful. Human Resources is getting the vacancy announcement ready for what would be a nice promotion and a longer-term contract for you. I'm on the selection panel, of course, and with all your experience you're highly qualified. The work would be in the same unit. I'm sure you would like that since you already know the staff. What do you think?"

"I think it would be perfect." But she couldn't put aside her suspicion that his words sounded canned, as if he had used them before on someone else. And would again, in the future.

FEBRUARY

LAURA WAS SICK. She shuffled to the bathroom where she caught sight of her green and disheveled reflection before she vomited. Was it the clams from last night's dinner? Maybe the salad wasn't washed enough. She made tea before she managed to dress and get off to work, though she wanted to climb back in bed and pull the covers over her head.

By noon she felt slightly better – until she opened the pocket calendar in her handbag. The red leather bag was a gift from Derrick after their latest encounter. The intertwined Gs of the Gucci logo made her feel fashionable, but the calendar itself gave her the discomforting news that her family would arrive next week.

She casually flipped the pages back several months while she tried to spoon down some soup. Her eyes fell on the regular monthly check marks. But she saw there wasn't one for the end of last month and the normal time had now passed by ten days. After she looked at the dates again she felt an uneasy sense that her life had reached another fork in the road. She told herself to wait a few days before doing anything. But what to do if the symptoms persisted? The office had a medical service, but what if word got out? Back at her desk, Laura stared at her computer screen while picking at her hangnail. She could not concentrate on editing while both sides of her brain contemplated the possibility of an unplanned event.

That evening Jake was out and she spent time researching "How to have a baby in Italy" on the laptop. Almost everything was in Italian. She gave up and went to bed early.

The same sensations of nausea and cold sweat hit her again the following morning. She began to panic. Despite her decision the day before to wait, Laura opened their dictionary to the English half to find what the words in Italian for "pregnancy test" might be. A pharmacy with its flashing green neon sign was not far from her apartment. She would stop in on the way home.

The day was interminable. The unpleasant symptoms persisted. She skipped espresso, sipping *camomilla* tea instead, and had another bowl of clear soup for lunch. Not knowing how late the pharmacy remained open, she left work on time.

Ads for products guaranteeing a great bikini body – summer was already on everyone's mind – filled the display windows of the pharmacy. Laura's mental picture of being fat and uncomfortable through the hot Roman summer only made the problem worse. Where could she find a doctor? Whose was it? Would she have to leave? She knew the answer to the last question. She visualized living in her parent's home in Seattle after Jake, incensed at her pregnancy, deserted her. But at least she would finally have a child. And perhaps having a child could bring them closer together.

She opened the heavy glass door, joining the line up behind the middle-aged and elderly people in front of her. Gradually the line moved forward. With each step closer to the counter her anxiety increased.

"*Prego?*"

She had reached the front of the line. The white-coated pharmacist looked at her with a stern demeanor.

"*Per favore, un test di gravidenza.*" She managed a weak smile but stammered with nervousness.

The man scrutinized her ring finger and his face relaxed, reassured she wasn't one of those women without a husband who were always wanting to know if they were going to need to find a way to relieve themselves of a problem. He waved her over to an aisle where boxes of condoms and gels were lined up on the top shelf. Laura found what she needed on the bottom shelf: an oblong box with a picture of a baby on it. She paid and stepped back out to the sidewalk, recalling a large sign posted by a religious oddball along the interstate south of Seattle: "The Wages of Sin are Death." She always saw the sign as funny whenever she and her family drove to Portland where her aunt lived in between her travels. Now she wasn't so sure.

On the way home, she stopped at the window of the baby store La Cicogna, The Stork. The sight of tiny suits and dresses, christening outfits, bassinets and strollers propelled her inside. A motherly-looking clerk approached. Laura shook her head. "Just looking." The clerk, rejected, moved on to welcome a couple. The woman flaunted her bulging belly and the man smiled with pride. They held hands. Laura left, taking care to shut the door gently. The memory of her frightening miscarriage loomed.

Nearly a year ago, determined to have a child, Laura went off the pill without consulting Jake. She wasn't far along in the undetected pregnancy, and despite the mess in the bathroom during the night, she didn't physically suffer much. The doctor in the ER said she was fine and that such events weren't at all unusual. Her own doctor said she would be able to conceive again but it might be best to wait a few months. It was in those intervening months that Laura had found the job in Rome, hoping that a change would take her mind off the incident and revive her relationship with Jake. The memory kept returning despite her will to put it aside along with her concerns about Jake's reluctance to even talk about having children. She knew that he had had a younger sister who had died but he never discussed the circumstances. His older sister was married with children, but there was something that had happened to make him wary of the commitment. Something so deep within him that he would never talk to her about it.

The fast-passing months of her life added weight to her concerns every time she remembered the scene in the bathroom in Seattle. She carried her confused mix of desires and fears back to the apartment, along with the white paper bag containing the package that would predict her fate.

Jake wasn't home. She headed for the bathroom and sat on the toilet seat holding the box. When she had enough courage she opened it. The instructions were all in Italian, beyond her capability to read. She went to their laptop to search for the proper method. The information was all the same: stick it in your urine in the morning and wait for a message.

She deleted her findings before trying to find the website for the hotel Derrick selected for her parents, but she couldn't bring to mind the name or where she'd stashed the information. She gave up, her efforts only bringing back the reality that they would soon arrive.

Jake was in one of his more pleasant moods and even amorous in the evening. She gave in reluctantly. He immediately fell asleep but she sat up, arms hooked around her knees, going over the events of the day and what the morning would bring. She remembered flipping the coin back and forth on their first night in Rome in the miserable *pensione,* wondering if the face with the Colosseum portended good news or bad.

Laura pulled the package from under the mattress and slipped into the bathroom at four after a sleepless night. Her stomach was in a knot of anxiety. After she locked the bathroom door she turned on the water to disguise any noise, and followed the instructions. And then she waited.

When the tiny window signaled negative, she sobbed from a combination of disappointment and relief. She wiped her tears before she began to worry: Is the test accurate? What is the success rate for these home tests? Should she take another? She vomited. As she washed up, she felt another twinge of regret.

The following day Laura began to feel better. A week later all was back to normal. She decided that her sickness was the result of worry about her parents who might see the rift in her marriage, along with Derrick, unfaithfulness, her job prospects, and the months passing so quickly they seemed to be part of a minute-long video clip. But the test's negative result didn't solve any of these problems.

As promised, Derrick brought his old Fiat to the apartment. It was one of the larger models with enough space for four people. On Saturday, she and Jake drove to Fiumicino to meet the incoming flight. It was behind schedule. Laura fidgeted with the wish to get the visit underway and then over. They waited nearly an hour until her parents came out the automatic doors from customs with their wheelie bags. They were both rumpled and gray with exhaustion. Laura gave them guilty hugs; Jake handled their suitcases after a brief handshake.

Laura had found the hotel's address but didn't recognize the name. When they arrived at the entrance, she was shocked. It was the same hotel where she and Derrick had enjoyed their first sexual encounter. She prayed the desk clerk didn't recognize her.

To Laura's relief, her parents were assigned a different room. It had a terrace with a lemon tree in a terracotta pot, and a marble bathroom with a waterfall shower and inlaid designs on the floor. Laura's mother eyed the bidet. "Oh – one of those! What do they use them for, I've always wondered? My friend Janet says she uses them to wash her nylons."

Laura, feeling European, didn't respond. She knew what they were for, even though she did not use the one in their apartment or Derrick's. Something about the fixture acknowledged her messy life too overtly.

"We'll leave you here for a rest and then come back for dinner. The restaurants here don't open until around eight."

"But that's really late – we're in bed by nine. What will we do?"

"You could go out for a walk and stop at a bar for a coffee down the hill."

"But I, we, don't know any Italian."

To her relief, her father stepped in to take charge saying, "Will do, but tell me where to go."

"Just walk down there and go into a place with a sign saying 'bar.' It's just on the corner on the busy street. Go to the cash register and say '*panino*' and '*caffè.*' Then pay and point to the sandwich you want." She gave her father a fifty-euro note. "This should be plenty."

"Are you tired, honey?" her mother asked. "You know I've never been to Rome before."

"Yes, I guess I am." Laura kissed them tentatively and said, "See you at eight."

Back in the Fiat, Jake said, "You're acting really bizarre lately. You could have gone with them."

"I'm tired and want a rest and don't know what to do with them for so long. And I have a lot on my mind about work."

"Yeah – but I'm the one having to take them around."

Laura was contrite. "I know. I'm sorry. I'll be better at dinner. Promise."

Laura curled up on the bed with her phone to listen to Zucchero and Il Volo before it was time for dinner. But the music didn't calm her as worries multiplied. Her fear that her parents would see the sham of her marriage and that Jake was as tired of her as she was of him. She worried about their opprobrium if she divorced Jake. She pictured herself again as a single mom, this time after some sort of hook-up or using a sperm donor. And there was Derrick. Her mother would die if she knew.

Through the maze of her thoughts she heard Jake say, "We need to get going to be on time." She put away the earbuds and went to the bathroom to clean up. She tried to avoid her reflection, afraid she wouldn't like what she saw.

They were ten minutes late. Her parents were standing in the lobby. "There you are, dear. We were getting worried."

"It's just Rome – the traffic is always a nightmare and you can't predict how long it will take to get somewhere. Let's go. We're just going to drive down the hill to a restaurant that's been around for ages. Did you see the pyramid when we came in? It's called Cestia, and that's the name of the restaurant as well. They serve food typical of Rome. And sorry about earlier. You were right – I needed a nap. Hope you found the place I told you about."

"No problem, your mom and I did fine, didn't we Dorothy?" She didn't respond other than to look at her daughter with hurt in her eyes.

The restaurant had opened up a few minutes earlier. The few patrons waiting to be fed were all tourists. Laura went over the menu.

"Dad, why don't you have the *penne all'arrabbiata*? It's spicy, but I'm not sure if this kind comes with a kind of bacon, *pancetta*. I can ask. Or *bucatini all' Amatriciana*, with cubes of pork cheek in a tomato sauce. The salads are good. Mom, there's a pork roast or chicken with rosemary. I'll order some of the house wine if that's okay with you."

Her mother fretted. Rome was nothing like a cruise ship where all was taken care of and the food was normal. "Nothing spicy – not good for my digestion. Don't they have plain food? I really don't think I would like anything so fancy. Could I have soup and maybe just a tiny salad, please? Isn't there a menu in English?"

Her father took the opposite approach. "I'll have the *bucatini* and then chicken, *pollo,* I think you called it. I'm really hungry. The food on the plane was so bad I couldn't eat it and the sandwich at the bar wasn't very substantial. What else is there?"

Laura, pleased that he wanted real Italian food, suggested he would also like a plate of grilled radicchio.

"Sounds great, but you'd better order in case I make a mistake. What's on for tomorrow? This is so much better than being on those damn boats all the time and being dragged around by a tour guide every time we dock. Thanks so much, hon, for having us. Hope it won't be too much trouble."

Laura's mother broke in: "See the cute baby in the stroller over at the next table? Such darling clothes. And look at the pink bow on her sweet little bald head." She sighed pointedly.

Laura interrupted. "Jake and I will take you around Rome tomorrow and have you to dinner at our apartment. You'll see it's not fancy. We thought of booking you for a few days in Florence after you see the major sights here. We'll take you to the train and tell you how to get to the hotel. Will you be okay on your own?"

Laura's father said, "Can't wait." Her mother, forgetting about babies, looked alarmed at the thought of going off unescorted.

Neither of them said much about the apartment when they visited the following day, although Laura knew by their expressions that they noticed the old furniture. Her mother didn't mention anything more about Laura being a diplomat.

Her mother also noticed the statue. Laura could see that Jake barely contained his amusement as his mother-in-law tried to ignore the naked faun with flute and goat's tail next to the wedding photo on the bedside table.

"I just love your wedding portrait," she remarked, picking it up to reminisce about the day she accomplished one of her two motherly goals. But her eyes insisted on turning back to the statue.

Later, Jake said, "Did you see your mother's expression when she looked at your faun? I wonder what she will do when confronted by Michelangelo's *David* in all his glory? She must have kept her eyes closed with your father."

"Stop it! Just try to be nice, Jake."

They fell back into their usual silence.

Laura's parents were back from their trip the beginning of the following week, both with rave reviews about the treasures of Florence, although *David* and his anatomy weren't mentioned. Jake took them to Tivoli, where Dorothy bought a picture of a fountain in the gardens of the Villa d'Este as a souvenir. He also took them to the major tourist sites in Rome but, because he was unhappy with his role as tour guide for two old people he didn't care about, he added in the church of the Cappuccini with its crypt filled with the bones and skeletons of thousands of Capuchin monks arranged in intricate designs as a reminder to visitors that they too will die. Dorothy told Laura later that she ran out of the crypt when she saw the bony chandeliers. Laura was furious when she learned of Jake's insensitivity.

By the time their departure date neared, Laura had become concerned about what more they could offer as entertainment. She was still full of guilt about her earlier childish behavior, but her mother hung back at most ideas and complained about being allergic to the mimosa flowers now blooming on the trees and the flower stands. Her father, on the other hand, was energized. So what might they like to do?

"Jake, what if I called Derrick to see if he would drive them out to his villa? They might like seeing how some people live here, more than just Rome and Florence. You'd have to go with them to make sure they are okay. My mother is so timid." She hated to bring Derrick into the picture but she was out of ideas and was sure he would keep his mouth shut about their relationship.

"This is absolutely the end. Don't ask me to do anything else. Understand?" Jake stood on their balcony to stare at the adjacent buildings, his arms crossed.

The next day Laura called Derrick's office and, as usual, was connected immediately.

"Derrick, sorry to ask, but could you help a bit more? My mother and father absolutely adore the hotel, but we're running out of ideas to entertain them. Could you possibly take a day off and show them your beautiful home? Our apartment isn't much and they can see the wonderful way people can live here."

Derrick assented without hesitation, but his agreement came with a caveat: "I don't have time to pick them up, so your husband will have to drive them out here." Then he added, "I'll have lunch for them. Would like to talk to Jake about the antique dealer he knows, anyway."

Jake agreed once Laura relayed the bit about antiques. Perhaps he might find out more about the odds and ends Derrick had arranged over his fireplace during the visit on New Year's Eve. "I don't have anything to say about the Nazi Muller, but yes, I'll drive them. But like I said: *Basta!* No more. Understand? I'm tired of shepherding them around to museums."

"You don't have to keep telling me it's the end. Please just be civil to them."

Jake collected Laura's parents late that morning, two days before they were to leave. Dorothy wanted the following day to rest. Jake thought it must be because she spent so much time wringing her hands, she wore herself out. What a nervous old thing. Laura forty years from now.

The weather cooperated with a warming spring sun. Hank, sitting in the front passenger seat, expressed interest in the passing villages and farms, making comments as they drove through the countryside. But, as they neared the villa's drive he changed the subject: "Is everything all right with you two?"

Jake glanced in the rear-view mirror. Laura's mother leaned forward, her arthritic hands gripping the seat back behind her husband, her mouth half open with anticipation at Jake's response. He was sure she put Hank up to the question.

"Well, we found getting settled hard, but now that we have been here for over six months, half our time, I think we're doing fine. Rome's not easy, but I'm tutoring and doing some art restoration, and even painting. We'll be back before you know."

Hank's expression showed he understood full well nothing more would be forthcoming about their lives. His wife, unsatisfied, relaxed her grip and sat back on the seat, silent and unhappy. Jake looked back at her again thinking, why don't you ask your darling daughter if you're so concerned?

Derrick stood at the front door waiting to meet them. "Welcome, welcome."

"Dorothy and Harold Johnson, this is Derrick." He couldn't remember his last name.

"Delighted to meet charming Laura's family. You are fortunate to have such an accomplished daughter."

Jake scowled at the overly-familiar remark, but Dorothy smiled with gratification. Hank briefly locked eyes with Derrick, blue on blue, before he curtly acknowledged the compliment.

Derrick escorted Laura's parents inside, suggesting they take a seat in the lounge. They looked confused. He explained, "Your term is living room, I think." He added that the maid would bring snacks. They sat down as directed.

"Let's take a stroll before lunch," he ordered Jake as he took his arm and steered him toward the door. Dorothy and Hank now wore bemused expressions, but Derrick closed off further discussion by saying, "Back in a tick," as he and Jake left the room.

Jake wanted to pull away, but Derrick's grip held him. He let go of Jake's arm only when they reached the barn.

"I might have items of interest for your Herr Muller. My manager, Antonio, found them and I don't have any need for them."

"He's not *my* Herr Muller, but I have his business card." He reached for his wallet and retrieved the card. "What kind of items?"

"My old pots and little sculptures. You were eying them the time you and Laura were here."

"So?"

"So I'd like you to take some of my collection up to Zurich to see if Muller is interested. I might have met him once, but I'll let you handle the arrangements since you know him. I'll reimburse you for expenses, of course. And some extra, too. Can't trust Italian dealers – they'll tell you your pieces are worthless even though they aren't. And who knows?"

Jake rubbed his arm which still bore the imprint of Derrick's fingers. "I thought the Italians were pretty picky about taking stuff out of the country. Saw something on the TV when we first got here." The proposition sounded a lot like that of Stella and her associates. If she was risky, adding another layer might be dangerous. But maybe there wasn't any problem.

"Italians don't care as long as you find the articles on your own property – ask Muller. He knows."

Jake was tempted to ask why he didn't take them himself. But on further thought, he realized the task might be interesting: The trip would give him another job and a chance to learn more about being an art dealer. And now spring had arrived, a few days away would be fun. Then another thought came to mind: he didn't have a car, assuming Derrick would want his loaner returned.

Derrick must have read his mind. "Have you bought a car yet?"

"Since we're only here for a year, I can't see buying one."

"I know how inconvenient life is without one. How about if I continue to lend you this one for the last half of your stay here? If you stay on, you'll have to buy one. I'll help you get something nice, tax-free."

The project now seemed even more appealing, especially since the trip offered transportation without being beholden to Stella. In fact, he didn't want Stella involved in this venture at all. After the disastrous last trip when Jake had asked too many questions and tried to take the initiative sexually, Jake's work had been confined to making local runs to pick up and deliver supplies and the occasional packages, well wrapped so he could not tell what they contained. He also ferried the silent Chinese women back and forth from the high-walled, and gated compound where they lived. Even so, his relationship with Stella continued although she controlled his access. Drunk with her foreign ways and creativity, he could not break away.

Jake had already decided that the opportunity Derrick presented could be a chance to establish himself as an independent dealer but, not wanting to seem too eager, he said, "Give me your number and I'll call in a few days."

Derrick looked satisfied. "Good. Time for my neglected guests and lunch." He walked toward the villa with Jake following behind.

Laura's parents were still in the living room. Her mother sat quietly in a straight-backed chair with her hands folded primly in her lap. Jake looked at her more closely. She and Laura bore a strong resemblance although her face was beginning to wrinkle and her thinning hair had suffered through too many futile efforts by a preening hairdresser named Raoul who told her that, "Madame looks lovely as usual," while he pocketed his overgenerous tip. Jake saw an aged Laura before him again. He turned away, uncomfortable with the future.

Hank stood in front of the fire, gazing at the sculptures. He wore his age well. Standing straight with no sign of a pot belly, he had a vigorous appearance despite his near-baldness. He remarked to Derrick, "Interesting objects you have here. I'd like to know more."

"Splendid. I love to talk about my little collection – not that anything is worth much. Lunch will be ready in a minute or two. Like a sherry?"

Dorothy shook her head. "I don't drink at this hour." Hank, pleased, said yes, he'd be happy to try one.

Derrick poured three glasses and said, "*Cin, cin.*" Jake couldn't stand sherry but accepted anyway in the interest of not making a scene in front of his in-laws. The men raised their glasses while Dorothy stared at the carpets.

The maid announced that the meal was ready. Derrick gallantly took Dorothy's arm to steer her into the dining room where a buffet of grilled vegetables, cold salmon, and a platter with cheese and fruit was arranged on a long table.

"You first, Dorothy," Derrick said, steering her toward the buffet. She took a few small spoons full. As she approached the table he pulled out a chair, even opened her napkin as if he was a headwaiter, and then tried to engage her in small talk.

Instead, she began to whimper, tears rolling down her face. "I can't leave Laura here. It's so awful with all these people and cars and noise, and I don't know what."

Hank tried to comfort her. "She's great, my girl, she's doing fine. You know she'll be back in six months." He put his arm on her shoulder.

Derrick interjected, "Yes, she's a real star with us. We'll be sorry to see her go. Here, have a serving of pudding." He pointed toward a plate of pastries at the same time Hank glanced at Jake as if to say, what's going on here? Jake shrugged, unable to think up a response without accusing his wife of actions he wasn't yet sure she had taken.

"Pudding?"

"Sorry, you Americans say dessert."

She didn't want any, but she daubed her face and apologized for the outburst. The conversation turned to the matter of antiquities – the ones that weren't worth anything much, according to Derrick.

He led them back to the lounge when the meal was finished. Switching from host to professor about to begin a lecture to his captive audience, Derrick lit his pipe. After he took a few puffs he pointed the stem in the direction of the fireplace mantel. "Found a new piece last month."

Jake, still seething with jealousy over Derrick's remarks about Laura being a star, reluctantly turned his attention to the mantel. Added to the antiquities he had seen over the New Year's visit was a small statue of a man wearing a helmet and breastplate, his private parts exposed for all to see. He wondered what Dorothy thought about this one after *David*, and Laura's statue too. But Laura didn't just spring out of nowhere, so she must have seen Hank's anatomy over the years. The vision of her eyes tightly shut during sex made Jake smile; that is if they had any after Laura showed up. But after the brief moment of satisfaction at his own wit, another thought sprung up: Why would anyone run around naked like that? Especially in the winter. The figure's lack of critical clothing reminded him of his own predicament with Stella – exposed and vulnerable. Time to get rid of her. Be on his own.

Ignoring Dorothy's pinched expression of offense, Hank expressed interest. "Tell me more. Where did you find it? Is it bronze? Is it real? Did they really dress in this odd fashion? I feel cold already."

Derrick got out a pipe cleaner and poked at his pipe before answering. "Probably isn't genuine. Actually, my manager found it somewhere. Anyway, the same junk is sold on those carts by the Colosseum and in the flea markets – just copies, you know. I like looking at Etruscan things. They are so much more distant than the Romans, really mysterious. I suppose that's the way warriors dressed. Maybe they wanted to show manhood in every sense of the word. Strange, yes?"

Jake was now sure the figure must be real. Otherwise why would Derrick make a show? And not knowing where it came from was ridiculous. He tried to give a signal that he wanted to leave when the antiquities lecture ended, but Derrick drew him aside and led him back to the barn. "Don't forget to call me as soon as you are free. Just a small favor. I only want an idea of what my collection is worth and I don't know anyone here who's trustworthy. Muller has a good reputation, I've heard. Bring them back after you get the information so I can decide what to do with them. Two nights should be enough time. Like I said, I'll pay your expenses, of course, and a little extra. You don't mind going up there, do you?" His voice had an undertone signaling he didn't care whether Jake minded or not. Derrick continued, "As soon as you call, we'll set a date for you to pick up my little finds." Derrick pointed toward two spare tires propped up against a wall. "They'll be safely packed."

MARCH

LAURA WAS ALONE AGAIN. Jake had gone up to the villa to pick up whatever Derrick wanted appraised before driving straight to Zurich. Silvia invited her to dinner on a Friday, confiding that she was worried her relationship with Giorgio might be ending, and that she needed someone to talk to. As they shared a pizza, it was apparent that Silvia really wanted to know more about Laura's relationship with Derrick. Giorgio's name didn't come up.

"I heard that an ad for a job you might qualify for is coming out. I have a friend with a temporary contract in another unit who is qualified, but I doubt she would get the job, what with you and Derrick."

"I've had lunch with Derrick a few times. Everyone here has lunch with other people." Laura knew she was on the defensive but her relationship with Derrick was not something she would discuss with anyone, especially Silvia. Despite an effort to appear collected, she felt a guilty blush enveloping her neck and face from shaving the truth down to the barest sliver.

"Oh, come off it. We all know about you and Derrick. And like I hinted before, when he's done, he'll drop you with a cheap parting gift." Her hand reached up to twist one of her diamond studs. She saw Laura staring. "Don't worry, they're from Giorgio."

Laura didn't want to hear any more warnings, especially from someone who was obviously lying about the source of her jewelry. Worse, Silvia was a regular Cassandra, "woe, betide," and the like. But her comments rekindled Laura's doubts about what Derrick's real intentions might be. He clearly wanted her company, but she could not imagine that their relationship could go anywhere, and she needed to learn to stand on her own. It was time to stop seeing him, job offer or not.

The dinner talk drifted to shopping. Laura said she would be going to the *centro* on Saturday. Silvia wanted to come along. Laura put her off.

Laura began her Saturday with cappuccino in Piazza Navona. While she opened a packet of sugar to sprinkle into her cup she thought of Stefania. She hoped somehow she and her little boy would magically reappear. When they didn't, she moved on to the Corso to wander. She explored side streets and paused in front of store windows. Rome was showing off spring styles: shoes in neon green or orange in one boutique, and another with delicate handmade sandals. Sports clothes and cocktail dresses for the warm evenings soon to arrive decorated mannequins in other showrooms. Laura resisted temptation until she came to a shop with a display of luxury underwear. Such wispy silk, far more beautiful than even the items she purchased several months ago.

The prices were gaspingly high. She tried to picture either Jake or Derrick in the shop. Maybe Derrick would think of buying her something but certainly not unromantic Jake, who came up with a vacuum cleaner for their anniversary present one year.

As if her hand was on automatic, Laura ran her hands over a nightgown and robe, imagining sleeping in silk and lace, before moving on to other, slightly more practical luxuries. She ignored the price tags when she picked out a lace bra and matching panties, blue-flowered with tiny pink bows. Adjacent shelves were stocked with garter belts and stockings. She associated them with her dowdy mother, who should have left them behind when pantyhose became available. But these looked so sexy on the model nearby she started to waver.

The shopkeeper rushed over. "You're so beautiful. Any man would be happy to see you in these." She ran her hands over the items Laura selected. Then she added one of the garter belts and a pair of lace-topped hose. "Come back later and tell me all about it."

Laura succumbed and fished her credit card from her handbag. She emerged with the fancy shopping bag in one hand and her Gucci handbag in the other to join the crowds of happy chattering shoppers strolling the cobblestoned street. Feeling like a real Roman, she wanted another coffee to celebrate her extravagance even if it was only to please herself instead of the two men. She looked at her watch. Perhaps it was time for an *aperitivo*. A glass of wine and a snack would be in keeping with her mood. She saw a sign advertising a bar father down the street. As she neared her destination, she was distracted by the sound of someone closing a shutter on a floor above street level.

She glanced up to see a round, red-rimmed dial affixed to the building wall next to the closed shutter. At first it appeared to be a clock. But as she squinted in the brilliant sun she made out words on the dial. Intrigued, she stepped back, bumping into another pedestrian. The word "OCULARIUM" was spelled out in large letters on the object's face. She didn't know the word, but it sounded like an eye or possibly something that predicted the future. Whatever it was, it did resemble a large eye, wide open in surprise.

The dial displayed the words *Pioggia, Variable, Bello,* and *Stabile* along with some sort of markings below them. Laura understood enough Italian to know the first word meant "rain." The rest must also refer to the weather. The pointer indicated *Variable,* a discomforting omen on the face's unblinking eye. She turned away and then back again. The thing seemed to be watching her.

She sat down at an outdoor table facing away from the eye and ordered a glass of Frascati, a white wine from the hills she saw from her office's terrace, and a plate of green olives. The forecaster's words floated in her mind.

Pioggia: Her mother's tears rained down her face as Laura and Jake took her family to the airport for their departure from Rome. "Will I ever see you again?" she wailed.

Hank had stared at Laura, who looked away, before comforting his wife. "Don't worry, Dorothy. She will be fine and home again in a few months. You know how fast time goes by."

Variable: Too much of Jake or not enough. The same with Derrick. Like the weather, her life didn't remain static for long. Soon there would have to be an end to her vacillation with either a reconciliation with Jake or a complete rupture. And Italy, too. If she got the job, she would stay on; if not, then another solution to her restlessness must be found. Going back to Seattle and freelance editing wasn't on the list. Jake was in ever more danger of slipping off it entirely.

Stabile: Desirable if it meant a happy life.

Bello: That's what life in Italy or anywhere else should be, beautiful.

Laura thought of her mother describing herself as "just a housewife." Maybe that occupation wasn't so awful. At least she probably would have never gotten herself into this mess. What about their marriage? She knew nothing of their relationship. Had they slipped into affairs, or were their lives truly as stable and serene as they appeared? She was unlikely to find out, although she couldn't help briefly trying to picture her with Derrick. Ashamed at the creepy thought, she finished her drink in one swallow to cancel the image.

At loose ends, she decided to visit the National Museum near the main train station, Stazione Termini, where she and Jake had arrived from the airport what now felt like a lifetime ago. Derrick was always insisting she improve her knowledge of art, so here was an opportunity on an afternoon when she had nothing else to do with Jake not returning until Monday. She was just like Jake, off doing Derrick's bidding, she thought as she pushed through the turnstile after checking her fancy package. The recognition made her angry at both men, even if she was the one who became involved with Derrick and who introduced him to Jake.

Laura sat on her balcony dutifully reading the museum's descriptive booklet, trying to fix in her memory the sculptures and frescoes she had admired the previous day. Whatever Derrick wanted, she realized that she was beginning to feel stirrings of her own interest in the artistic glories of Rome.

Her cell phone emitted its marimba ring. Surely not her parents at this hour. Jake never called so it couldn't be him unless he was in trouble. The number on the screen was unfamiliar.

She put the book down and pressed "Accept Call," and said, "*Pronto.*"

"Is this Laura Miller?" an Italian-accented male voice asked.

"Yes?"

"My name is Francesco Moretti. I believe you met my mother and father last New Year's. My mother suggested I call you if I came to Rome."

"Yes, I recognize your name." She thought back to the charming foursome whose personal warmth livened up the otherwise cold New Year's Eve at Derrick's villa.

"Is there any chance you and your husband are available for dinner this evening? I know I'm suggesting a last-minute arrangement, but I've been tied up with work here and am just having a moment to take a breath. If not, don't worry. Maybe another time would be better?"

"I'm sorry, but Jake isn't here." Then, after a slight pause: "But I'd be happy to have some company if you don't mind just me."

"What part of the city do you live in? Perhaps we could meet at a local restaurant? I don't want to interfere so I'll understand if it is inconvenient."

"I'm not so far from San Giovanni and it isn't inconvenient at all."

"Right. There's a good one on Via Capo d'Africa. I've found the food is always good. If you are okay with the idea, I'll see you there at eight." He gave her the name.

"I'd be delighted."

"I look forward to meeting you. I look a bit like my father. How will I recognize you?"

"Well, I'm short and blonde and I'll have on a black suit with a red scarf." She was tired of the outfit but didn't have anything else appropriate for meeting a stranger.

"See you soon. *Ciao.*"

Laura held her cell phone, thinking. Did he know Jake was gone? What was he like – a Latin lothario or just a bored man who wanted company for an evening? What was it his mother had said about him? She recalled giving the woman her phone number. Now she worried her agreement to meet him at dinner was another foolish idea in her ever-lengthening list of mistakes.

She arrived fifteen minutes early to make sure she didn't miss her unexpected dinner date. She stood outside the restaurant watching patrons arrive. She tried to appear at ease and confident but was unconsciously chewing her lip as she fretted he wouldn't show up. At eight o'clock a man in his mid-thirties approached her. He wore a dress shirt, sport coat, slacks, and polished loafers.

"Are you Laura?"

"Yes, are you Francesco?"

"Yes."

They smiled uncertainly at each other. He opened the door to the restaurant. The maître d' escorted them to a reserved table.

"Very pleasant to meet you. My mother thought it would be a good idea since I hardly know anyone in Rome anymore, even though I went to La Sapienza."

"Sapienza?"

"The big university here. And then I did a year of graduate work in New York, along with an internship."

The conversation lapsed when Laura couldn't think of anything interesting to say in response. The waiter presented the wine list and menu. The conversation began again with decisions on wine and dinner.

"I'll have the *prosciutto con melone* and then *spaghetti allo scoglio* with an *insalata mista.*"

"Sounds good. I'll have the same." The faint smile lines around his brown eyes crinkled as he added "I see you have been learning to appreciate Italian food."

"I want to try it all if I live long enough. And I'd like to write about it if I can get going."

"For sure you won't run out of topics."

They nibbled at breadsticks and sipped the wine, a white from the Trentino area, while occasionally glancing at each other. The silence began to feel forced until Laura ventured: "So tell me what you do."

"I'm very lucky. Jobs are so hard to get in Italy, but I work in a small studio – that's a professional office – with two other architects. We design villas and apartment buildings."

Although Laura had decided she would not talk about her personal life, she changed her mind. A brief mention of her personal situation was best just to be safe. "My husband, Jake, is an artist."

"I'd like to hear about his work. Next time the three of us can meet if you would like."

She was pleased to learn he already wanted a next time and didn't try to separate her and Jake. "Yes, I'm sure Jake would like to meet you."

They slowly worked their way through the starter; the seafood pasta, which came with a generous portion of scampi, clams, and mussels; and the salad. As the conversation flowed, Laura warmed to Francesco's easy demeanor, like that of his parents at the New Year's party. She relaxed and told him a little about Seattle, her background, and how she wanted a change. She gave her impressions of Rome and said that, along with trying all the food, she wanted to see all of Italy.

She kept Jake out of her narrative, deciding she had done her duty with the earlier mention.

Francesco smiled. "Even I haven't seen all of Italy. And be careful of Stendahl's Syndrome. But I'm sure you would appreciate Milan. So sophisticated compared to Rome."

"What kind of disease is that? I've never heard of it. Is it fatal?"

"Fatal only in the sense of being so overcome with Italian art, you get sick. Not real of course, just an expression."

"Well, I haven't seen enough yet to even get a temperature. I'm working on it, though."

"If you want, I can give you and your husband some ideas of sights you might not have seen yet."

"I'll tell him." She stirred her espresso. She knew she wouldn't. A brief moment of sadness at their failing relationship passed over her.

When the espresso cups were empty Francesco asked, "Where is your car? I'll walk you to it."

"I took a cab. I'll ask someone here to order one."

"Please, let me drive you. And I have a thought. Have you seen the Colosseum lit up at night? We could take a quick walk. It's just a block or two from here. And my car is in that direction."

"Actually, we haven't really seen it at night yet." Laura had caught a glimpse of the Colosseum their second evening in Rome but didn't pay much attention. The prospect of taking a closer look with someone so accommodating was interesting.

The arcades of the three tiers were lit with a golden light, turning the bloody ancient stones into a panorama of peace. A few fake gladiators lingered with hope that tourists would take their picture for a fee. Nearby, the Arch of Constantine stood solitary waiting for a triumphal march. In the background the Roman Forum was bathed in a ghostly glow as if the reincarnations of ancient Senators were gathering to debate the state of the Empire. Tiny bats flew in irregular patterns in search of their evening meal in front of a full moon. The sight was enchanting, until she thought about their first days in Rome. She and Jake had eaten in a tourist trap not far away, their problems already evident.

She tried to imagine herself in the past wearing a draped gown and sandals, a Roman senator's wife, watching a hunky gladiator. But if she had been married to an ancient Jake, she would probably be in the top row broiling in the sun and turning thumbs down.

"It was a pleasure, but I think I'd better go."

They walked to his car, a modest but new Alfa Romeo. When they arrived at the apartment, he didn't offer to accompany her beyond the lobby door. "I enjoyed our evening very much. Would you mind if I called you again? I'm back to Rome in May." He shook her hand formally.

"Of course," she answered. She wished she dared to give a more enthusiastic answer. Francesco gave her his business card. She stashed it in her wallet to study in the morning. As the elevator ascended, she went over Francesco's attributes: polite, amiable, well groomed, reasonably handsome, speaking good English. Not at all like Jake, with his slouch and sweatshirts. She already wanted to see him again, although Jake would probably veto any contact, so there wasn't much point in getting overly excited. Anyway, May was a long time in the future.

Lost in daydreams, she opened the door to find her sullen husband sitting in front of the TV.

"I thought you weren't coming back until Monday."

"I said maybe Sunday evening. And I thought you'd be here when I came home." He looked at her outfit and fast-fading happy expression. "And where the hell have you been in your fancy suit?"

His outburst infected her. "What exactly were you doing for Derrick, anyway?"

"If you want to know, I took your old fart's junk to Zurich to see if any of it was worth anything. Nazi Muller laughed in my face. Said he didn't need to waste any time with fakes. The stuff is no better than what you find in flea markets."

"Fake?" Laura found this piece of news hard to believe. For all his faults, Derrick wasn't dim-witted, and he said he found the pieces on his property. Didn't he say so?

Jake's voice lowered to a confessional pitch. "But now there's a real problem. I was told to bring the stuff back with an appraisal, but Muller changed his mind at the last minute and wouldn't let go of the pieces. Said he knew another guy who might want to see them just in case he made a mistake in the valuation. Didn't want to hang around. They'll let me know."

"You mean you left Derrick's things with a man you don't know?" She heard her voice rise again to the level of a harpy. She knew the neighbors would hear.

In a hesitant voice Jake admitted he left them. "What could I do? Beat him up? Steal them or stay in Zurich forever? I'll call Muller first and then Derrick tomorrow to explain."

"I think you made a big mistake. So stop accusing me of wrongdoing. I did nothing wrong. I had dinner with the son of the people we met at Derrick's. If you were here you could have come as well. You were invited specifically, and I wasn't sure what day you were coming back. I'm just supposed to sit around waiting? I'm going to bed." She slammed the bedroom door. Shortly after, she heard the apartment door open and close. She was alone again.

Jake stared at his glass of Guinness. The bar was temporarily quiet, the early crowd having headed out to dinner and the late drinkers still absent. The barkeep, Sean, stood in front of him, wiping glasses as usual.

"Trouble with the wifey again?"

"You don't know the half of the story. I think I'm in the shit, not only with her but with her boyfriend or lover or whoever the old bastard is."

"Yeah?" Sean said in an encouraging voice.

"Need another beer."

"This one is on the house," Sean said as he handed over another glass. He crossed his arms to lean on the bar, waiting for Jake to continue.

Jake took a swallow and wiped the thick foam from his upper lip before he began. He knew it was dangerous to tell a stranger about the mess, but he was out of ideas and desperate for advice.

"Well..." He hesitated before he made up his mind to tell the whole story. "I took my in-laws out to a villa in the country, near Viterbo, where Laura, that's my wife, and I spent New Year's. I made the mistake of admiring some old pots and pieces of stuff – not even sure what some of it really is. I've been working for some guys here who repair and sell similar junk, which is why I was interested. And then, I had to take Dorothy and Hank out there – they're my wife's mom and dad – and Laura's old whatever-he-is asked if I could get them, his stuff I mean, looked at by this guy in Zurich, where the junk I restore is sold."

Sean's eyes grew round and his mouth gaped as if to swallow more of this news.

Jake downed the last of the beer and continued even though he knew he was talking too much. He had to tell someone. "So I went in the car Laura's friend is lending us. No trouble at the border, but when the dealer saw the stuff, he said they were all fakes. Then he said he'd show them to a friend who deals in tourist junk and reproductions and let me know if he could get any money for them. Didn't know how long an appraisal would take, so I left the stuff even though I was to bring them all back. And when I came home, Laura wasn't around. She finally comes in all dressed up after having dinner with a man I don't know, not the old one. To top it off, I told her about the trip and she got mad. So now I'm in trouble with Laura, Laura's old guy, and maybe even the crazy woman I work for, if she finds out."

"You really know how to fuck up, don't you?"

Jake pushed the wet beer mat around with a finger as if he was contemplating a deep plan when he had no ideas at all. "What to do?"

"Don't have a clue. Don't think I'd mess with antiquities, if that's what they are. The authorities here can be downright nasty."

"God, what a mess."

"Have another, pal."

But Jake needed to think about what to do instead of getting drunk, although that was what he wanted. He left the pub to walk down the dark street toward the apartment. A car pulled up beside him. The window slid down silently. Jake saw Nando leaning over the passenger seat.

"Stella wants to see you. Get in."

He thought about running but knew it would be useless. They'd find him wherever he went. He climbed in. The car pulled into the garage under Stella's building. Nando remained close behind him as they walked to the elevator. Jake worried that he might have a knife.

Stella waited at the open door to her apartment. Before Jake could open his mouth, she launched into attack mode. "What the hell did you think you were doing, you jackass?" She followed up this remark with a string of words, few of which Jake understood. He got the message anyway.

She took hold of his shirt and shoved him down into a hard wooden chair, standing above in a menacing manner.

"I didn't do anything wrong and you know it, you bitch. This guy just asked me to take the stuff to be valued because my wife told him

I worked at a restoration lab. I never told him where I worked, I never told him about you, I never...."

Nando interrupted his story by hitting him in the face. The blow brought tears to his eyes and blood from a cut lower lip.

"Quit bluffing. I want to hear all about how you came to be involved with this man."

"Why do you care so much? Just because you wanted to buy the things? The stuff isn't worth zilch according to your pal Muller."

Stella laughed. "Is that what he told you? He called, and believe me, the goods are not worthless. You listen up, I know how to deal with Muller and you never will."

She dropped into an armchair and lit up. She sat silently as the smoke curled around her face. Jake waited for whatever was coming next.

"Now, little boy, I want to know everything, and I mean everything."

Jake daubed the welling blood with his knuckle and began with a summary, leaving out his suspicions about Laura's relationship with Derrick, although Stella would get the picture. She kept pressing for details: exactly where Derrick lived and where he found or bought the pieces. Jake tried to respond but knew little; no doubt exactly what Derrick intended.

"And now tell me what you've told your pal, this Derrick, your wife's lover, I think, about what Muller said."

Jake acknowledged he hadn't talked to him yet. Stella interrupted with orders: "You call him tomorrow and tell him you're waiting to hear from Muller. You understand? Tell him you need to get back home for an emergency. You've got family in the States, don't you?"

"Yes. Okay."

"Now get out."

"But I live miles away."

"So walk, *stronzo*."

As Jake stumbled out her apartment door, he heard her say to Nando, "You were right. I never should have used him."

Stella's apartment was several miles from his home on the other side of the city, and although there were bus routes, Jake didn't feel like waiting until a bus on a night-owl run might pass by. As he walked head down between the cones of light from the streetlamps, he saw his shadow stretch before him to beckon him onward, before it retreated as if he was being pulled back each time he approached the next light. The empty streets echoed with his footsteps.

When he neared the *centro,* prostitutes, men and women, pale-skinned Russians to ebony Africans, young and middle-aged, all dressed in revealing outfits, stood along the curbs. He watched as they bent down from their platform shoes to openly negotiate with drivers stopping by to inspect the merchandise.

By the time he reached Santa Maria Maggiore, dawn overcame the night. Freshly-washed streets glistened in the rising sun. Jake trudged past the basilica's obelisk and along Via Merulana with aching feet and a headache pounding in his temples. He tried to convince himself the headache came from the beer, but he knew it was from fear. Fear he would be rejected by both Stella and Laura before he could reject them, cut loose from his newly exciting life to slink back to Seattle, tail between his legs. So much for luck like he'd always had in poker games. So much for his efforts to help rescue abandoned art treasures.

He came to the basilica of San Giovanni after walking for more than an hour. He was back in familiar territory not far from his own apartment. But he didn't want to crawl home in case Laura hadn't left for work yet. Commuters were already up and about, aiming for bus stops or the Metro. Cars were beginning to compete for space. One of the basilica's massive doors swung open as if inviting him to find shelter inside. Jake walked up the steps.

The church was softly lit by the early morning sunshine with only the sound of a few echoing footsteps to break the peaceful spell cast by the nave's grandeur. He found a folding chair near the back and sat down, head in his hands. He heard footsteps.

"Do you need help?" The voice had an American accent.

Startled, Jake jumped up. "No. I mean, maybe."

"What do you need?" The young priest's voice was quiet but firm, probing.

"I'm not Catholic, not a believer at all. But I need to talk."

"Come with me."

The priest led him to a small office, produced a coffee from an American-style drip coffeemaker, and suggested that he sit down. Jake took the mug, happy to see the watery liquid, a reminder of home, his Seattle home.

"I'm Father John. Please tell me about the problem."

"Not a *problem*, I've got *problems*, plural. Nothing is going right and I don't know what I'm doing in Rome."

"Why?"

The question produced a torrent of pent-up words. "My wife wanted to move to Italy and I didn't really want to but went along with it, and I don't ever see my family, and I hated my job but now I don't know what to do, and my wife doesn't love me, and..."

"Maybe you should begin at the beginning," the priest said, interrupting him. Jake paused to take a slurp of the now-cold coffee. The priest dumped it out and poured fresh before asking, "So, where are you from?"

Jake began at the beginning: his childhood in rural Washington, the fights with and flights from his violent father, his hope to be an architect but his inability to excel at the courses, his unhappiness with teaching, and his neglected attempts to become a painter. He left out the part about his little sister. Some feelings ran too deep even for a priest to hear.

As he was beginning the story of his unsatisfactory marriage and the move to Rome, Father John stood up, breaking his flow. "Sorry, I'm on for confession soon. If you want, you can come back any day. I'll be in the nave at the same time as today."

Jake put down his mug and walked out of the church into a blast of morning sun.

Laura was long gone to work. As usual, he fell asleep while listening to his country favorites. He dreamed that he, Stella, and Laura were involved in a sex game but no one enjoyed themselves, least of all him. Then a marble foot missing its little toe fell to the ground, shattering. He woke up to see Laura dropping her bag on the dining table.

"My God, what happened? You look like hell."

Jake pulled out one earbud. Laura could hear the whiny music twanging from the dangling earpiece.

Rather than a pretense that life was calm after their argument the evening before, he said, "You wouldn't look any better if you had to call Derrick today and let him know you left his *ar-te-facts* with Muller and the other man." His mouth distorted in derision as he pronounced the word.

Laura saw the small tear of dried blood on his chin. She softened. "Maybe I can help." She tried to sound conciliatory but the thought of getting crosswise with Derrick was alarming. Who knew what power he had whatever the state of their relationship?

"What happened to your lip?" She could not resist asking even though she knew the answer would likely be a lie. His lip was swollen but the rest of him looked deflated, nothing like the confident Jake she'd briefly seen after his first trip to Zurich.

"I tripped. Just help me talk with Derrick." He turned toward the television but not before Laura saw his abject expression.

She knew he wouldn't divulge anything more. He never did.

"Let me think a bit before you talk to Derrick. One more day isn't going to make a difference." While she tried to come up with a plan, she pulled a package of premade polenta from the refrigerator, sliced it, and threw it in a frying pan with sausage links. The grease spattered and burnt her hand. She doused the pain with cold water.

Jake ate in silence, head down to avoid his wife's eyes. To find a way out of the situation, she suggested, "Why don't you let me talk to Derrick instead? Since I don't know anything, it might go better. Did you say Muller would call at some point?"

"He didn't give me a date. But I could call and ask if you think I should." Jake talked to his plate rather than his wife.

"Well, my dear, you just call him tomorrow morning. Okay? I'll take care of Derrick." With nothing more to say she gathered up the dinner dishes and hustled into the kitchen to clean up. She regretted calling him "dear."

She spotted her journal next to the flute player. It was dusty with disuse. Instead of opening it, she dropped the book in the bathroom wastebasket to go out with the trash in the morning. What was the point of recording her life? Anything to do with Jake was now too painful, and her affair with Derrick made her feel sleazy. When life got better, she would restart her blog about her *dolce vita,* if she ever found one.

Jake called Laura at work the next day to say he talked with Muller, who put him off, telling him not to worry and he would hear something in a few days. The information made Jake sure the man was negotiating with Stella on how to split the spoils. He couldn't decide whether or not to return to the priest for more talk therapy, although if he continued his tale, "confession" would be the more accurate word even if there would be no absolution. Instead, he entered the church on the Via dei Fori Imperiali with the staring Christ.

Just as he entered the church, his cell phone rang. Stella's number showed on the screen. He denied the call. Then he received a text message. He hit the delete button. "A first step," he said aloud. He stared at the unblinking figure above the altar. Christ looked concerned.

Not far from the altar a teacher desperately tried to control a group of noisy, giggling schoolchildren. Her lecture went unheeded. Jake watched her fruitless efforts. That's what he could look forward to if he went back to Seattle. He switched his attention to the few worshippers, all old women attempting to concentrate on their prayers in spite of the din.

Her spiel over, the teacher managed to corral her charges and herd them out of the church. In the quiet Jake couldn't avoid reflecting on his blundering, how he let himself be duped. He didn't like what he had done, any of it, but he couldn't change the past. So what about the future?

While Jake was staring at the silent mosaic of Christ, Laura was staring at her office telephone. She picked up the receiver after several minutes of hesitation. "Derrick, hi." Laura tried to sound upbeat, but her voice betrayed nervousness.

"Yes, my dear? What may I do for you?"

"Could we have a quick coffee?"

"Well, I'm rather busy, but how about after work – say at six?"

Laura was concerned at his disinterested response. "Okay, Derrick. I'll meet you in the lobby." He had already hung up before she finished her sentence.

She put on fresh makeup and a smile before entering the lobby in hopes he'd already arrived. He hadn't. Fifteen minutes went by before he walked up to her.

"Sorry I'm late. Telephone call. Spot of bother."

Laura hid her concern. But the wait had been an eternity. "I just need to talk to you about a problem for a few minutes. Can we go across the street to the bar?"

"How about just over here?" He pointed to a corner where two armchairs sat at right angles.

Laura was now thoroughly alarmed. How could it be that he didn't even want a drink with her?

They sat down. Laura leaned toward him while he stared straight ahead. "My husband, Jake, you know, told me he took your antiques up to Zurich. You asked him to, remember?"

"Of course. Why wouldn't I?" He looked indignant.

"You need to know that the man, I think his name is Muller, said he wanted to keep them for a while, even though they weren't worth anything and I'm worried you'll be cross. And…I don't know. Jake is sorry for the mix up." A lame ending, she knew, but she *was* worried. And she shouldn't have suggested he might not remember.

"Bloody hell, Laura, I'm neither senile nor gullible. I called Muller before your husband even left. You don't need to get involved. He and I will work a deal. I just wanted your dear and I must say, naïve husband, to transport the items. It was a test to see if he could follow directions, which he obviously can't."

"I'm sorry. I'm sorry," she repeated. "You're right, I don't want to be involved."

Derrick stood up. "Must leave. Small trouble with my wife. Will call soon." He walked out.

Laura sat stunned at this development. Livia, whom he hardly ever mentioned, was now so important? And poor Jake, nothing but a conduit to whatever anyone wanted. They could ask him to do anything, tell him anything. He was a sheep. And what am I? She didn't care to find an answer.

On the way home Laura thought about Derrick's wife. What did "bother" mean? Was she sick, or could the problem be related to her antique business? She must be somewhere on the Internet if she had a business. Her first name was Livia, and Laura assumed she went by Clawson. She'd look her up if Jake was out.

Jake was waiting for her.

Laura noted his apprehensive and expectant expression. "I talked to Derrick. He says no problem, he talked to Muller. So he must have known the guy all along. So relax. I don't know what this is all about, but I've done my duty. That's it – don't expect me to get involved." Then she added, "Don't you dare get me in trouble. I don't know why you couldn't have taught English or painted like you wanted to do. There are so many things to do here."

Jake opened his mouth for a retort he hadn't quite formed. Laura cut him off. "Why don't you go home, I mean to Seattle, for a while to get away and think things over?"

Jake spiraled out of control. "Why don't you go instead? You're never here. You're having sex with that disgusting man and now you're seeing this Italian guy you were out with the other night. I know what you're up to, you're just a tramp. Getting ahead on your back. Do you keep your eyes closed like you did with me? Like your mother? And I'm not going back to Seattle. You go. Who the hell do you think you are, anyway?" He gasped after the outburst, ever more worried he was becoming his father.

Laura blinked, stung by the accusations and the core of truth. "But…at least he's interested in my career. You said you wanted to stay on. And so far I'm not getting ahead and you're involved with Derrick, too, so leave me alone."

Jake flipped on the TV and stared blindly at the screen. Laura got out a bottle of wine from the rack and, in a futile effort to make a conciliatory gesture, poured two glasses. He took one without acknowledgement. As she sipped the wine, she contemplated his profile: weak, indecisive. She knew her own face was damp with tears of disappointment. The wine tasted as if it had turned to vinegar.

"What now, Jake?" He didn't respond. Laura reflected on the article she read shortly before arriving in Rome, and the office talk she heard about other people's partners trapped in the undertow of expat life. They spent their time consorting with prostitutes, took too many pills or drugs, hid in their apartments, refused to participate, or just gave up and returned to wherever they came from. And she knew plenty of her officemates were also having affairs with their coworkers. Was there a hex on expat life that brought out the worst, or did the same problems happen at home and she didn't know about them? How would her old friends in Seattle, the ones with all the advice, react to Rome if they weren't tourists? Probably the same as she.

But Doug and her colleague, Raj, appeared to be content with their lives, and from what she saw of their wives, they too were adjusted to the vicissitudes of Italian life. So being an expatriate wasn't the reason, she comforted herself.

Her truce with Jake had fallen apart. What about tomorrow or the next week, or month? She saw Jake adrift in Rome, unable to find satisfaction in any of its wonders. But her own life, a child, Derrick, her job, and the possibility of staying on were up in the ether, too. Any illusion about her marriage was gone forever, but what to do? Surely something to clarify the situation would happen soon.

APRIL

JAKE WAS A REGULAR at his neighborhood bar. Mario, the owner, was always on duty, ready to pour an espresso or a shot of *grappa*. A group of old men perpetually hung around. They sat on shabby white plastic chairs pulled up to the few chipped Formica tables, or stood at the counter to argue about politics or soccer, the comments and complaints never varying.

Jake thought the bar must not have been remodeled since shortly after the Second World War. Its very fustiness gave him a welcome feeling of continuity in the face of so much change in his life. The aroma of coffee wafted out the door to welcome him whenever he approached, and the hiss of steam, the noise of heavy cups slapped on the counter for impatient patrons, and the hard rap as the grounds were emptied from the filter, offered a haven of unthreatening routine. Last year's calendar hung on a wall. A curling poster of Padre Pio in his brown robes hovered over the espresso machine. Jake had never heard of the priest before coming to Rome, but his picture was frequently displayed in restaurants, shops, and bars. He presumed the old guy was a local guardian angel.

This month Jake saw a few leftover chocolate Easter eggs wrapped in yellow, blue, and red foil, and two boxes of dove-shaped cakes gathering dust. Another holiday come and gone.

Mario did a double take at Jake's lip, which was still slightly swollen with a small scab remaining, before he began to fiddle with the espresso maker, a new Gaggia, full of shiny knobs and spouts. Jake was disappointed to see that even here, life moved on. But could Seattle really have been as stable as he thought, now that he looked back at his former life? Like his time in Rome, life in Seattle lacked definition or clarity, as if the mirror needed wiping.

He ordered an espresso and sat down at a vacant table to think about Stella and Derrick fighting over the artifacts. In some ways the whole situation was almost funny, except that he found himself trapped between them. In an effort to divert his thoughts, he scanned the headlines of a *La Repubblica* discarded by another patron. More political scandals and articles about corruption. At least there was no change on that front. He paged to the culture section to review the listing of exhibits. There were always new ones. Rome was a city of artists all competing for gallery space alongside old and not-so-old masters.

Bitter dregs remained at the bottom of his cup – yes, bitter, *amaro*. The word reminded him of Stella and the lunch where she first offered him the liqueur of the same name. Like Eve and the apple from his childhood Sunday school lessons.

He put the cup back on the bar and left, turning his footsteps toward San Giovanni. When he saw the church was not yet open for visitors, he walked to the nearby Via Sannio market to wait. The area was already animated, reminding him of how much color Rome offered. Not just of its buildings, but of its inhabitants. Maybe he wasn't crazy enough like other artists who would kill to get to Rome to paint. He visualized cutting off part of his ear and showing the bloody remains to Laura to get her sympathy.

The church door was open by the time Jake headed back. He walked in, hoping to see Father John. He lingered in the same corner as before. After a few minutes the priest approached him. This time Jake started the conversation by asking him where he was from.

"I'm from Idaho, here for a couple of months."

"Would you mind if I talked some more?"

The young priest led him to the same small office with the same coffee pot. Jake slumped in the hard plastic chair.

"Yes?"

"I'd like to finish my story – the one from the other week."

Father John didn't say anything, so Jake, uncomfortable with the silence, took up the thread of his tale.

"You know, at first I didn't want to leave my job and home, and then I wanted to. But now, I don't know. I find it hard here and Laura, well, we don't get along much now. Things were okay in Seattle, but since we got here everything's changed. She's got a new life and I don't have anything, can't find anything good. I've tried to paint but can't get going. That's what I thought I wanted to do here, but now I don't know. I'd like to become an art dealer, too. And sometimes I think I still love my wife, but other times..." He stared at the posters on the wall asking for donations for the poor in Africa. There was an idea: He could go to Africa, some outpost in the jungle with just a few dried-up old nuns around.

The priest poured more coffee. They drank slowly without speaking until Father John said, "I obviously don't know much about marriage except for my parents' happiness, and I haven't taken many counseling courses, so I have no concrete advice, other than you must honor your vows and talk to one another." He added an afterthought: "I realize I don't know you well, but from what you have told me, you do seem quite self-centered. Perhaps that could be part of the problem."

Jake hadn't gotten to the part about Stella yet, the worst part of the whole sorry tale. If he continued, he would need to shape the narrative very carefully. Adultery, along with being an accessory to probable art theft, might be too much for his naïve young confidant dressed so uptightly in black.

Father John shot a shrewd glance in Jake's direction. "What's the rest of the story? You surely aren't in all this anguish over your brush with Italy."

Jake became alarmed. His desire to unburden his mind by talking to the priest vanished. He would settle his problems by himself. "Back some other time. Got other stuff to do." He put down the cup and stood facing the door.

"Wait. Please."

Jake stopped with one hand on the doorknob.

"You don't have to tell me anything. This isn't confession. I like to have the opportunity to talk with people from the U.S. There hasn't been much time to do that since I arrived a month ago."

Jake hesitated.

"Do you know Idaho at all? I am missing my old home and family. I attended seminary in Pennsylvania. Haven't been back home in a long time."

Jake sat down again. The priest looked pleased to have someone to listen to. Jake looked at him. About his own age, short with red hair, looking like he might become fat if he didn't get some exercise. His coloring made Jake think he was Irish.

"I've been to the Idaho panhandle a few times. Nowhere else in the state." Curious about a man who knew what he wanted, Jake said, "How did you decide on being a priest?"

The young man told him about growing up in Boise, his family of Basque extraction, his calling from earliest childhood to become a priest even though it was against his family's wishes, and his recent arrival in Rome for a short stay. After he heard John's condensed life story, Jake took his turn to offer up a few more edited facts about his life in Rome all the while wishing that he had a real calling – artist, or even another go at becoming an architect if it wasn't too late. Maybe sometime he could talk more about Laura and his fear of having a child. Nevertheless, he was relieved to find a man, even if he was only a priest, with whom he could carry on a normal conversation; no probing, no scoffing at his status.

Jake turned to a safe subject. "Will you tell me more about San Giovanni?"

"I'd be delighted. You mentioned becoming an art dealer. Well, you've come to the right place as St. John is their patron saint. Now, let's begin with the cloister."

Jake didn't want to see any more of the scene of his original sin. The echo of the past with Stella was too unpleasant. And he recognized his illusions about becoming a dealer were never to be realized. He said, "Sorry. Gotta go. I just remembered an appointment. Maybe I'll see you again." He made a show of looking at his watch before walking into the sunshine thinking about his first encounter with Stella in the cloister. Country boy in the big city. He knew he must get away from her tentacles. Sure, the sex had been exciting and he'd earned five thousand euros for doing almost nothing; hush money, he knew. He fingered the remains of the scab below his lip. What to do? Lying low for a while was probably best.

Their affair had come to an abrupt end in the wake of the mess with Derrick, and he no longer bothered with driving. She hadn't tried to contact him again since he refused to respond while he was in the church staring at Christ's eyes. But could a rejected phone call and text convince her to let him go and find someone else to follow her orders?

As Jake walked toward the apartment, the sensation of being followed crept over him. He turned around but couldn't see anybody unusual. The feeling persisted until he entered his building. Once inside, he locked himself in the apartment and went to the window to check the street below. Cars and pedestrians passed. Nothing looked amiss, but his nerves pulsed with foreboding.

His phone rang. An unfamiliar number showed up on the screen. He answered, but whoever called hung up without speaking. The cold sweat of fear drenched his body.

Neither Jake nor Laura had made any more moves to revive their marriage. Instead of talking, Laura brought more work home. Jake stared at the TV and slept in the guest room. But when she received a party invitation she decided to ask him if he wanted to participate.

"We've been invited to Doug's country house for lunch. Do you want to go? I can find someone else to go with if you don't."

"I'll drive." Jake knew she was only trying to disguise the state of their marriage and had no real interest in his company. But he saw the invitation as a way to engage normal people for a change. People who were as normal as expats can be. And he wanted to check out the countryside for possibilities of shelter from Stella if necessary.

The drive took them north to Lake Bolsena. When they arrived cars were already parked on the grass outside a small farmhouse in the throes of remodeling. A cement mixer stood on one side of the house, along with debris and discarded lumber. The golden-colored stucco on the exterior walls needed repair. Beyond the house were two more structures: a lean-to sheltering more building materials, and a shack with cobwebbed windows and a half-open door sagging on rusted hinges.

Doug came out to welcome them. He invited Jake and Laura inside to take a tour before they joined the other guests. Laura admired the flooring, reddish tiles in an antique style, and the airy linen curtains. Unlike Derrick's villa with oppressive draperies, this home was filled with light. But the kitchen was antediluvian with an ancient stove, a tiny refrigerator, and open cabinets, even worse than her place in Rome.

A woman wearing a flowered apron over a black dress busily stirred something on one burner before she lifted the lid to test something else on another. An array of fruit and vegetables sat on the stone counter. The woman waved a long spoon and smiled in greeting, undaunted by the inadequate appliances.

"That's our wonderful neighbor, Gina. She helps us out when we have a party. She's a great cook. The kitchen remodeling starts next year," Doug offered by way of explanation of her presence and the state of the house.

"You are so fortunate. I'd love to have a place like this. I'll say hello to Helena."

Laura left Jake to face his host alone. Jake never had any interest in getting to know Doug, and their exchanges at the few Friday evening pizza parties he had attended were limited to pleasantries. Stuck face to face, he knew he had to make an effort at small talk. The only subject he could think of was the house.

Doug responded to Jake's questions, describing how he and Helena had searched for several years, the complexity of the transaction, the problems of remodeling, and how they wished the property was closer to Rome. They hadn't known about the spotty cell phone service until they purchased. "But just see the view over the lake with the villages scattered around."

As Jake wandered around the house with Doug, he saw it as a refuge to work on, to live in. A refuge from Rome and Stella, a problem sticking to him like his shadow. Jake shifted his attention to the open French doors. He saw the lake with an island resting not far from one shore and a hill town flowing down the far slope: a church at the top surrounded by large buildings, smaller ones scattered below. A resort occupied a large piece of property near the water. The blue surface of a swimming pool flashed in the sunshine.

"I'd like to paint around here."

"Now I remember. Laura said you were an artist. Well, I like to have someone around during the week, so if you want to come up, you're welcome. Let me know and I'll give Laura a key for you." As an afterthought he added, "Could use a little help around here if you're interested."

"Hey, that's great. Thanks." He tried to make his response seem casual but the possibility of using the house as a hideout was exciting.

He took a closer look at the interior before he felt obligated to join the other guests, an international crowd in contrast to the Fergusons' Christmas party. The living and dining room took up the greater part of the house. A long wooden table and six chairs, pushed against the wall to allow a buffet to be set up, occupied one end. A fireplace with bookshelves on either side filled the other end of the room. Jake inspected the books. There were numerous guidebooks to the local area and all of Italy, memoirs and histories of the country, and a set of Gibbon's *The Decline and Fall of the Roman Empire*. Jake hadn't read a book for years and certainly none of such depth. Sitting on top of a stack of home design magazines were some black pottery fragments. Is this yet another person involved in buying and selling? Puzzled, Jake wondered if Derrick and Doug were working together in some scheme. He walked out of the French doors with his mind on how he could have a country home and what he could do with one, with or without Laura.

Doug, who had gone outside before him, was chatting with several guests. When the conversation paused, Jake took the opportunity to interject a question about the fragments. Doug chuckled. "They're a few odds and ends Derrick gave me as a housewarming gift. I think he gave some to Raj, too. The pieces don't even fit together. I should get rid of them – it's illegal to have them. Don't want to toss them until Derrick retires, though. Then I think I'll just bury them for a future archeologist to discover. What a laugh it will be when someone tries to figure out how the pieces got here."

Jake digested this information as he kept an eye out for Laura. She was not far away, chatting happily with other guests, including Helena. Behind them stood Derrick, his face shaded with a battered Panama hat and his body enclosed in a wrinkled and yellowing linen suit. He was trying to light his pipe. Jake watched him fumble. Derrick made a show of not seeing him.

Jake overheard Laura ask Helena about her daughter. Helena said, "She's at UC Davis, in vet school of all the strange things because we've never even owned a dog. Never know what your kids will do. She'll be here for a month this August. Do you have children? I forgot what you said earlier."

He also heard Laura respond, "No, not yet," and watched as she turned to engage the Fergusons. Jake tried to keep one eye on Derrick without being too obvious.

While Laura was engaged in inconsequential small talk, she was mulling over what she'd found on the Internet after her last conversation with Derrick. She had been searching for references to his wife. Livia Clawson wasn't obscure with a professional website advertising her antique store in Belgravia, a wealthy section of London. She also had a blog where she wrote about the various antiques she found. Many of the items pictured on her site were Georgian silver or Meissen porcelain, but one page was devoted to antiquities similar to the items Laura had seen at their villa on her only visit. She searched further until she came to one of the scandal-mongering newspapers' websites. There she found a short article indicating an unidentified woman being investigated for selling antiquities with provenances that were doubtful at best. Laura checked the word "provenance" on Wikipedia to be sure she understood its meaning.

Still thinking about the information she found earlier, she approached Derrick. "How are you? I've missed your company. Everything okay with your wife now?"

He said, "Let's walk."

Laura knew Jake was watching as she and Derrick strolled along a path past a vineyard and on through a sunlit grove of olive trees. Wildflowers carpeted the ground. Brilliant red poppies and other blooms in purple, white, blue, and yellow, competed for the bees' attention. Small white flowers that would eventually turn into olives peeked out between the pale green and silver leaves of the trees, their trunks contorted with great age as if they suffered from arthritis.

The path led them near the edge of a steep hill. Derrick, perspiring, took off his hat. Laura looked at the red ring around his forehead from the too-tight headband. He wiped his face with his handkerchief. He looked haggard, his face gray and slack.

She sat beside him on a bench overlooking the water and took his hand. His signet ring faced the wrong way. She turned it back while saying, "Is there anything I can do?"

He put his hand on top of hers. "Livia's healthy as a horse, but there's another problem. Tell your husband he should stay out of the way. I shouldn't have asked him to help me. I'm probably going to have to go back to London for a while. Livia hasn't committed a crime, but there's a mess to deal with all the same."

"I'll tell him, and I'm glad your wife is healthy, but...how long would you be gone?"

"Don't worry, my dear. I've already written a strong recommendation and I know Doug will also. Good help is hard to find. Let's have lunch next week. I'll be flying back Friday evening for a few days."

"Yes, let's." She tried to sound bright, but she saw how the effects of continuing stress had aged him. She suggested they rejoin the others. People might talk or, embarrassingly, Jake would be sulking in a corner. Derrick continued to look at the lake.

"Derrick? We need to head back now."

He stood up and obediently followed her back to the party.

The other guests, Jake among them, were sitting or standing on the terrace talking, glasses of wine in hand. No one acted like they missed either Laura or Derrick.

"How's it going?" Laura said as she took Jake's arm. He ignored her as he continued to talk to Helena about a canvas she had seen in a gallery in the town of Bolsena. Laura heard him ask for the name of the gallery, saying he might want to check it out.

Gina, the neighbor hired for the day's festivities, interrupted the small talk to tell Helena lunch was ready. Helena clapped her hands together to get her guests' attention while saying, "*A tavola!*"

They trooped inside to the now heavily laden dining table to serve themselves. The array was a feast: a whole prosciutto on a stand, with slices already cut; a bowl of fresh mozzarella, the round balls floating in milky liquid; salamis; melon slices; baked tomatoes filled and decorated with basil; deep-fried zucchini flowers stuffed with ricotta and herbs; grilled mushrooms; coarse Roman bread and *grissini* sticks; a cheese board; smoked salmon. As the guests lined up, Gina came out of the kitchen with an enormous bowl of steaming *linguine ai frutti di mare,* clams, mussels, shrimp, scallops, and calamari, decorated with red pepper flakes and parsley, the colors of Italy. Bottles of wine and water were at one end of the table, along with the plates and silverware.

Laura thought of the lunch party she hosted months ago. What on earth had she been thinking, inviting these people to her apartment? She hardly knew them. How they must have laughed afterward. Putting the red wine in the ice bucket, serving that disgusting chicken.

As she filled her plate, Laura took mental notes on how to host an Italian party. She wished she had enough nerve to take photos with her phone for reference for the blog or in case she ever hosted another party. Another fiasco would be unbearable.

As they ate, the group continued their conversations about local and international politics and scandals, the UN and its policies, and where they were going for their summer holidays. The beach, the mountains, Norway, back home, Buenos Aires. Laura kept her portion of the conversation to generalities. Jake remained silent.

Gina emerged from the kitchen bearing dessert. Several tortes, accompanied by a perfect *tiramisu* and a *semifreddo*, beckoned. Laura couldn't bear to see the *tiramisu*, thinking of the mess she'd produced, but she tried the *semifreddo*, a pistachio-flavored custard and gelato mix.

She spooned up the calming dessert, content for the moment.

"I want the key."

Laura was dozing on the way back to Rome. Too much food and wine, but a satisfying day except for Derrick's problems. When Jake's voice reached her she sat up.

"What are you talking about? I don't know about any key other than the one to our apartment." She was now wide awake looking at Jake's profile. He looked determined, an unusual expression.

"Doug said you could get me the key to his place so I could go up there and paint. And I'll offer to do some work, if he wants."

Laura was surprised. "Why? Are you planning to move out? Did Doug say anything about the job?"

"Doug didn't say anything specific but he wants me to help out, and there's a lot of work to do, so I don't know. But I've put aside my work for too long. I'll just be gone for a few days at a time if Derrick will let me have the car."

She was pleased that he finally wanted to paint, the original reason he agreed to come to Rome. But it seemed awfully sudden after months of delay. There must be something more but it would be a relief to have him gone. "Yes, I'll ask Doug tomorrow."

An envelope was lying on Laura's desk the following morning. She opened it to find an advance copy of the long-awaited job announcement. The duties were similar to her current work and she met the basic qualifications perfectly, a degree in English and extensive editing experience. But there might be a catch: the selection panel would like the candidates to have a second official language. She felt her stomach sink with this bit of unexpected information.

She began to draft the section on the form requesting information on her past experience, all the while waiting for Doug to arrive. Her editing assignment was forgotten.

He came in later than usual. "Stayed at the farmhouse last night and it was a long drive in. Traffic hellish." He looked distracted.

She thanked him for the party and added that Jake would like to go there from time to time. Then she moved on to her immediate concern: "Doug, I received an advance copy about the vacancy and I see one of the desirable qualifications is a second language. Do you think I should apply anyway?"

"What vacancy?"

"What do you mean? It's the one I want to apply for, you know, I want to stay on if possible. I thought…" Her sentence trailed off into silence. He surely knew the vacancy was in his own office.

Doug was already staring into his computer screen as if she didn't exist. He looked up after a minute, unaware she still stood in front of his desk. "Oh, right, I forgot. I have a bunch of things on my mind. Don't worry, the phrase about another language is standard, doesn't mean much." Then he continued as if thinking aloud, "Although I understand the selection committee being interested in bilingual staff. We are the United Nations, you know. And we have other official languages besides English." As she turned to leave his office, Doug emerged from his thoughts to add, "I'll bring in a spare key tomorrow along with info on the utilities and what to do in case of problems."

Problems. Everyone had one damn problem or another. Including her. She phoned Derrick's office. His secretary answered with the news he wouldn't be in the office today. Maybe he would come in tomorrow. Jake was fiddling with an easel when she arrived home.

"What's up?"

"Well, if I'm going to have a chance to paint out in the country I need more supplies."

His watercolors, brushes, and paper were piled on the table accompanied by a new palette, palette knife, a few small canvases, more brushes, about twenty large tubes of acrylics and a sturdy easel. Laura knew then that he'd been squirreling money away because every month they had spent her salary and the five hundred he said he was paid for his work. He must have lied about his earnings. Where could he have kept it? No point in asking; he'd never admit it.

"Jake, I did ask Doug about the key. He said he would bring it to me. He will try to get it to me this week." She debated whether to tell him what she found on the Internet. In the end she let the subject rest; enough for now. The article didn't actually mention Livia's name, anyway, so she might be wrong.

Jake interrupted her thoughts by saying, "Sooner is better." Then he yelled, "Goddamnit, *merda, merda, merda.*" He had caught his thumb in the folding leg of the easel.

Doug brought keys to the buildings on his property and a sheaf of instructions the following day. Silvia asked Laura if she would like to have lunch. Knowing she couldn't find a credible excuse to avoid her any further – over a month had passed since they even shared coffee – she accepted. Laura didn't bring up the weekend party, thinking Silvia wasn't invited.

Silvia immediately began talking about her friend's need for the job. "I told her you'll get the job even though she knows French and Spanish besides her diploma in English. She needs the money, you know."

Laura didn't know, nor did she care. Silvia went on with her laments, saying that she and Giorgio had split up. She was too depressed to attend the Sunday party. Laura tried to appear concerned, although she thought Silvia better off without a man who apparently did nothing but smoke. No doubt there would be other parties with other men.

"For heaven's sake, Silvia, if your friend really wants the job she should go ahead and apply. I'm not going to sabotage anyone." Undeterred, Silvia continued with her complaints: Derrick was unfair; what an old lecher he was; the job had been wired for Laura. Laura finished her soup, a thick *pasta e fagioli*, and salad as fast as she could to get away. The cloud of concern over the competition for the job gathered in intensity with each of Silvia's remarks.

Someone had stuck a note on her computer monitor over the lunch hour. Derrick called and would like her to call back. Her mood leaped with the hope that he would not leave before she got the job. She rang his extension. He said he wanted to meet her at his apartment for lunch the following day.

Trying to be light, she responded, "Do you want me to cook?"

Derrick took her question as sarcasm and reverted to a business-like voice. "No, no, of course not. I'll have the maid pop down to Volpetti. See you at one."

Laura held the beeping receiver for another minute before she carefully hung up. She hoped no one overheard her end of the conversation, especially the part about cooking which sounded like they were married. She was sure their meeting would be the end of their relationship with another handbag as compensation. She tried to imagine how it would go, who would take the initiative, but she was too agitated to think clearly.

Jake was out again that evening. She poured a glass of wine and fired up the laptop to search the Internet again, looking for references to Derrick's wife. This time she found one on a website about antiques with a link to an article naming names: a Ms. Clawson, among others, was under investigation for trafficking in stolen antiquities. Laura clicked back to Livia's own website to take another look at the photos. No picture of the imperious woman showed up, but there couldn't be two people with the same name in the same business. The information convinced Laura that Derrick was linked to his wife's problems.

The next day Laura took a cab for the short ride to Derrick's apartment. He buzzed her into the building and stood in his own doorway, waiting. Given his attitude the last few days, she wasn't sure what to expect and hesitated before entering. He grasped both of her hands and pulled her into the apartment, where he began kissing her with more passion than usual.

They moved to his sofa where he began his tale. "Think I'm going to have to take a longer break than I thought to take care of business. Don't worry, my dear, Doug will be on the selection panel. No – no worries for you, I think. And don't worry about the car either."

"Derrick – tell me, please." Her curiosity needed to be assuaged.

"There might be problems with some of the items Livia and I have sold lately."

"Items?"

"You remember when your husband took the things I found up to Switzerland? You see, that idiot Muller knew they were genuine and sold them to a buyer in the UK without asking and before I could do anything. Worse, for some reason, he wasn't careful about the papers showing provenance. The buyer hired an expert to review the papers. The expert suggested the artifacts didn't have a valid export permit, and now the police are involved. They were already investigating several London dealers, including Livia, although she isn't involved in this batch. The police probably will be contacting the Italian authorities, and if they do I could be in real trouble. Ghastly, what?"

"This batch? You mean there are others, and you and your wife have been doing something illegal?" Laura was put off by his fake-sounding British clichés but astounded by the frank admission even though it confirmed her suspicions. "But you said what Jake took to Zurich was old stuff you found. I don't see a problem. Why would *you* be in trouble?"

Derrick didn't respond directly. "I might have to retire and leave. I don't want to but there you are. Like you lot, I mean you Americans, say, 'shit happens.'"

"So how can I help?" She didn't want to help. She wanted to get away from him and anything to do with antiques.

"Just need a friendly ear. But this must never go beyond these walls. Let's have our lunch and a rest and I'll cheer up. Must muddle through." He tried to laugh.

His hands were shaking slightly as he wielded his knife and fork to take small bites of a plate of prosciutto and figs. His jowls worked with the effort. Laura watched with sadness as he tried to drink his glass of Verdicchio without sloshing. She saw him as an old man when only a few weeks ago he was the ideal European companion. A better lover than Jake, but just as ineffective in everything else.

He led her to the bedroom, undressing her first and then himself. He began to caress her. She tried to relax but after the sight of his nakedness it was all she could do not to turn aside. When she saw his fear of a decline in his sexual powers she began to help him with words and touch. It did not work and his repeated and almost frantic efforts at consummation were futile. Laura saw tears of frustration in his watery eyes.

He managed to control himself, throw on a robe, and go to his dresser. He pulled out a small shopping bag with the name "Bvlgari" on the side. "I wanted to wait to give you this, but I think the time is now." He looked at her with an anxious expression. "You have given me such joy. I can't tell you how sorry I am that I'm leaving."

"Derrick I can't accept anything. I'm not proud of my behavior." She knew she needed to say more but what do you say when an affair is over?

Derrick thrust the bag into her hands and folded her fingers over it. "Take it, take it. I won't let you leave until you do." His words had a tinge of anger as if her refusal was a refusal of all their meetings and the help he had offered.

Laura reluctantly untied the ribbon binding the unwanted box inside the bag and lifted the lid. A pair of earrings rested on tissue. Each had a blue topaz at the top, connected by nearly an inch of pavé diamonds that dropped down to an equally large amethyst.

She tried to think of appropriate words in thanks for the reward for sex and solicitous listening to his lectures on art and history. She came up with the truth. "Derrick, oh my, oh, these are fabulous. I didn't do anything to deserve them."

She fondled the earrings, watching the light catch the gems. Her own loneliness and deceit had culminated in a gift from the most famous jewelry store in Rome. What a laugh: she had nowhere to wear them.

"Try them on. Just as you are."

She put them on. Reclining on the pillows she tried to picture herself as the glamorous mistress in an Impressionist work or in a gallery of Old Masters. Instead she saw herself as a tramp. Like Jake said.

Derrick admired her. "You're just like a Rubens, one where the woman wears only her jewelry." He reached to the floor to retrieve his underwear. "Just lie there while I get myself back together. Might be the last time for a while that I can enjoy looking at you."

His comment made her feel even more indecent, adding to her discomfort at the sight of his sleeveless undershirt like her father wore. She pulled up the sheet. What was it about moving to an unfamiliar location where she knew few people that changed her behavior so dramatically? Was engaging in an affair with a man nearing her father's age typically European, or had she read too many novels? Or did she need her father? She was both shamed and relieved that it was the end of her time as a mistress. There had been erotic moments, but never romance.

She dressed while Derrick rummaged about the kitchen, throwing the remains of the lunch in the garbage and putting dishes in the sink.

"I have to get back to work."

Derrick called a cab. He stood in his doorway with an expression of regret as she gave him a tentative wave and pressed the elevator button.

She locked the box containing the earrings in her office desk drawer.

MAY

LAURA LAZED on her balcony on a blue and gold early summer morning. Her mind floated, pleasurably vacant, until the thought of Derrick and the earrings intruded. She would miss him, with no one in her life to provide support and companionship. But the gift? Would she ever find herself in an appropriate setting to wear them? Too expensive and a reminder of events she wanted to forget. She momentarily considered a blog post beginning, *Who would believe I have a problem with jewelry?* She discarded the idea as juvenile.

A bird landed on the railing, cocking its head to inspect her. Slowly turning her own head to get a direct look, Laura saw it was a dove. She tried to put her coffee cup down quietly but it flew off at her movement.

She had enjoyed the antics of the swifts late last summer, and the millions of restless starlings, swooping in endlessly morphing geometric patterns in the waning winter daylight were spellbinding. Depending on her mood the designs were either beautifully ephemeral, or menacing, a black funeral veil floating in the wind. The starlings had long since flown off to wherever they went in the spring. Perhaps their departure also signaled life would become more settled.

The dove was a welcome visitor, maybe even a good omen. Much better than the little coin with an imprint of the Colosseum she'd found in the airport the day they arrived. The dove didn't carry an olive branch in its beak, but it conveyed a sense of peace nonetheless with its soft beige body and elegant jet-black necklace. Surely she could find an area with trees to attract birds when she got the new job. If she got the job.

Once in her office Laura booted up her computer and scrolled through her inbox. It contained critiques of her work and new assignments. As she checked them for relevance and priority, she saw an e-mail from Francesco buried near the bottom of the incoming messages.

Dear Laura, I must come to Rome next week for a few days.
I'll visit my family but afterward I would enjoy meeting Jake
and seeing you again. I was sorry we all could not meet the
last time and hope both of you will be available next
Saturday. If you are, please let me know. Francesco

Did he really want to see them both? Her mind lingered on the message for the rest of the day. She approached the subject with care after dinner. Jake, who had returned from a short stay at the farmhouse, watched a game and twisted his ring without noticing her. "Earth to Jake," she said. He tore his eyes away from the television. She told him about Francesco's invitation.

"Yeah, whatever. Let me know how it goes."

He returned his attention to the screen. Laura's exasperation was mixed with relief at not having to share Francesco.

Dear Francesco: I'm sorry to say Jake won't be available, but I'd
be delighted to meet with you again. Let me know where and
what time. Thanks again for the invitation. Laura

The next day Francesco replied that he'd meet her at the Galleria Borghese at three o'clock. They would view the galleries, then have an *aperitivo* and dinner. Laura knew of the museum but hadn't visited. Instead of working, she pulled out the guidebook stashed in her bag and looked it up: a beautiful Renaissance villa once owned by a cardinal, now a museum displaying famous paintings and sculptures. The pictures and narrative made her think of Derrick who always wanted her to get more cultured. She unlocked her desk drawer and took a quick peek at the earrings to reassure herself they were still there. At that moment Doug walked by and glanced at her and then the computer screen with the museum's home page.

Laura colored. "Sorry, just taking a quick break." She exited the website and went back to work. Doug didn't make a remark, but she was rattled at her stupidity. Maybe he didn't see.

That evening, a grunt was Jake's only acknowledgement that he'd heard her say, "I'm home." But as they ate dinner, he broke the silence by saying, "Think I'll go back up to Doug's tomorrow. Probably going to stay quite a while this time. Don't know when I'll be back."

"Okay, Jake. You do what you want."

So that's it, she thought. Not with a bang but with a whimper. What had she seen in him other than good looks and someone to demonstrate she could make her own decisions even if her mother disapproved? No longer frightened at being left alone in the city, Laura welcomed his departure.

When she went to bed, she stared at her faun. He was unconcerned with their problems as he played his soundless tune.

Jake had already decided Laura didn't need to know how much he wanted a place to hide out, or about his feeling of being followed. He hadn't actually seen any of the gang since the night when Nando gave him a cut lip, but the sensation of being watched whenever he came back to Rome after a few days at the farmhouse was grinding him down. Sometimes a mysterious car slowly passed by. The driver, barely visible through the tinted windows, reminded him of Nando. Other times Jake sensed an unseen presence several paces behind. But when he turned around no one nearby looked suspicious.

However, one day the previous week as he was walking home from the art supply store, the eyes in the back of his head told him a watcher lurked somewhere close. He ducked into a *tabaccheria* and stood behind the customers near the counter, where the clerk was busy selling cigarettes, plastic lighters or lottery and bus tickets.

Jake peered around the shoppers and through a streaked window cluttered with trinkets and boxes of candy. Nando was across the street, swiveling his head back and forth to survey the area. Jake slipped to the back of the shop and spent twenty minutes pretending to be examining the goods before making a selection, until the clerk gave him a look clearly saying *if you don't leave, I'll call the cops*. Jake left, walking in the opposite direction from his apartment. He didn't see Nando as he glanced in shop windows to catch reflections, but remained on red alert.

Jake had begun to have nightmares in the last few months. The morning he was to leave for the farmhouse he woke up in a sweat on the hide-a-bed with the sheet wound around his knees. He felt trapped by the bed linens, by Laura in their bedroom without him, and by Stella. And Derrick. The latest nightmare involved a row of marble heads wearing masks. He was forced to put on one of the masks before having sex with a faceless woman. He was sure the figure represented Stella, and he was equally sure she wouldn't just walk away from their business relationship.

Unable to return to sleep, he dressed and headed for the bar. Mario was off to the dentist, according to the pensioner filling in for the morning. The old man, who looked like he'd once been a boxer, reminded Jake of his father. If he had known his son contemplated fleeing to an isolated spot to escape Stella and Company instead of staying to fight "like a man," Jake would have been beaten and locked out of the house. But what had acting like a man ever done for his father, a gyppo logger and unsuccessful small-time rancher with a wife whose life became controlled by liquor?

The memory of his younger sister's death by drowning poured into his consciousness. For once he let it remain.

Lisa had just celebrated her fifth birthday with a party, kindergarten friends, chocolate cake and balloons. After everyone left she had gone to play near the creek running through their property. Jake came home from school to see an ambulance in their driveway, his older sister crying on the steps to the house, and his mother collapsed on the ground, sobbing uncontrollably. The party balloons, taken by a breeze that had sprung up, drifted skyward and disappeared behind the trees. Jake listened with eyes wide as his mother screamed and screamed, raging against God, against her husband, against Jake and his older sister, who were alive when her favorite was dead. "I don't want any more children. I hate children. They always disappoint you. Never, never, never again."

His father, helpless, stood with head down, fists clenched, for once with nothing to say, no one to hit.

Now that the memory was out in the open, Jake wondered if his sister's death might have influenced his decision to become a school teacher. Children, but none that required his personal responsibility after they left the classroom. No need for love and worry. But he'd found he wasn't good at that job either.

The released memory and the possible rationale for his actions floated like the party balloons, urging him to seek someone, the only one, who perhaps might offer some solace. It was long past the time he could talk to Laura who would see his weakness. He threw a few coins on the bar counter and walked to San Giovanni hoping the young priest might be available. As usual, there was no one around so early in the morning. Jake sat in the back, waiting. An elderly, white-bearded priest approached. Jake said, "Father John?"

"*Aspetta per favore.*" Wait, please. The man walked through a doorway and returned with another priest, somewhat younger with sandy hair.

"I'm Father John." The voice sounded English, like Derrick's.

"No. Sorry, I wanted another John. Younger, American. Is he here?"

"Oh, yes, I knew him. Unfortunately, he left to go back to the U.S. last week. Can I help?"

Jake shook his head and turned away. The last thing he wanted was to talk to a priest who spoke like Derrick. Feeling jilted, he walked out of the church and turned back toward Mario's bar, no longer caring if he was being followed. He rammed his hands in his pockets and damned everyone who had ever crossed his path: his father, Laura, Stella, Nando, Derrick, and now this Francesco character, whoever he was, and the students he might have to see again in Seattle.

Any remaining hesitation over actually putting his plan of escape into action vaporized after Jake downed his second *caffè corretto*. He hurried home and packed his duffel bag and art supplies, leaving the insipid watercolors behind. "*At Doug's.*" He stuck the reminder note to the refrigerator with one of Laura's magnets, a little ceramic tile decorated with a dove that she'd bought the one time they went to the Vatican Museum. He locked the door and walked to Derrick's car.

As he drove up the Via Cassia, the detritus of suburban Rome gradually faded, along with his anger. He stopped for a coffee in the tiny town of Sutri. The white marble remains of a Roman arena rested in a verdant field. The ruins made him think of old bones, a skeleton bleached by the sun of centuries. Nearby, a sign described a church carved into the rock of an Etruscan tomb, closed for the midday siesta. He considered the silent setting while trying to remember the lessons in color and composition he took while in university. So long ago; a time when he believed the trajectory of his life would move steadily forward in a positive direction.

Jake pulled a fat stash of euros from his wallet, the money taken from the envelopes he'd taped to the back of the picture of the Appia Antica. He looked around to be sure no one was watching. Not seeing anything unusual, he hunched down in the driver's seat and counted out the fifties. Enough to keep him going for several months if he was careful and Doug let him stay. A few cars drove by, unnoticed.

In the next town Jake stopped at a supermarket. He bought meat, pasta, coffee, fruit, and vegetables, along with red wine and beer. If he couldn't stand his cooking, at least he'd have drinks to enjoy in the evenings.

It was windy by the time Lake Bolsena, deep in its volcanic crater, came into sight. There were so many whitecaps the lake looked like it was pushing its island toward the far shore. Jake had read about a princess being imprisoned on the island in medieval times. If there was a way to get there he could do a few canvasses. What a refuge an island would be if he needed one.

The farmhouse was cool and damp. Without turning on the lights he hauled his duffel, art supplies, and the sacks of food and drink inside before lighting a fire, bolting the door and checking the locks on the windows and French doors. He drew the curtains, uncorked a bottle, and poured a tumbler of wine. Then another. The ruby-colored liquid glowed in the light of the fire. He relaxed for the first time in months.

He awoke, stiff and cold, to the sound of an owl hooting outside. The fire had died and the bottle and a half-filled glass rested on the floor. Jake found a blanket and lay down on top of the bed fully clothed. He dreamed of his childhood on the ranch, where owls called to him to creep outside and watch them swoop silently onto unsuspecting field mice.

The air felt cold in the morning's early light even though it was late spring. He lit another fire before making coffee and sitting down to plan the day and plan his future. Going back to teaching was now unthinkable. He had hated the daily interaction with students, who returned the favor. But if he and Laura divorced, how would he sustain himself? She was "head of household" according to the UN and the Italian government. He would need papers if he stayed on, unless he remained under the radar like all the other illegal immigrants. If he got arrested for involvement in shady dealings with Stella and maybe Derrick, he'd soon be thrown out of the country, or worse, sent to prison. Giving up trying to find a resolution, he opened the door to look for a good spot to begin his career as an artist. The future would be whatever arrived. At least for today.

Laura was relieved to be alone. If marriage was supposed to be about a couple helping each other, they hadn't been much good at it. First, ignoring their problems in Seattle. Now in Rome, failing to face up to reality as their relationship slid over a precipice, and doing nothing to change course. She thought of the dove, hoping it would return with a message of peace, and then she thought of the earrings she had brought home from the office, no longer worried about Jake seeing them. They reminded her of her adultery but Jake had been so devious she was sure he had also broken their marriage vows. Whatever love they might have shared was finally dead, buried in the dusty ruins of Rome.

She met Francesco at the Galleria Borghese on Saturday afternoon. He was unfailingly polite and showed enjoyment in describing the art works to her. Bernini's depiction of Apollo and Daphne fascinated Laura. The marble looked as though Daphne was still soft and warm – remaining human even though she was changing into a laurel tree to escape her pursuer. Canova's cold sculpture of the haughty Pauline Bonaparte reminded her of her boss at Boeing.

Francesco said, "Your name is from Latin, meaning 'laurel,' as in 'crowned with laurels.' And our poet, Petrarch, dedicated his love sonnets to his muse, a young woman named Laura."

"I never liked my name before, but now it sounds Italian. How wonderful to be someone's muse."

They moved on to other rooms, lingering long at two canvasses. The first was Dossi's *Circe*, with the enchantress wearing a brilliant blue and red dress with gold insets and a gold turban. She dipped a candle into a brazier while holding a tablet inscribed with geometric designs. A dog rested beside her as she looked in the direction of several small figures bound to a tree trunk. The landscape in the background shimmered with bronze hues. Three men lounged in a field, unconcerned with the muse or the bound figures. Beyond them rose the buildings and towers of a hill town and a threatening sky.

"No one knows what the picture means – enigmatic, don't you think? Even the title is uncertain."

"I love her outfit, whatever she's doing. Real Italian fashion. Wish we still wore clothes like that." Not wanting to get emotional, she didn't add that the picture reflected her view of Italy: gentle tamed landscapes, a heightened sense of style, and unrevealed truths.

They strolled on at a relaxed pace through the rooms until they came to Titian's *Sacred and Profane Love.* Laura stood transfixed. On the left side, a woman dressed in a white gown with red sleeves rested beside a fountain. She grasped a small bouquet in her right hand and held a vase with jewels in the other. On the other side of the fountain, a nearly naked woman with a white cloth over her lap and a red robe over one arm held up an incense burner. In between the two figures, a Cupid dangled his hand in the water.

"Do you know what this one means?"

"It was commissioned to celebrate a marriage. There are two interpretations. The first claims the bride with the jewels symbolizes fleeting happiness on earth, while the woman holding the small pot of smoking incense represents eternal happiness in heaven. The second theory states that it's meant to be an exaltation of both earthly and heavenly love, although no one knows which woman represents which kind of love."

She contemplated the picture as she heard Francesco add, "I prefer the second story."

"Yes, a dream to wish for." She kept her eyes on the picture although she wanted to look at Francesco. To see his expression.

Evening was approaching. They walked along the Via Pinciana until they reached the beginning of the Via Veneto. They stopped at a bar to sit outside, nibbling and sipping while hoping to see the rich and famous as if they were all part of a film from the 1960s. Afterward, they continued to Piazza Barberini. Francesco showed Laura the two Bernini fountains. The first, the Fontana del Tritone, was composed of dolphins supporting a Triton. The sea god with scaly legs held up a conch, through which he blew water up into the early evening sunlight. The Triton reminded Laura of her flute player, bound by eternal time to his music.

The second and smaller fountain, the Fontana delle Api, was a simple scallop shell with three bees, each resting above a spout from which water descended into a basin, also scallop shaped. Francesco told her the bees were the symbol of the Barberini family and the fountain was originally a horse trough. To Laura, the modest fountain represented the Rome she wanted to enjoy, a city where even horses could drink in beauty.

"Let's continue – we'll make a detour to the Trevi Fountain. Most of the tourists should be gone because they all eat such early dinners. Afterward, we can go to a trattoria on the other side of the Corso. A friend of my parents owns it – he's a nice guy. Does that sound good?" He linked his arm in hers.

"Yes, I'd like that." She didn't object to his arm.

They reached the gushing waters of the fountain. Laura felt as if she had never seen the monument before, even though she and Jake visited that first day in Rome. The rushing spray brought forth even more longing to live an Italian life surrounded by all the artistry before her. In this heightened mood she threw a coin into the basin. This time it was a euro with a wish to stay in Italy. Francesco handed her another euro. As the coin spun upward to catch the last rays of the sun, she wished to continue seeing Francesco. It splashed with a sound that sounded like, "Yes."

The shadows lengthened as Earth slowly turned its back to the sun for a nightly rest. Laura walked with care, trying not to get her heels stuck between the *sanpietrini*, the small cobblestones paving the streets. She also tried to memorize the route by watching the shops and street signs posted above them. When she caught sight of the weather forecaster high on the wall, she recognized the location. The red eye was still immobile, but the formerly baleful expression on its face now seemed benign, watching her without judgment. Its pointer was at *"Bello."*

They arrived at a small trattoria where a few tables were set outside under an awning. The owner came out to greet Francesco. They embraced before Francesco introduced Laura. Beppe, all smiles and wrinkles, shook her hand and then raised it near his mustache for an air kiss. She tried to follow as he asked about Francesco's parents' health and how he was enjoying the cultural attractions of the North. After the conversation concluded, Beppe showed them to one of the outdoor tables before hurrying back with water, bread, and the wine list. "I'll leave everything to you." Beppe looked pleased at the vote of confidence. Francesco explained to Laura how the owner, who was from Sicily, knew his family, who were Tuscan, through a mutual relative.

Beppe suggested a red or a white wine, both from vineyards in Sicily. Then he recited his recommendations for their dinner: *pasta con le sarde*, followed by *tonno alla marinara, caponata,* and *cannoli* for dessert.

"What do you think? Would you like to try real Sicilian food? It's distinct from Roman or Tuscan, because many of the dishes are Arabic in origin."

By this time Laura was so overwhelmed with her day that if Francesco proposed calf innards like Derrick ate, she would have agreed. After Francesco selected the white wine, a Bianco d'Alcamo, Beppe saw to the cork and poured a measure for Laura. She could taste mineral and citrus. She smiled and said *"Sì, buono."*

Beppe responded, "You must tell me if you taste the ocean spray."

Francesco raised his glass in a silent toast. "How is your Italian? If you want to remain here, you should learn." Laura admitted her Italian was still poor. "Don't they have classes at your office? Many do. You might find out."

Laura agreed she would, unhappy with herself at her minimal efforts so far. They fell silent until the pasta arrived. Francesco explained the ingredients: sardines, anchovies, fennel, raisins, and pine nuts served with spaghetti. Salty and sweet at the same time, like much of life.

Francesco talked about his parents. His father was a retired engineer who had worked at the port in Livorno, and his mother had been a teacher. They bought their retirement home not far from Derrick's villa and occasionally saw him. "Of course, they don't have money like he does. I think my mother said you and your husband were friends."

Friends. Laura ruminated over the word. Should she admit that he might have been more than a friend? Best not to play any more games, especially with someone who appeared to be honorable. She cautiously responded. "He was a good friend for a little while. No longer." She knew he had noticed her hesitation and probably the spectacular earrings she'd decided to wear at the last minute. "It was a bad mistake," she said to her wine glass, unable to look at him.

Francesco's response comforted her. "Well, we all make mistakes. Made plenty myself."

The main course arrived. The tuna steak was decorated with basil and black olives. The *caponata,* a mixture of eggplant, tomatoes, celery, olives, and onions blended into a sweet-sour sauce, was strange to Laura's tongue. As they ate, Francesco told her about his childhood. He spoke warmly of how his parents encouraged him in his studies. "All in all, I had a happy time."

Laura was grateful he didn't ask about her family. She thought back to her own youth. A few scrapes and bruises, both physical and mental, but otherwise the same as all her classmates. Neither anguished nor joyful, there were braces and pimples, dreams of being a model in *Seventeen,* a few boyfriends in high school, and a brief, unsatisfactory affair during her freshman year at university before she met Jake. Her one stellar event was the trip to London after she graduated from high school that finally and unexpectedly set her on the long path leading to Rome.

She studied Francesco: smiling, at ease with his past and maybe even his future. She wanted to know more about his life, one that seemed organized and fulfilling. His relaxed and pleasant manner was appealing. He seemed to have his feet on the ground, a quality she never saw in Jake. An adult rather than a man-child.

Sensing that Laura wanted to know more about him, he told her about his work, how the architectural firm was gaining a solid reputation for creativity. He described Milan, with its more northern culture, and how the city differed from Rome. He summed up by saying, "Doesn't have the ruins or the Vatican, but it's much more European in sensibility. Some even say Africa begins at the Tiber although I don't agree."

Although the hour had nearly reached midnight when Beppe brought the bill along with small glasses of sweet Marsala, Laura didn't want to end the evening and was gratified when Francesco suggested they walk a while. They joined the crowds filling the streets to enjoy the seductive warmth of a Roman summer night, a time when no one needed sleep. But eventually it was time to bring their evening together to a close. Dawn would soon be breaking. Francesco found a cab to take them back to Laura's building.

When the cab pulled up by her apartment building. Laura toyed with asking if he would like to come in for a coffee but refrained. She offered effusive thanks. He squeezed her hand and said, "Shall we do this again?"

She dared not say anything more than, "Yes."

Laura awoke with the Sunday sun. She turned to look at her earrings dangling from the flute player's two reeds. They blazed as her movement made them swing just enough to catch the rays peeking through the neighboring buildings.

She pulled the espresso maker from the shelf, filled the bottom with water, measured the coffee into the top, and put it on the burner, her fear of the steam's pressure long put aside. As the brew began to puff and gurgle, she stared out the glass door to the balcony, her mind vacant until she saw a collared dove and its mate. They were both pecking away at crumbs she'd scattered. The sound of cooing came through the glass until, seeing her, they flew off. She poured herself coffee and took the cup outside, along with her phone full of Italian songs. Her tiny herb garden flourished with basil, rosemary, thyme, and oregano all happy in their pots. The geranium on the table expressed pleasure in being alive by producing ever more scarlet flower clusters.

The peaceful sight lulled her, but as she poured a second cup, reality intruded: the near-term future with her job and her husband, if he could really be called that any more. Decisions not hard to make in Seattle, with their clear pros and cons, were so much more complex here with all the unknowns. She knew she had changed since coming to Rome, but her quest for new experiences must have begun well before, or why else would she have tried to find a job in Europe? The miscarriage had been the turning point. So many questions plagued her, and still no answers. Maybe she would return to the gallery and ask Circe.

She went over Francesco's remarks about learning Italian and his parents, how he valued them and they him along with their other children. She would like to see them again and meet his siblings, too.

Laura made two resolutions. First, she would call her parents more often, even though they didn't call her. If her efforts didn't work out at first, she would continue for at least a month or two. Second, she must become proficient in Italian. But how? She needed intensive lessons. Should she call or e-mail Francesco for help? She again decided to take it easy. No more mistakes.

That afternoon when she knew they would be up, she called Seattle. Both were glad to hear her voice, but neither had much to say of substance. Laura described her visit to the Galleria Borghese without bringing up Francesco's name. The memory made her think about his explanation of her own name. Did her unimaginative mother know the derivation? Maybe she had a bit of a romantic streak unknown to Laura. A pleasant thought.

Following up on her second resolve, she found their Italian-English dictionary. Jake must have spent a lot of time using it, with the pages dog eared and coffee stained. She reviewed some of the words she already knew. Each one was followed by expressions associated with the word. She began to copy out the various usages to memorize:

buono, good;

un buon dizionario, a good dictionary;

un buono scolaro, a clever pupil;

una buona stella, a lucky star;

buona fortuna! good luck!

That's what she wanted: a lucky star, and to be a clever pupil of Italian and Italian living. She bought a newspaper at the local *giornalaio.* She spread it out on the table and slowly began to read, scribbling translation notes in the margins.

Laura arrived at her office on Monday to see Doug looking distracted, Raj pleased, and Silvia definitely smug.

"What's going on?"

Silvia answered. "Your friend Derrick won't be back for a while, Doug's going to fill in for him, and Raj is taking Doug's job." She looked triumphantly at Laura. "And I'm going to do Raj's work."

Her cocksure statement shriveled Laura's hopes. She stammered out her congratulations and then hid behind her computer, worrying about what all these changes meant for her. Little work was accomplished with the news whirling around in her head.

Near one o'clock she asked Silvia if she would like to go to lunch with her. Silvia, eager to enlarge on the office news, accepted. They went across the street to have a salad. The restaurant was crowded, but they found a table on the wide sidewalk. Laura waited expectantly for Silvia to begin.

"Well..." Silvia paused for effect. "You won't believe all the stuff that happened over the weekend." Laura was sure she would believe it. From the day she got off the plane, nothing went as planned. So why not another twist in the plot?

Silvia launched into her tale. "Rumor has it Derrick is involved in funny business. And his wife, who sells antiques in London, is also implicated. The police in England have been investigating her, and another rumor has it she will be arrested in the next day or so. I'll bet Derrick will be next."

Laura thought about the items from the British newspapers she read on the Internet.

"You wouldn't know anything about all of this, would you?" Silvia asked.

"Of course not. How could you even think that? It's ridiculous."

Silvia scrutinized her with a sharp expression. Laura concentrated on her meal even though her appetite had vanished.

"Like I said before, the whole office knows Derrick has, shall we say, taken an interest in you. So I thought you might have information."

"I assure you and anyone else who might be doubting me that I am not involved in anything. I'm really offended by this, Silvia. I have to get back to work. I'll pay for both of us at the register." She shouldered her bag and stood up.

"Oh, don't be silly. I just asked if you knew about Derrick's problems. Don't be so sensitive. Besides, I haven't told you the rest of the story."

Laura sat down to await the next salvo.

"The big shots suggested to Derrick that he should, or maybe must, take a leave of absence while he fixed whatever was going on. No one knows how long it will take – if the investigation was in Italy, it would take forever, but maybe the Brits move faster. Anyway, as I said, Doug has been asked to sit in, and of course Raj, as next in line, will be doing Doug's work. Since I've got a regular contract, I'll be helping Raj. You needn't worry about your job, at least for the few months you have left. But then, of course, I don't know about the job you wanted. You know how things are."

Laura didn't know how "things" were; likely not good, she was sure, but she did know Silvia now used the term "we," and having Derrick's support for the job she wanted was poison.

For once she wanted to talk to Jake, tell him that she might have to leave Italy. She tried to contact him that evening on his cell phone, but the call would not go through. She got on the Internet to see if she could find more about Derrick's wife, or maybe now Derrick himself. There was nothing specific, but she came across a database of stolen art and antiquities maintained by the Italian authorities. Some of the items looked similar to Derrick's collection, but then she thought there must be thousands of other pieces just like his.

She sat down on the bed thinking about Derrick and Jake, two flawed men who amplified her own failings. Her bronze youth on the table beside her went about his musical business. She pictured him propped up on her mantel back in Seattle, lonely for his home in Italy, his goat tail drooping in dejection.

JUNE

JAKE SPENT HOURS in the nearby olive grove trying to catch the colors of the green leaves with silver undersides and the contorted trunks against a deep blue sky. He saw himself as one of the Impressionists, standing before his easel to paint *en plein air*, wearing a straw hat and smock, though he actually dressed in an old Seahawks cap, a ragged tee shirt, and paint-spattered jeans. His style was slash and burn, not at all like the blurry work of the nineteenth century masters. The aggression he expressed with his brush gave him a sense of release. Release from Laura and release from the oppressive city where everything was off balance in his life.

As he slathered vermilion on a section of his canvas meant to represent poppies, Jake thought about his talk with Doug who had shown up the previous Sunday without notice, but with good news. First, he would be taking over work from Derrick, who'd gone to England on an indefinite basis; second, he and Helena thought it would be useful to have Jake around the property on a regular basis, as a sort of caretaker/handyman. Especially since Doug was now so busy he wouldn't have time to come up very often. This meant Jake was free to remain on the condition he renovated the old shack so he could move in when the main house was sufficiently restored to be rented out to paying guests, or when Doug and Helena were staying at the property. As compensation for the work, Doug would pay him a small amount for food and incidentals, along with the free rent.

Now tanned and taut from working on the shack and painting in the sun, Jake saw himself as useful and decisive. Masculine. Virile. His worries were forgotten.

Jake occasionally drove into the nearest town, Marta, to stock up on food. Every time he thought about contacting Laura from a shop with wi-fi, he hesitated. In the end, he never got around to making the call, sure that she would ask Doug to relay a message if she had concerns. He had nothing to say anyway.

He was busy hauling old junk out of the shack when he heard a car coming up the road. He dropped his armload of materials and craned his neck to see who was approaching. It was a weekday and he wasn't expecting a visit from Doug. The dust on the unpaved road plumed and obscured his view until the car came to a stop in the yard. Jake stared at the black Lancia.

Nando emerged and opened the passenger door. Stella swung her legs sideways and slowly stepped out. The legs were shapely and far more inviting than her expression. In the bright light Jake saw the lines around her eyes, and there were new furrows running from the sides of her nose down past a pinched mouth. The smoke from her cigarette coiled around her head like the vipers he occasionally found behind the shed.

He didn't bother to consider how she found him. She and her pals somehow always knew his whereabouts.

"We've work to do."

"What do you mean? What are you talking about? You know I'm done and don't want your money. Whatever you and Nando and Robert and Muller are involved in, I don't want to be a part of any of it. Just leave me alone. I'm not going to rat on you. I mean, who would I even talk to here? I don't even know anyone." Jake heard the uncertain waver in his voice, an echo of their last encounter when Nando hit him. He wanted to run, as if he were back on the family ranch and his father was about to pummel him for some nonexistent misdeed.

"Just want to make sure you don't do anything you'll regret now or in the future, *caro*."

"What do you want?" Jake heard the weakness in his voice even more.

"I need a driver for a quick operation near your wife's friend Derrick's place. There are interesting tombs around."

Jake was so stunned he backed up, tripping over a board before he caught himself. "Grave robbing? You must be kidding, huh?" He hated his pleading whine, but he couldn't manage to change it to something more assertive. "For Christ's sake, you don't expect me to dig up the dead, do you? Do you?" Finally working up some courage he added, "Well, I'm not going to. You're crazy."

"Don't get so agitated. The tombs are over two thousand years old and no one but a few collectors are interested in the stuff. All you have to do is drive the van tonight."

"Then what?"

"Then what? Then you've earned the money we gave you and we know that you will be considered part of our group if anyone investigates. We won't forget you. You didn't work out well, so don't try anything funny or we'll be back. We'll pick you up at ten tonight." She waved to Nando to fire up the engine. He complied while leaning over to open the passenger door for her. Stella jumped in and slammed the door. Her Lancia roared off in a cloud of the same dust kicked up by its arrival.

"Fuck off," Jake screamed at the dust cloud. A fist of anger filled his chest, but he knew bluffing his way out of the situation was impossible. His gamble to be a player in the art world had come to an end and he had to fold.

He went into the house to get a beer. He dropped the can, which rolled into a corner. He kneeled down to retrieve it and went outside to sit near the cement mixer. When he popped the can open, foam erupted all over his hands. He threw the container into the trash pile. His anger at himself, that cow Stella, and especially Laura for bringing up the whole idea of leaving Seattle boiled over like the foaming beer. If he was home, his real home, Seattle, he would be looking forward to the end of the school year and the summer off. Instead, he was in the shit again.

Jake knew the name for tomb robbers, *tombaroli,* and he also knew that whatever Stella told him, the Italian authorities did prosecute if they were caught. But they weren't often discovered so there might be hope. Maybe he really would be left alone if he did this final job. He could not think of any other solution. He got another beer, the last in the refrigerator, gulped it down and crushed the can before pitching it into the trash next to its mate still dribbling its remaining liquid.

A half-moon was rising in the night sky when Nando drove the van up to the farmhouse. He told Jake to put on dark clothes. Jake got out his black leather jacket. Nando handed him the keys and said, "Drive." Despite his fear, Jake began to feel a thrill, like he was a character in *Raiders of the Lost Ark*.

He followed Nando's directions without having any idea where he was going, although the countryside looked familiar. They passed several signs pointing the way to Viterbo, but Jake became disoriented by all the turns, first one way, and then the other as the road deteriorated from pavement to gravel to nothing but a dusty potholed track.

Nando told him to pull over at a wide spot and extinguish the headlights. He opened the van's door for Marco and Gianni to climb down from the back where they had been riding in silence. Trees and thick brush covered the ground, obscuring the weak moonlight. Nando turned on a small flashlight, clipped the wire fence surrounding the property, and directed the others to bring their shovels and a long steel rod. Jake nearly fell into a hole as they stumbled along.

They came to a spot where a wild fig tree grew, surrounded by summer-dry grasses. Jake stopped at a cairn made of nearby rocks. "This is the place," said Nando. He grabbed the rod and stabbed it into the ground. The metal penetrated the void below with ease. "Just want to be sure, even though I marked the spot earlier." He put the rod down and said to the others, "Now, dig."

He looked at Jake and said, "Don't try anything funny. Understand?"

Jake pulled on a pair of gloves and gripped a shovel, but despite Nando's threat, put as little effort as he dared into the work. Marco and Gianni put their backs into the task. No one worked fast enough for Nando who grabbed an extra shovel and drove it into the dry ground as hard as he could. The earth gave way. Nando plummeted into the hole, pulling dirt and grasses and a terrified scream along with him. There was a dropped-melon thud, then silence.

The other three threw down their shovels and carefully edged toward the gaping hole. Marco found the flashlight and pointed the beam into the cavity. Nando was at least fifteen feet below ground, lying face up on top of a stone sarcophagus lid, the carved head of the former occupant overlooking his battered skull. Nando's eyes were open, but he didn't move. A trickle of blood seeped from his silent mouth and more was beginning to puddle beneath his head.

Jake panicked. He ran for the van, jerked the keys out of his pocket, and slammed into the driver's seat. Marco and Gianni were screaming, "*aspetta, aspetta,*" but he didn't wait. He drove as fast as possible on the rough road, hoping he could remember the route and that the van didn't break an axle and strand him. He reached the main road and kept driving until he found a sign to Viterbo, some ten miles farther on. He pulled off into the bushes and got out, leaving the keys in the ignition.

The road was deserted. Jake could hear his heart racing, blood pounding with adrenaline. He tried to think, but the image of Nando's broken head kept intruding, a parody of the stone one. He wished it was Stella's. He began to walk, figuring he would eventually get to the small city and then the farmhouse. About a quarter of a mile down the road, he stopped. Would the police dust the van for prints? Probably, yes. Were his on record? He couldn't remember ever having been fingerprinted, but everyone's were on file in databases. And he went through a security check before he got the teaching contract. And what about DNA?

Jake retraced his steps back to the van. He found an old rag in the back, dampened it with roadside mud, and wiped the steering wheel, dashboard, keys, handles, and other places he might have touched. The gloves he wore while digging were on the passenger seat. He stuffed them along with the rag into his jacket pocket and set on his way again. Fear seeped through his body like groundwater, filling every empty crevice.

By dawn he neared Viterbo. A local bus came along. He climbed aboard with a crowd of early risers. Even though he worried someone might remember him if the police opened an inquiry, there was no way else to get to the farmhouse. The bus reached the depot. Jake downed a coffee and caught another bus going north. Several miles from his destination he descended and hiked the remainder of the way. As far as he could tell none of these passengers, who were intent on their own business or talking with seatmates, had even glanced his way, nor did any of the traffic slow down as he walked along.

Jake was worn out and sweaty by the time Doug's property came into sight. He cleaned up and slept for several hours. Later, he showered and drove into town to get supplies and pick up the local paper to check whether any news about the accident had come to light. Nothing yet. For the first time since coming to the farmhouse he regretted not having a television or his laptop. Surely finding a body in a tomb would be news of interest. But then, it might take a long time to find the hole. Maybe months, until some hunters came along in the fall. Or, even better, maybe years would pass and the body would be so decayed the remains would be unidentifiable. Or maybe Nando wasn't dead. He didn't know which could be worse: involvement in a death or Nando, on the warpath, coming after him.

He visited the *giornalaio* in town the following day to buy the latest paper. Returning to Doug's farmhouse, Jake sat outside drinking a beer while he combed through the pages of the *Corriere di Viterbo*. The story was on page eight:

The Carabinieri are investigating the death of a suspected tombarolo found two days ago with a broken skull and back in a tomb he was apparently about to loot. Looking at the footsteps around the dig the authorities believe others were with him, although no traces of anyone else have yet been found. Investigators are attempting to determine if the death could be linked to an abandoned van found near Viterbo the morning after the body was discovered by retiree Massimiliano Rinaldi, on whose property the tomb is located. Archeologists are now surveying and securing the tomb, which appears to have a number of valuable antiquities inside despite the collapse of the tomb's roof sometime in the distant past.

Jake's fear abated with the knowledge that Nando had met a suitable end. Surely that would be the last of the gang's operations and he would be safe. He got out the shoes and gloves he had been wearing that night and buried them deep in a far corner of Doug's property. He washed the jeans twice and wiped his jacket to be sure no dirt remained.

Laura worked hard editing during the day and trying to learn more Italian in the evenings. Her thirtieth birthday came with a call from her parents, dinner with Silvia, and a night of insomnia.

Francesco called the following week. He'd been tied up with the bidding on a new job but would be coming to Rome for the following weekend. Would she be available? Laura said yes without hesitation. If nothing else, he was easy to talk to.

"I promised my mother I'd visit. Do you want to come along? My mother is a great cook so I'm sure you will enjoy a good lunch."

Laura's heart gave a small skip at this news.

He arrived early on Saturday. "We'll go up the coast road, the Via Aurelia, and come back on the Cassia – a roundtrip so you see more of the countryside. If you like, we will make a quick stop at Cerveteri and Tarquinia on the way up. Do you know about the Etruscans?"

"Yes, let's stop and no, I don't know about them, but I have a request. I'm trying to learn more Italian, so could we try not to use English? Except when I get stuck. *Per favore?*"

Francesco looked pleased at her request. Using simple words, he began to tell her the history of the area. Laura took in about half of the narrative but was gratified to have even managed a basic understanding. They stopped at both sites to study the tombs, rounded above-ground structures at Cerveteri and underground painted chambers at Tarquinia. Laura bought a book in Italian at the museum bookstore after they toured the collection of decorated pottery and sarcophagi. The lids depicted the former occupants as life size figures, raised on one elbow and intently observing life around them.

She would translate the guidebook, although it would take a long time with her rudimentary knowledge. Perhaps she could ask Francesco to correct her mistakes. The translation would be another step in the right direction. One that pointed toward becoming a real expatriate instead of a sojourner. Still an American, but a full participant in Italian life.

Francesco's mother had said they lived not far from Derrick's villa, but to her relief she didn't see any evidence of his property as Francesco drove to their home. Both parents rushed out the door to embrace their son before warmly welcoming Laura with a kiss on both cheeks.

"Lunch is nearly ready. Sit on the terrace and have a glass of wine – the grapes are from the Rinaldi's harvest three years ago. There's the corkscrew."

Laura followed Francesco to the terrace where large pots held lemon trees bearing bright yellow fruit set among shiny green leaves and fragrant white flowers. Rosemary and lavender bordered the area, adding more scent and combining with that from the roses flourishing in nearby beds. Enticing aromas also emanated from the kitchen. She watched Francesco pull the cork and pour four glasses, taking one into the kitchen for his mother before he sat down beside Laura to await the call to eat.

"What do you think?" he asked in Italian as he handed her a glass before raising his in a toast.

Laura stumbled a reply, trying to express her delight at the opportunity to meet his family again and to be in their home. Francesco's father, Salvatore, joined them and practiced his English on Laura until they heard the standard call for lunch: "*A tavola!*" They left the shaded terrace to sit down while Francesco's mother, Cristina, brought out a steaming bowl of risotto with asparagus. "*Buon appetito,*" she said as the bowl was passed around for them to serve themselves. Next came a platter of sizzling grilled lamb chops, garnished with rosemary and surrounded by potatoes. Green beans were in a serving bowl. "From our garden," Cristina said with pride.

The talk flowed at times in Italian, with Francesco translating when necessary, and more often in a mix of Italian and English, as Cristina, Salvatore, and Laura used their limited skills between sips and bites. Laura was as charmed by his mother and father as she had been at Derrick's over the New Year's holiday.

Dessert was *frutti di bosco*: tiny wild strawberries, gooseberries, currants, and blackberries. Talk lapsed as they enjoyed the finale to the meal.

Laura helped Cristina carry plates and silverware into the kitchen. "My son has come to like risotto since he went to Milan. They eat a lot of rice there. Maybe you will visit sometime and he can cook. I taught him how to make this dish. And he's a pretty good cook now." Laura didn't know how to respond since Cristina knew she was married. Or maybe she thought Jake was only a friend, or maybe she meant "you" as plural. She asked Francesco's mother if she would show her how to cook it correctly another time. And she would make notes for that blog she always meant to write.

Cristina made espresso and Laura carried the tray of cups outside, where father and son were chatting. She watched them interact, always puzzled at how some people were at ease with their parents and others weren't.

A contented silence reigned until Salvatore said, "Oh, I forgot to tell you earlier. The strangest thing happened over on the Rinaldi's property. You know they rent out a big section of land to boar hunters in the fall? Maybe you saw the story on the Internet or TV a couple of weeks ago. One of those idiot *tombaroli* was digging around and found an old Etruscan tomb. The roof of the tomb had fallen in so there was only loose dirt on top. I guess the man didn't watch what he was doing and dug down straight instead of sideways and fell in. Killed himself right on top of an old sarcophagus. No great loss, but now the Rinaldis are worried that with the news, there will be others trying the same trick." He added, "Maybe there are old pots on our property. Might talk to the archeologists working over there to see if they can find anything here. It would be interesting to think we live on top of treasure. The State would get everything, of course, but I think there's a finder's fee."

Seeing that Laura didn't understand the word *tombaroli*, he explained, "Grave robbers, lots of them wherever there might be old tombs."

Laura thought of Derrick's artifacts, the trip Jake took to Zurich at his request, and his sudden departure surrounded by rumors. She now knew what Derrick had been doing. He must have found tombs on his property.

The coffee cups were empty, the dishes put away. Francesco suggested it was time to get back to Rome. She reluctantly assented. When they reached her apartment, she invited him to share a snack in her apartment before they parted.

Laura put out a plate of cheese and crackers, glasses, and a bottle of Chianti. They sat on the terrace talking about the day, and then Laura asked where he stayed when he came to Rome for work.

"The company maintains a small apartment near the Pantheon. We frequently have to come down to Rome to settle problems with the authorities. Endless, but that's Italy. I meant to tell you, we're considering opening a branch office in New York. I doubt there would be so many problems there with hiring and permits, from what I have been reading."

Laura tucked this information away to mull over later, along with the brief exchange about cooking risotto. Francesco asked her again why she came to Italy from Seattle. She admitted she only came because the job she found happened to be in Rome, but now she loved the city and Italy even though there was so much more to learn. Jake came to mind and, to her embarrassment, her eyes began to tear up. She added, "But I don't think my husband likes living here. He's, he's...gone away and I'm not sure he will return. I'm sorry, all this blubbering. Sorry."

"Don't worry. I know it's hard to move and takes a while to get settled. We can talk more sometime later if you need to. Shall we go for a walk on the Appia Antica tomorrow? Cars are not allowed on Sunday, so it should be pleasant." He stood up, ready to depart.

"I'd love that," she said as she blotted her eyes and nose.

Francesco pressed the call button on the *citofono* Sunday morning. Laura was ready to go in walking shoes, jeans, and a tee shirt, with a backpack carrying bottles of water, grapes, and a package of sandwiches. They parked near the start of the ancient road and began to walk along the massive paving blocks. They had grooves carved by chariot wheels from officials and generals traveling to and from the south end of the Italian peninsula over the centuries.

Laura and Francesco were surrounded by other walkers, many with baby carriages or strollers. Laura regarded Francesco, so reassuring with his quiet good manners and ready smile compared to her coworkers, Derrick, or Jake. She knew she could easily fall in love with him.

They passed up the entrance to the catacombs of St. Callistus, neither wanting to spend time in the dark thinking of death on a light-filled day. They paused at the Circus Maxentius. With the ruins of two tall brick gatehouses overlooking the ancient racecourse, now only a long grassy oval, the Circus slumbered with its dreams of long-ago chariot races and shouts of touts and other onlookers stilled by time.

Next was the tomb of Cecilia Metella, the ruined round tower set on a square base standing firm despite two thousand years of weather and war. Francesco pointed out the architectural features, saying the ones he found most interesting were the *bucrania*, ox skulls, separated by swags of fruit and flowers, the combination signifying sacrifice. The strange mix of dead animals and live vegetation reminded Laura of how little she knew about the people who originally built the city and the empire, and how much time she wasted being caught up in her own turmoil.

Francesco went on to relate what was known about Cecilia: her father-in-law put down the slave revolt of Spartacus, her father brought

Crete into the Roman Empire, her husband served with Julius Caesar in Gaul, and her son became a colleague of the great emperor, Augustus.

"But is much known about *her* – not just the men in her family?" she asked while thinking of her mother's statement about being just a housewife.

"She was a true Roman matron, virtuous and obscure. What would she think of us today?" Laura cringed at the word "virtuous," a quality she left behind with Derrick, before she shared a laugh with Francesco, thinking of their casual dress and that of the nearby families – women in shorts and tank tops, men carrying their babies or guiding the strollers, all talking to each other or on their cell phones, or both at once. He continued, "If Cecilia was somehow resurrected, she would have to sit in modest robes watching the world from the sanctity of her room as she tried to deal with bank statements, cell phones, airplanes, and Twitter."

"I'll bet she would have loved smartphones and Skype to talk to her family on the front lines. And I think she would have loved the Via Condotti." Laura pictured the woman wandering into a shop in her matron's drapery to view the new fall fashions. "Ferragamo for sandals, don't you think?"

Francesco put his arm around her waist and pulled her to him as they shared visions of Signora Metella trying to cope with twenty-first century life. Laura didn't move away.

They stopped to sit on an ancient chunk of marble to enjoy their lunch. Laura told him about the time she cooked spaghetti and meatballs to encourage her husband to agree to move to Italy. Francesco laughed when he told her that it really wasn't an Italian dish. Americans just thought it was. Then he became serious and spoke about his work and the small firm's plans. He asked her about the long-term job she applied for.

"What will you do if you don't get the job?"

"I don't know. I haven't gotten that far, but I know for sure I'm not ready to go back to Seattle. I've got some money saved from the rental of our house in Seattle, but it wouldn't last long. I've heard there are a few other United Nations offices in Rome, and some American companies have offices here as well. Maybe they would have a job I could do." Although the sky was clear, Laura felt as if a rain cloud momentarily passed over the sun as she wondered what she would do if no job turned up.

He took her hands in his. "I'm asking for two reasons. The most important is I'd like to continue seeing you. The second is with the proposed expansion of our firm, we might need help from time to time getting the New York end organized. If we do, and if your Italian is good enough, translating our marketing materials into proper English would be a great help. I don't know if you would be interested in either offer. Or both? And of course I don't want to interfere with your marriage."

She looked at him in surprise, wondering if it was all too good to be true. It was a lovely thought that perhaps there might be some *buona fortuna* in her future. But after all that had happened since she arrived in Rome she was wary.

"I've never felt so comfortable with anyone, but I don't want to rush. I want to continue seeing you, but I need to earn enough to live on. And there's my husband. Like I said earlier, we've got some big problems. I think we will be divorcing, but I don't want to make any more mistakes." A further thought came to mind: "Would the work be in Milan?"

"Milan, Rome from time to time, and maybe New York once in a while if we do set up an office there. New York isn't certain; depends on the economy. Have you considered freelance editing again? I don't see why that kind of work couldn't be done away from Seattle."

The possibilities were more than she could take in. "Let's walk," was the only rejoinder she dared make lest she stumble. They moved on, talking about the ruins strewn along both sides of the old road. One was an ancient milestone marking the distance from the Roman Forum, not far from her office. While one part of her mind took in the scenery, another part, deeper inside, processed the possibilities of another change in her life. A milestone even more dramatic than the move to Rome.

"I can make some salad and pasta at the apartment, if you like," she said after they finished their walk, perspiring and thirsty. "My cooking won't be as good as your mother's, I'm sure. I confess I bought the package at our supermarket."

"Whatever you're serving sounds good to me. I'll share dinner on one condition. You have to speak Italian the whole time."

"*Certo.*" For sure. Then she said in her shaky Italian, "Do you know how I could get intensive lessons? I'm not leaving Italy." Bravely said, but she knew her declaration was perhaps unrealistic.

"I'll check with an architect I know here. If she isn't available, maybe a student from La Sapienza will be interested in trading English and Italian lessons."

When they reached her apartment, Laura said, "I think the news is on if you want to watch while I get dinner ready." Francesco turned on the television while she went to the refrigerator to get salad fixings and a package of readymade *ravioli di zucca,* which she planned to top with a little browned butter and sage to set off the flavor of the pumpkin. The pot of water began to boil while the butter melted in the frying pan. She tuned out the newscaster's voice.

"Laura, come here!" The urgency in Francesco's voice made her hurry into the living room. A journalist was talking too fast for Laura to understand, although she caught the word *tombaroli.* There were pictures of the police standing around a hole in the ground, medics carrying a body on a stretcher, and an abandoned van, the photos taken several weeks ago. The newscaster continued her rapid commentary over a photo of Carabinieri standing behind a table loaded with pots, both decorated and plain, along with fragments of sculptures. A photo of a disheveled woman and three slovenly men resembling bouncers gone to seed flashed on the screen, followed by pictures of a gallery in Zurich and an antique shop in London. Livia's shop.

Laura remembered the television news story she and Jake watched their first evening in the apartment. From the pictures she had thought some gangsters might be under arrest for stealing antiquities. Could it be the same group? She could not remember what they had looked like. "Tell me, in English, what is this about?"

"Well, this is really odd. You remember yesterday my father was talking with us about the fool who died trying to loot a tomb. This is him. And the police were able to trace his accomplices through fingerprints. They are known criminals. They're from Romania and had already fled before the authorities here could arrest them. They were probably also involved in bringing in old icons and other stolen artifacts from Eastern Europe to be restored here and then sold illegally. The Carabinieri recovered a lot of items at a farm near Ravenna, although the guy who owns it is missing. The government will try to get them extradited, but I doubt anything will happen any time soon, if ever. It's strange, you know, some people mistake Romanians for Italians because the languages can sound similar."

"What are the Zurich and London connections?" Laura felt sick. She didn't need to be told but wanted to be sure.

"From what I understand, most of the antiquities were being sold to a man in Zurich, and then he must have sold them on to people in London. Always been trouble with a few Swiss dealers. And there might be an American middleman."

Laura collapsed into a chair with her head in her hands. "Oh my God, oh my God," she moaned.

"What's wrong? This sort of crime goes on all the time. What's wrong? Do you know these people?" He stared at her without comprehension.

Laura wrung her hands. "It can't be, it just can't be," she repeated over and over. She was afraid for Jake and maybe even for herself. But surely the Italian authorities didn't have Jake's prints, did they? Or would they go to Interpol? "Oh my God," she said again.

A burning smell came from the stove. She leaped up to turn the burner off, but the butter was already blackened.

Francesco switched off the television and came into the kitchen. He put a hand on her shoulder. "Forget cleaning up and come sit with me and tell me what is going on."

Laura allowed herself to be led to the sofa. She began to talk, expanding on the situation with Jake. She said she didn't know much in the way of specifics, but she had suspicions Jake was involved and also a man in her office, the man who gave her the earrings.

The words gushed out as she related to Francesco how Jake had told her he worked at a restoration lab and from time to time he went to Ravenna and to an art dealer in Zurich. She was sure he also took artworks up there for the man she knew, her former friend who went to England, but Jake would never tell her anything. She added that Jake had been secretive during the last few months, and he was living in the countryside at her boss's vacation house, supposedly painting, but now after hearing the news, she thought he was probably hiding.

"I never dreamed these things could happen. It's a nightmare." She started to cry, hiccupping and feeling her nose run. Humiliated, she ran for the bathroom.

Her face was still blotchy when she returned. Seeing her distress, Francesco said, "Laura, you don't need to worry about what your husband may have done. It is his problem. Nor do you need to be concerned about your affair. I have had a few relationships along the way. We're adults, not children, and the past can be put behind. We need to look to the future. Forget cooking dinner. Let's eat nearby. We'll have Roman comfort food. What I always ate before exams when I was at university. And if you want, I'll stay with you tonight."

Laura was swept with temporary relief. She needed his calm company, terrified this mess would drag her into a criminal investigation even though she had no role.

The waiter at the local trattoria served up bowls of *cacio e pepe*, the Italian version of macaroni and cheese, but with a richer flavor. Laura found the dish comforting, like Francesco. The taste made her think of her mother opening a blue box of Kraft Macaroni and Cheese on those occasions when she suffered a childhood adversity or slight. The memory of the packet of impossibly orange-colored powdered cheese mixed into the old red bowl full of overcooked pasta softened her feelings toward her mother. And the contrast between the two meals finally gave her a subject for her first food blog. It would be about the effect food and the setting it is served in has on mood and desire.

Francesco didn't refer to her situation or that of her husband any further, and Laura had said all there was to say for now. They shared a comfortable silence until he said, "Shall we?" as he signaled for the bill.

He turned toward her when they entered her apartment. "Laura, please don't think I'm pressing you. I can wait if you wish."

But Laura needed to embrace him, mentally and physically. Their lovemaking was as unhurried as if it was an event long foretold in the stars, an event that was a prelude to their future. Dawn arrived before they fell asleep, dreamless and still entwined in each other's arms. Though ignored, the faun gently watched over them.

Laura awoke in the morning unable to stop thinking of the gyrations of her life. From the time she raised the subject of moving to Italy while she and Jake ate the overcooked and over-sauced pretend Italian dinner in Seattle, to her life in Rome with uncertain job prospects, a husband gone missing, and now to the man resting quietly next to her.

She put on her robe and went to the kitchen to make coffee. The dove and its mate were back on the balcony, looking for a handout. The espresso maker began to work its magic. She got out two cups, pouring hers to take outside to sit in the morning sun and think. The doves remained.

She was tired of thinking but couldn't stop. What would be the outcome if she accepted Francesco's offer? Should she divorce Jake now, or just leave things as they were for a while; could she even do the work for Francesco's firm successfully; and what if she found that he or the job didn't work out? And what about children?

She heard Francesco stir, her signal to bring him coffee.

"About last night..."

"I'm happy, don't say anything more now." She kissed him and they fell back on the bed. Her eyes were open but they didn't see the coffee spill.

A few days after he returned to Milan, Laura received an e-mail from Francesco with the name of a fellow architect who would be willing to give her intensive Italian lessons. Laura contacted her, a woman named Anna Luisa Zen, a Venetian "exiled to Rome," as she described herself. They agreed to meet four times a week in the evenings. Anna Luisa's English was excellent, but she forced Laura to speak and gradually to think in Italian, along with reading several daily papers online. Often the subject was architecture, ancient and modern, subjects Laura hadn't much interest in prior to the walk on the Appia Antica, where she connected Cecilia Metella's tomb to a real person and to Francesco.

Reading and speaking became easy, but writing remained another matter, with slow progress and many red marks on her work. In between work and the exhausting lessons, Laura searched the Internet for Derrick's name and the art thefts she was sure he and Jake were involved in. But she could not find any further mention of Derrick or Livia. She assumed the investigation continued.

Francesco took the fast train from Milan to arrive early each Friday evening for a weekend of explorations of Rome and of themselves, their hopes, their fears, their future plans. Laura knew that for the first time in her life, her feelings were called love. The proposed job might not work out, but she began to nourish hope that Francesco would want to remain with her even if it didn't. That what he had said about wanting children was true. Despite her intentions not to get caught up in romantic dreams so soon she had done exactly that.

Laura heard nothing more about the UN vacancy. She refrained from asking for any news, not knowing whether she would accept if offered the job, even though her contract was expiring at the end of August.

Near the end of June, Francesco asked if she wanted to come to Milan for a visit. "I'd like you to see my home and the city, and to meet the partners to talk about how we could structure your work with us. I don't think it could be full time, but we would pay you a decent salary and get your legal status arranged. The firm's doing quite well now, and we are eager to get commissions in the U.S. My two partners have never been there, and when I did my graduate work and internship in New York I didn't have time to see more than a few places. There are many Italian companies doing business in the States, and branches of American companies in Milan and elsewhere in Italy, so they might be able to use you. And as I said earlier about freelance editing, I don't see why you couldn't work from Italy. Why don't you send me a few samples of the type of work you do so I can show my partners?" Then he added, "If you come next weekend, I will have a special treat to introduce you to the city."

Of course she would come, Laura assured him. Her interest in working for the UN was waning and her interest in moving to Milan, whatever the city might offer in the way of work, waxing with the same speed.

She dug through her files on the laptop to find the names of her former contacts for the freelance editing jobs. They weren't so unimportant now, nor did the idea of freelancing seem so tedious. During her lunch breaks, Laura studied a guidebook to Milan and tried to avoid Silvia, who would be sure to ask why she wanted to know about the city. Anna Luisa came to her apartment as usual for rigorous Italian lessons.

Wednesday was Anna Luisa's day off. Instead of time to catch up on her Italian homework, Laura came home to an intruder. Jake stood in the living room with a can of beer in hand.

"Hello, Laura. I came for the rest of my belongings. And I'd like to talk."

She sat down to wait for whatever was coming. He'd lost weight, put on muscle. A few days of stubble made him resemble one of the Italian models for Armani or Hugo Boss suits. His manual labor was reflected in calloused hands, without a ring, she saw. His whole demeanor gave the impression of being assured and in control. He looked like he did when they first became lovers in university.

"What do you want?"

He took a swallow of beer before answering. "I've been painting, and I've got a gallery showing my pieces in the town of Bolsena. Lots of Germans come there and they like my work. I'm staying."

"But, what about the art thefts I read about, and how are you going to stay in Italy if I leave?"

"I don't know what you're talking about. I know Derrick went back to England. Doug's going to talk to him so I can keep the car for a while since I need it for the work I'm doing on the house and shack. He's also paying me. As soon as I'm done with the house, he's going to rent the place out when they're not staying there. I'll help build another one so I can stay on indefinitely. My idea is to run the whole place as a bed and breakfast." Then he added, "I don't need you. Italy's full of people without papers. Who do you think does all the work?" He took a few more gulps of beer. "Now, help me find the rest of my stuff."

"Find it yourself." She saw that despite his physical appearance he was just as evasive and negative as he was after their arrival in Rome, after that day he came home with the odor of smoke on his clothes.

Surprised by her sharpness, he took out one of their suitcases from under the bed and began to clear the dresser and closet of his clothes. She decided to help in case he took things she wanted. She found the picture Jake bought for her at Tivoli. She held the little picture, thinking of their excursion and the purchase of her flute player. Underneath the picture was a black turtleneck sweater, but the one she bought him on the day they moved to the apartment was missing. "Where is the sweater I bought you?"

Jake became agitated at the question. He pushed Laura out of the way knocking over the bronze statue in his haste. It fell, the heavy base bruising his foot and the goat tail gouging his ankle.

"God damn stupid thing." He kicked it into a corner. Laura knelt to pick up her treasure. Jake grabbed the remainder of his clothes, stuffed them into the suitcase, and limped out, slamming the door behind him. An old beer mat from a restaurant in Zurich with a ring where a glass once sweated, the painting on papyrus, and the wedding photo put away in her underwear drawer were now the only physical reminders of his former presence in the room.

Laura sat on the floor, cradling her sculpture. She thought back to the time in Seattle when she asked Jake if he ever wondered what would happen if they went to Europe. And she remembered the entry in her discarded journal about the day they arrived in Rome being the first day of her new life. This day, she saw, was yet another first day. She looked at her hands. The hangnail had healed but her engagement and wedding rings remained. She removed them, dropping the final residue of her marriage into the handbag Derrick had given her. Tomorrow she would toss all of them in the trash container outside the apartment building on her way to work.

JULY/AUGUST

WHILE THE TRAIN SPED northward toward Milan in a straight and smooth line, Laura's thoughts went in circles. The days were flying by and her work contract would soon be up. Jake was definitively out of the picture. She felt a sense of regret that it all went so wrong, but he seemed content with his new life when he came to pick up his clothes. She wondered if she had ever really understood him. What little she knew of his family made her sure they were dysfunctional, and it now appeared as though he was the same. But to have someone disappear from her life after more than seven years of marriage was disconcerting. It was the mark of failure, a stain on her character that she hoped would fade out with time.

And now Francesco would be waiting for her at the station. If she couldn't find work in Rome, or if this weekend with Francesco in Milan and its possibilities of a long-term relationship and work for his firm didn't work out, the small amount of money she had would not last long.

She went to the bar car to get a coffee. Returning to her seat, she opened the *La Repubblica* she'd purchased that morning and tried to concentrate on reading. The complexities of Italian politics were still confusing, but she could read international news and the arts and culture pages with ease thanks to Signora Zen. She turned to the local news for the area around Rome. There was a review in the arts listings about a gallery showing work by several expatriates, among them Jake Miller.

The train began to slow as the landscape changed from small towns and agricultural vistas to industry and apartment buildings. More and more tracks joined and separated like strands of spaghetti until the train pulled into *Milano Centrale*. Francesco was waiting with hugs and kisses. "We can drop off your bag before walking around the city center, and later we'll have dinner with the partners. Tomorrow morning I'll have the treat I promised before you leave."

He parked his car in the apartment block's underground garage. When he opened the door to his flat, Laura found herself in a light-filled living space with polished parquet floors, a fireplace with a marble surround, and the comfortable furniture of a midcentury design she saw in interior design magazines. A bookcase filled with volumes on art, architecture, and history filled one wall, floor to ceiling. Canvasses and a few sculptures from the 1930s reflected his interest in the recent past. The small kitchen was sleek and efficient, thoroughly Italian high style. A festive Franciacorta chilled in a bucket on the counter with two glasses nearby. He opened the bottle and poured. "Come and see the view."

Laura stepped out onto a small terrace where jasmine vines and a lemon tree perfumed the air and framed the very top of an enormous white building spiked with Gothic spires and statues. She briefly remembered looking at the statues on the top of San Giovanni when she and Jake moved into their apartment an eon ago.

"This is heavenly. How fortunate you are. My house in Seattle was never really decorated. It just wasn't important to me. When I look back now, I don't see that we were ever settled." Looking over neighboring apartment buildings, she asked: "Is the building with the spires the Duomo? I read about it in my guidebook and I'd like to see it."

"Yes, the Duomo. We'll go there and walk on the roof. I have a few snacks here for us to eat in case you don't want to go out yet. I could make you some risotto."

Laura said, "Let's stay in."

"With pleasure."

They left the apartment in the afternoon to begin their walking tour with the Duomo, Milan's central cathedral. They ascended to the roof to admire the view of the city rooftops and blue hills beyond. In the distance Laura could see the snowy Alps. She turned her attention downward to the cloister of a monastery. A few monks walked with their heads down as if they were reciting prayers.

"What do you think? Could you be happy here?"

"I think I could be very happy." She rested her head on his shoulder and closed her eyes to dream. Francesco gave her a hug.

They had coffee in the glass-domed Galleria Vittorio Emanuele before perusing the playbills outside La Scala, and window shopping on Via Spiga and Via Montenapoleone. Laura's impressions mirrored those of so many other visitors: a city of style and business. The city center didn't have the chaotic atmosphere of Rome with its hordes of tourists, multitudes of religious adherents, and endless ruins. Milan appeared altogether more rational and organized.

Laura was apprehensive about meeting the partners. Francesco assured her they were anxious to greet her, but she knew the dinner would be an interview of sorts, both for work possibilities and to be sure Francesco hadn't gone off the deep end emotionally. They set off just before eight for the home of one of the men, Claudio Mengoni. He, his wife, Marisa, and the other partner, Lorenzo Barbiano, were relaxed and welcoming. Laura spoke in Italian as much as she could and they all responded graciously by speaking more slowly than normal or switching to English. She learned Claudio and Marisa had two children and that she worked as an industrial designer concentrating on office furniture for a big company. The two partner architects were eager to hear what work Laura had done in the way of editing.

They also wanted to know her opinions of Milan, Rome, and Italy in general. Did she want to attend La Scala? Was viewing *The Last Supper* on her schedule for the weekend? Had they had time to visit any of the galleries displaying works by their friends? She managed to respond in a manner seemingly acceptable, offering comments on the beauty of the city and her hopes to partake in all its many cultural offerings in the future. The table talk advanced to American politics and social issues. Laura couldn't picture her former friends sitting around discussing European policies during a dinner party but she joined the conversation based on newspapers and other websites Anna Luisa had insisted she read.

The conversation flowed around *bresaola*, the slices of dried beef complemented by lemon juice, olive oil, parmesan and arugula; risotto redolent of saffron, and *vitello tonnato*, cold veal slices in a mayonnaise-like sauce flavored with tuna and capers. To complete the meal, Marisa offered a fruit bowl laden with peaches, plums, and grapes, and a chocolate *semifreddo,* along with espresso and liqueurs. Laura was in bliss with the food, the intelligent conversation, and the prospect of participating in these people's artistic lives, all of whom knew more and had accomplished more than she ever dreamed. Not only did her Italian need more improvement; her knowledge of the arts and contemporary issues was still woeful. She saw how insular her friends and family in Seattle were, and even some coworkers in the United Nations.

Laura and Francesco sat on his terrace later that night, holding hands and watching the lights illuminating the city. After a time, she ventured, "Do you really think these people would accept me? I know nothing compared to them."

"I'm sure they will, but you will have to give them a little time. And tomorrow I think you will see this should be your home. If not with the company, then with me alone. I do so love you Laura, for your beauty, your intelligence, and because you love my country and people."

Laura didn't respond directly for fear of making a commitment too soon.

Mid-day on Sunday they joined a small group of Italians standing in a gate house waiting to tour a villa. "This will be a tour of my favorite house in Milan. It's called the Villa Necchi. If you've seen the film, *I Am Love,* this is the setting. I love the architecture and I hope you will also enjoy it."

The guide approached to lead them into the villa. The large windows of a sitting room opened onto a tree-filled garden. Pale green upholstered furniture complemented the lush color of the tree ferns and other vegetation. A lapis lazuli table held blue and gold Chinese vases. The sliding door to the library was made of German silver. Works by Italian artists from the 1920s and 1930s decorated the walls and tables. Inlaid marble or parquet floors emphasized the spaciousness of the elegant, serene, and comfortable rooms.

After, they lingered by the pool. "This villa is my style, not that I could ever have it. I hope you might feel the same way." He looked at her with a question in his eyes.

Laura reflected on Francesco's apartment. His furnishings and design expressed the same sentiment. Yes, serene was the word in comparison to her carelessly furnished house in Seattle, a builder's special that always gave the impression of impermanence, and the apartment in Rome, decorated with the landlady's discards.

"Francesco, I'm in love with you, with the villa, and with the possibility of moving to Milan. But I need to think – this is an even bigger step than moving to Rome. Jake and I are done, but I don't want to hurry. It's too important and I've made a lot of mistakes. I couldn't survive another one."

"I understand. We'll take things slow." He stood up. "We need to go back to the apartment for your suitcase and get to the station. All I ask is please think about our future together."

Before Laura saw the inside of her Rome apartment again, she put aside all her doubts about Francesco being too good to be true. He was a caring and well-educated man who knew what he wanted from life. He had a loving family. What more could she expect? She made her decision. She would have to tell her parents, Doug or Raj or whoever was in charge, and also the landlady. And Jake, to begin the process of formally ending their marriage. To avoid having to think about resolving all these problems, *if* they were problems, on Monday she found a video store and rented *I Am Love*. The settings were a poem to the Villa Necchi, although the plot centered on the owner's wife, a foreigner like herself, who left her husband and the villa to follow her heart. The passionate love scenes made Laura long to be with Francesco again.

What the future would bring was unknown, but like the woman in the film, she made the decision to love above all. Would they marry, would they really have a child or children, would there be heartbreak? If heartbreak was the result, at least she made a conscious decision. The years of operating on automatic were finished.

Not wanting to wait until morning, she called Francesco at midnight to say, "Yes, yes, yes."

The following afternoon she overcame her trepidation to place the call to Seattle. "Hi Mom and Dad. I have some news." She paused to be sure she had their attention before plunging ahead after deciding to get it out all at once. "Jake and I have split up after realizing we should never have married. You were right all along. And I've decided to stay on in Italy. And I've met a wonderful man, an architect. He lives in Milan, in the north, and I'm moving there." She paused again for their reaction. A long silence was all she got. She continued, "I'll come to Seattle once in a while and maybe there will be some trips to New York and we can meet up. His name is Francesco and he wants to meet you."

After her mother overcame her shock, she said in a quavering voice, "But I don't understand. Why don't you and Francis, isn't that his name in English, move here? What's wrong with Seattle? Are you getting a divorce? Are you going to marry him? We haven't met him, never heard of him before."

"I want to be here, in Italy, and this is where Francesco works. I met him last March and we fell in love. And I want to share my life with him. We will probably marry, but for now I'm content. I'm thirty now, and I want to live my life in my own way before everything good passes me by. I have found a life that makes me happy. And I hope you will be happy for me."

"What about Jake?" This time her father interjected.

She didn't have the heart to tell them the whole story, so she selected particulars to put a positive slant on the situation. Jake wanted to go his own way to become an artist. But when they finally asked more about Francesco she was delighted to tell them all about his wonderful qualities.

She could tell her father was unhappy although he would come around eventually. But even after her description of Francesco and her expressions of happiness, her mother sounded inconsolable. Laura knew she would eventually suppress her feelings, but having her only child decide to remain abroad with a foreigner must be a terrible blow.

When Laura ran out of things to say she promised to call them again as soon as she could, to tell them more about her arrangements. After the conversation, if it could be called that, she felt a sense of sadness mixed with hope. She wanted to be more emotionally close with her family but never managed to cross some invisible barrier. Jake's poor relations with his family didn't help, but now, with Francesco's easy manner, there might come an opportunity. Maybe the two families could meet at some point, build an understanding, even a friendship over time. She put her thoughts aside to worry about how to tell Raj.

She invited him to coffee to tell him the news. He was neither shocked nor unhappy. In fact, he looked relieved, as if a problem was off his hands. He asked her to stay on through August, the month when most of the employees took their vacations, leaving the office short-staffed. She said she would. She and Francesco had already agreed that moving at a slower pace than they both desired was best. There were plans to make, stories about their pasts to share, and he wanted to take her to see his family again before the move to Milan.

"I wouldn't have gotten the job, would I?" Laura couldn't resist asking.

"Well – you know, Derrick became a bit of an annoyance with all his protégées. Got tiresome, although we liked your work. After Silvia, we tried to call a stop to his recommendations, which we couldn't refuse, but he pressed and pressed about you. He's gone now, finally retired. Guess the selection committee wanted someone without ties to him."

"Silvia, too?"

"Of course, what did you think? English isn't even her mother tongue and we're stuck with her. But we won't be hiring her friend."

She thought of her earrings. They were a relic of her past life, almost an antiquity. She would keep them safe for now as a memento and only wear them when she could match their style. Probably not soon.

She contacted her landlady, who wasn't disturbed that the rental contract would not be renewed. United Nations people came and went regularly. She'd put another notice on the office bulletin board for the next new arrival to see.

Laura and Francesco alternated their weekends between Milan and Rome. On the mid-August holiday, the Feast of the Assumption of the Virgin Mary, he drove to Rome to pick her up for an overnight visit with his parents and to meet his two brothers and their families. Francesco had told them the news beforehand and they all enthusiastically hugged and kissed her on both cheeks. His mother said in Italian, "Anything that makes Francesco happy, makes me happy. You're part of our family now and I'm going to teach you to make risotto tomorrow. And I can't wait for another grandchild." Laura felt a flush of pleasure at the warm welcome. Finally, an authentic family. The glories of intrigued-filled Rome would soon be gone, replaced by family warmth and a loving partner.

She and Francesco drove deep into the countryside late that night to watch the falling stars. Francesco told her about the traditional Night of San Lorenzo, just a few days earlier, when people make a wish for each star they see shooting across the sky. Laura treasured the memory of the glorious evening when they went to the Trevi Fountain and she wished to stay in Italy and be with Francesco. And now as they lay on their backs on a blanket Francesco spread in a field, Laura made the same wishes in the hope the reinforcement would ensure they came true.

Near the end of August Laura began to pack. She tenderly nestled the flute player in her clothes to keep him safe from adversity. From now on he would be her constant companion, her talisman. She found the forgotten wedding photo as she emptied the dresser drawers and heaved it into the trash, the same fate her journal met months ago.

Telling Jake was the last chore.

He never answered his cell phone, even if the connection worked, and she didn't want to ask Doug to contact him on her behalf. In his temper the last time they met, Jake neglected to take their laptop. She pulled up the gallery's website. Several photos of his recent pictures were on the section devoted to his work. She expected to see pastoral landscapes, but instead her senses were assaulted by aggressive thrusts of crimson, green, and dark blue.

Using the contact page she sent a message with a disguised name, saying she was a potential buyer and would like to meet him at a piano bar on the Via Veneto near the embassy. She knew he would be curious enough to come.

Jake arrived well before the appointed time. Even though the workday was far from over, a few of the nearby office workers were already hanging around, drinking martinis. He ordered a Jack Daniels with plenty of ice and sat back to watch the crowd, mostly American. He thought some of the arrogant and over-confident men must be CIA agents poorly disguised as aides to the many attachés or other diplomats populating the embassy. Maybe he could offer his services as a mole in the antiquity trafficking business. He laughed bitterly to himself at the idea, acknowledging his gullibility and illusions. Well, he knew better now.

Laura came through the door. He was startled and angry, expecting an eager admirer of his work and a sale. "What are you doing here?"

"I'll have a pinot grigio." She sat down opposite him at the small table. He waved up a waiter giving him her order. Then he waited to hear what she wanted to say. Must be important, otherwise, why would she have bothered? She looked happy, younger with a new hairdo, and, from what he could tell, stylish Italian clothes. Not like his Seattle wife dressed in casual clothes less than a year ago.

She began. "Jake, I don't know what happened to us. I guess the problems were building all along. I thought a change of scene would help our marriage but it only made it worse. I regret deceiving you with Derrick. It was wrong of me. Now my life has changed. I will be moving to Milan and hoping to get a sponsorship for a work permit to stay on at an architectural firm. Then I'll be starting divorce proceedings, unless you want to go first. We'll have to talk about the house in Seattle at some point. I am truly sorry our marriage didn't work out, but I've found a new life and you'll have to make your own way. I assume you still have friends here."

"You have someone else."

"Yes. He's an architect. I'm really in love. A good feeling I've never had before, and I hope you find someone. I thought we were a pair, like you said, but I was wrong, really wrong. I can see that now." With this, she finished her atonement.

Jake wasn't shocked at the news, although the part about her lover being an architect upset him. He knew that they had drifted so far apart that their marriage was irretrievably broken. Laura had presented him with a solution. Now he could move on with his own new life.

He drained his glass before responding. "You can contact me through Doug if you ever need to." He didn't tell her about his newfound contentment with the rural life: about Mirella, to whom he gave English lessons in exchange for her companionship and help cooking and housework; about her teenage son, Dante, who showed artistic promise and whose company he was slowly learning to enjoy; or about how his own style was becoming less violent and more reflective of the Italian countryside. Nor did he tell her he never bothered to contact the school district, which now represented a life past and best forgotten. There was no point. He and Laura were never close enough to talk about their hopes and worries.

Laura put her half-full glass down and rose from the table. Jake watched her walk through the door and into her new life. As the door closed the pianist began the evening entertainment with an old Cole Porter standard. Jake recognized the tune, "Smoke Gets in Your Eyes."

Jake stared into the bottom of his glass thinking what if his sister hadn't drowned, what if he had been an architect instead of a teacher, what if he hadn't gotten married to Laura, what if they had had a child, what if they hadn't come to Rome? It was all pointless. He could not change the past. He consoled himself by thinking maybe something good would come along now. It was his turn.

He ordered another drink before deciding he would stop by a computer store to find a game for Dante before he returned to the countryside. He was hopeful for the future, resolving this time there would be no dishonesty, no lies with Mirella. He stepped out into the hot Roman summer afternoon. The sound of a siren assaulted his ears. Turning toward the noise, he saw the Carabinieri's car screeching to a stop in front of the bar. The driver and another officer jumped out and headed in his direction.

TWO YEARS LATER

LAURA STIRRED SUGAR into her cappuccino as she looked at Piero sleeping in his stroller. He clutched a plush rabbit next to his check. A little drool spotted his tiny Inter Milan soccer jersey. She took a sip of her coffee before she opened her briefcase to take out the draft of her latest article on trends in Italian cuisine, commissioned by an international magazine aimed at luxury travelers. Below the draft she saw a page her mother had torn from a Seattle quarterly focused on the arts and brought to Milan the last time she and Hank had come to see their grandchild.

The article had a photo of Jake standing beside a display of his latest work. Jake had grayed and was beginning to bald. The article implied he had studied in Italy and the author either didn't know or chose not to write that Jake had been thrown out of the country after the Italian police determined he was such a low-level trafficker he wasn't worth the time it would take to prosecute. The exhibition was titled "A Labyrinth of Echoes and Illusions." The paintings were abstractions of scenes in Rome, really quite pleasing. Laura thought about asking Francesco if they should buy one when they went to Seattle next month.

Laura had been in Rome for several days. Francesco had some bureaucratic work with the government to complete and she came along so she could revisit some of her favorite places. The Piazza Navona was too crowded and noisy for Piero to take his morning nap so Laura decided on her coffee break in a nearby café.

She looked up to see Francesco entering the café. He sat down after ruffling Piero's fine baby hair and took Laura's hand. "I finished up early. Let's go home."

ACKNOWLEDGMENTS

I owe countless thanks to the many friends who suffered through hours of reading earlier drafts. They all provided valuable comments and critique.

The story could not have been finished without the assistance of my excellent editors, Sarah Kishpaugh and Kathryn Schipper.

Julie Simrock, my book manager at Booktrope has been patient and understanding throughout the process, always providing me with good advice.

And of course, I thank my family who have to put up with so much. You know who you are.

MORE GREAT READS
FROM BOOKTROPE

A State of Jane by **Meredith Schorr** (Contemporary Women's Fiction) Jane is ready to have it all: great friends, partner at her father's law firm and a happily-ever-after love. But her life plan veers off track when every guy she dates flakes out on her. As other aspects of Jane's life begin to spiral out of control, Jane will discover that having it all isn't all that easy.

How to Un-Marry a Millionaire by **Billie Morton** (Contemporary Women's Fiction) A girl with nothing from Nowhere, Arizona is determined to reinvent her life, even if it means making a deal with the devil and marrying a rich old sonofabitch with a crazy family.

Thank You For Flying Air Zoe by **Erik Atwell** (Contemporary Women's Fiction) Realizing she needs to awaken her life's tired refrains, Zoe vows to recapture the one chapter of her life that truly mattered—her days as drummer for an all-girl garage band. Will Zoe bring the band back together and give The Flip-Flops a second chance at stardom?

Next Year I'll be Perfect by **Laura Kilmartin** (Contemporary Fiction) Sarah's discovery of a list her younger self put together outlining what she wanted to achieve by the age of 30 turns her world upside down.

Grace Unexpected by **Gale Martin** (Contemporary Romance) When her longtime boyfriend dumps her instead of proposing, Grace avows the sexless Shaker ways. She appears to be on the fast track to a marriage proposal… until secrets revealed deliver a death rattle to the Shaker Plan.

Caramel and Magnolias by **Tess Thompson** (Contemporary Romance) A former actress goes undercover to help a Seattle police detective expose an adoption fraud in this story of friendship, mended hearts, and new beginnings.

Discover more books and learn about our
new approach to publishing at **booktrope.com**.

18369610R00127

Made in the USA
San Bernardino, CA
11 January 2015